Gordon Carfax did not believe that pseudo-scientist Western's machine, called MEDIUM, could communicate with the dead. Carfax thought it might just possibly be alien messages that the machine was receiving. In any case, he had publicly challenged Western and since Western was making a handy living off MEDIUM it was up to Western to prove Carfax a liar. So Carfax found himself invited to inspect and even to use MEDIUM – a privilege which would normally have cost a great deal. But Carfax had his own private reasons for testing the weird machine – quite aside from exposing it as a fraud. For Patricia Carfax, his cousin, had come to him in distress claiming that Western had murdered her father, Rufton Carfax, in order to get the machine. Gordon Carfax was understandably sceptical of all parties concerned. He was all the more astounded, therefore, when he finally used MEDIUM . . .

Also by Philip José Farmer

Doc Savage: His Apocalyptic Life
Lord Tyger
Strange Relations
Tarzan Alive
Time's Last Gift
The Stone God Awakens
Flesh

To Your Scattered Bodies Go
The Fabulous Riverboat

Alley God
Behind the Walls of Terra
Blown
Gates of Creation
Image of the Beast
Maker of Universes
Night of Light
Private Cosmos
Wind Whales of Ishmael
Feast Unknown

Philip José Farmer

Traitor to the Living

PANTHER
GRANADA PUBLISHING
London Toronto Sydney New York

Published by Granada Publishing Limited
in Panther Books 1975
Reprinted 1978

ISBN 0 586 04200 8

First published in Great Britain by
Panther Books Ltd 1975
Copyright © Philip José Farmer 1973

Granada Publishing Limited
Frogmore, St Albans, Herts AL2 2NF
and
3 Upper James Street, London W1R 4BP
1221 Avenue of the Americas, New York, NY10020, USA
117 York Street, Sydney, NSW 2000, Australia
100 Skyway Avenue, Toronto Ontario, Canada M9W 3A6
Trio City, Coventry Street, Johannesburg 2001, South Africa
CML Centre, Queen & Wyndham, Auckland 1, New Zealand

Made and printed in Great Britain by
Hazell Watson & Viney Ltd
Aylesbury, Bucks
Set in Linotype Plantin

ONE

Gordon Carfax moaned.

He was sitting up in bed and reaching out for Frances.

The blinds were graying with dawn, and Frances had left with the night.

There were no fowl in the neighborhood, only barking dogs, but he was sure, at that moment, that he had faintly heard a crowing. He had read too much, he told himself later. Hamlet's ghost and all that. But his explanation was too soft to turn aside the knife of reason.

Out of the dark grayness, Frances had appeared. The grayness had swirled, as if it were ectoplasm arranging itself around her. Slowly, silently, she had been gliding toward him. Her arms were stretched out to him. She was unmarked, as he remembered her just before the accident. She was smiling, but behind the smile was hurt and anger.

'Frances?' he said. 'If only I had known . . .'

And then the cock had crowed somewhere in his mind, and Frances, also a mental configuration, had evaporated. She had not just disappeared; she had seemed to boil away in little gray clouds.

He lay back sighing and with the breath that followed he sucked in reality. But weren't dreams a part of reality?

And wasn't it only through dreams that the dead could return?

Raymond Western had said that that was not so. No, give the devil – Western – his due. He had made no claim that the dead could return. He affirmed only that they could be located and they could talk with the living. Western could prove his claims with MEDIUM, which crouched metallic and humming in his house in Los Angeles.

Carfax was not alone in dreaming of the dead. The whole world was dreaming of them; the dreams were troubled or joyous or frightening, just as the conscious life of the world was troubled or joyous or frightening.

There was little doubt that MEDIUM could be used to speak with somethings or somebodies. And many accepted Western's statements that these entities were dead human beings.

Gordon Carfax had another explanation, and from this a great uproar had resulted. Sometimes, he wished he had kept his mouth shut.

Now he was the center of world attention and might just possibly be involved in a murder. In its aftereffects, rather.

He closed his eyes and hoped he could go back to sleep. He also hoped that, if he did sleep, he would not dream. Or, if he did, he would dream pleasantly. He had thought he had loved Frances, but when she came to him in dreams, she scared him.

TWO

PROFESSOR SAYS SPOOKS REALLY SCIENCE-FICTION MONSTERS

Carfax forced himself to read the article under the headline. Disgusted, he threw the paper down on the floor with several others.

Trust the yellow dog the *National Questioner* to give that turn to his lecture.

Yet, he thought, as he picked up the *New York Times* from the pile on the table by his chair, the article was essentially correct.

He was front-page news. Even the *Times*'s writeup on him was on the front page. In pre-MEDIUM days, it would have mentioned him – if at all – some place deep within its massive body.

'It can't be denied that we are getting communications from another world, another universe, in fact,' said Gordon Carfax, Professor of Medieval History at Traybell University, Busiris, Illinois. 'We need not, however, depend upon the supernatural for explanation. Using Occam's razor . . .'

The *National Questioner* had defined Occam's razor. Its editors had supposed, and rightly, that most of its readers would think, if they thought at all, that Occam's razor was some sort of barber's tool.

The *New York Times* had not bothered to explain the term, leaving it to their readers to go to the dictionary, if they needed to do so.

However, the *Times* had also used 'science-fiction' in classifying his theory.

Carfax was exasperated by this, but he had to admit that it was almost impossible to get away from that word; the temptation was too great for journalists. The moment you spoke of the 'fifth dimension' – reported as the more familiar 'fourth' by the *National Questioner* – you invoked science-fiction. And when you went on to talk of 'polarized universes,' of 'worlds at right angles to ours,' and 'alien sentients with possibly sinister designs on our Earth,' you ensured that the reporters would mention science-fiction.

You also ensured that your opponents had a solid launching base for ridicule.

But even the newsmagazine *Time* had refrained from its almost-compulsory policy of sacrificing truth for the sake of witty sarcasm. At the end of a series of articles supposed to devastate MEDIUM and Western, *Time* had admitted that Western might be right. Shortly after this, Carfax had presented his theory. Eager for any explanation other than the supernatural, *Time* had then backed Carfax. Once again, it was attacking Western.

Carfax had stated in his lecture that his theory owed a certain debt to science-fiction. But it did not derive from that field of literature any more than space travel or television did. Men, not books or magazines, had originated these. Carfax was advocating that scientists consider all theories to explain the entities which MEDIUM had contacted. The theory to be developed first would be the simplest one. And this, according to Carfax, was the theory that the 'spirits' were actually non-human inhabitants of a universe occupying the same space as ours but 'at right angles' to ours. And these entities, for no good reason, were pretending to be dead human beings.

Western, via a series of news media interviews, had asked how these entities had gotten such detailed and valid knowledge about the people they were supposed to be impersonating.

Carfax had replied, also via the news media, that the entities probably had always had some means of spying on us. They had not been able to communicate with us until MEDIUM opened the way. Or, possibly, they could have communicated at any time but preferred, for some reason, that we do it first.

Carfax put down the *Times* and unfolded the local morning

paper, the *Busiris Journal-Star*. It contained an article which capsulized, for the dozenth time, his lecture and the 'riot' that followed. Actually, the 'riot' was a fist fight among six men immediately after a man was knocked down by a huge, heavily weighted purse swung by a woman.

It all started when Carfax gave the final lecture in the Roberta J. Blue Memorial Lecture Series. One stipulation of the memorial was that the final lecture be given by a member of the Traybell University faculty. Moreover, the speaker must talk about a subject outside his/her specialized field.

Carfax had volunteered to speak. He had, in fact, used his pull with the dean of education, a Wednesday night poker partner, to get the appointment. Ordinarily, he would have avoided this as a chore, especially since it was scheduled for a Thursday night and final examinations began the following Monday.

But he believed fiercely that there had to be a simpler and more scientific explanation for Western's findings. And so he had notified members of the Busirian press and TV stations of the tenor of his lecture. He had expected to get only local publicity, but the manager of a TV station had notified the *Chicago Tribune*. When Carfax had entered the lecture room, he had found, not the usual fifty or so students and faculty but five hundred people from the university and city. Moreover, four Chicago reporters and a Chicago TV team were present. The *Tribune* reporter had discovered that Carfax was first cousin to Western, and this was to be played up in the news media. It had no relevance to the issue, but the implications that the dispute was a family quarrel were pushed by the media.

It did no good for Carfax to explain that he had never met his cousin.

Carfax gave a lecture much punctuated and, from his viewpoint, nearly ruined, by both cheers and boos. Afterward, he answered questions from the audience.

Mrs. Knowlton, tall, angular, middle-aged, possessor of a very loud and commanding voice, was the first – and last – inquisitor. She was the sister of the publisher of the local newspaper, and she had recently lost her husband, daughter, and grandchild in a boating accident. She was desperate to believe

9

that they were still living and that she could talk to them. She was not, however, hysterical, and her questions were intelligent.

'You keep referring to Western's theory,' she said after Carfax had tried to answer her satisfactorily. 'But it's not theory! It's fact! MEDIUM works just as Mr. Western says it does, and some of the greatest minds in the United States agree with him, even though they were prepared to call him a quack when they started the investigation!

'Professor Carfax, just who is the quack? You or Mr. Western? You tell us that the scientists should be using Occam's razor! I suggest that it's about time you used it yourself!'

'Cut your throat with it!' a large and hairy student had yelled.

He was looking at Carfax, so Carfax supposed that the advice was for him, not Mrs. Knowlton.

Mrs. Knowlton's voice rose high and clear, overriding the hubbub.

'Professor Carfax, you say that we who believe in Western do so only because of emotional factors! We're supposed to be operating on highly subjective factors! Well, Doctor Carfax, why are you so emotional, so subjective, in your denial of our beliefs, when all the evidence is on our side? Isn't the blind emotionalism, as you call it, all yours?'

Carfax had gotten angry then, perhaps, no, undoubtedly, because her accusation was based on solid ground. He was not entirely objective; his theory sprang from a hunch. It was true that hunches often were the forefathers of hypotheses that later turned out to be excellent theories and often ended in proof. But he could not say that in public.

As it turned out, he was not able to say that or anything.

A man leaped up and yelled, 'Carfax hates us! He wants to deny the greatest thing since creation!'

The man was quoting Western's famous phrase. Carfax had a reply to it, but the man was knocked forward by the ten-pound purse (a reporter retrieved it and weighed it before returning it to the owner just after she was bailed out).

The noise and melee were not stopped until some time after the police came. But the furore had not ceased there. Carfax had become a national figure. As such, he received many phone calls from all over the country. The two he was most concerned about at this time were from Los Angeles.

One was from Raymond Western, who had invited him to fly to California for a free session with MEDIUM.

The other was from Patricia Carfax. She was the daughter of Rufton Carfax, who was the uncle of Western and Gordon Carfax.

Miss Carfax had been somewhat hysterical but evidently sincere. She believed that Western had murdered her father so that he could steal the schematics for MEDIUM.

THREE

Gordon Carfax sat in an easy chair in the glassed-in sun porch and sipped coffee. It was delicious, a blend of six special South American coffees which he prepared himself every two weeks. He watched the tiny wrens diving in and out of the little round entrance to the tiny wooden house hung from the limb of the big sycamore tree in his backyard. He enjoyed the red beauty of the cardinal perched upon the edge of the white birdbath beside a mulberry tree.

The house was comfortable and quiet, though he often felt lonely in it. It was in the middle-class Knollwoods division on the edge of the middle-sized, mid-Illinois city of Busiris. Carfax had purchased it shortly after being hired by Traybell University. It had needed some repair and much interior decorating. He had finished the repairing but had not yet gotten around to the interior by the time he had married Frances. She had been happy to quit her job as secretary to the dean of women at Traybell, and to plunge into fixing up the house according to her excellent tastes.

And then, as she was about done with the decorating and was looking for another project, she had died.

On that twilit summer evening, Gordon Carfax had commented that he was out of cigarettes. Frances had refrained from her usual answer that she wished he would give up smoking. Instead, she had offered to drive to the shopping center for him. There she would also stop in at the book emporium and pick up a paperback mystery. This had irked him because the house was full of books, ranging all the way from the heaviest of classics to the lightest of murder mysteries. There must have been at least a score of the latter which she had not yet read.

He said something about this, and she had replied that she wasn't in the mood for any of them. She had then asked him if he'd like to go along for the ride. It would do him, and her, some good to get his nose out of a book.

Somewhat crossly, perhaps because he felt guilty, he had said that the book was one which he could use for tomorrow's class in Medieval English History. And if she was hinting again that he did not talk to her enough, she should remember that he had taken her out last night to a show and a few drinks at the Golden Boar's Head.

Frances had slammed the door hard enough to startle him. She was justifiably angry, he told himself later, since they had not talked during the movie, and in the tavern they had been joined by the head of the English Department and his wife and so had exchanged only a few words.

A few minutes after she left, she was dead. An old man had driven his large, heavy car at fifty kilometers an hour through a stop sign in a 30-kph zone and rammed through the door of her German import and into her.

Frances went underground. Mr. Lincks, a very solid citizen and very rich, went into the hospital overnight for observation. He had a cut on his head and a ticket for going through a stop sign. Lincks claimed he had not been able to see the stop sign because of an obscuring bush.

It was true that the city had failed to keep the bush cropped and that a stranger might have missed it. Carfax could, however, prove that the old man had driven this route many times. The only witness was a seventeen year old who, it turned out, was drunk and driving with a suspended license. And he had twice been charged though not convicted of car stealing. The last car he was supposed to have stolen had been from one of Mr. Lincks's car lots. It was Lincks's own testimony, given shortly after the policeman showed up, that had resulted in the ticket for failure to stop. The claim that Lincks was doing fifty was based on the youth's testimony, and nothing he said was likely to be believed.

Two weeks ago, Mr. Lincks had flown to Los Angeles and purchased three hours of MEDIUM's time. On returning to

Busiris, he had been interviewed by Mrs. Knowlton of the *Journal-Star*. Her article had quoted in full Mr. Lincks's over-whelmingly favorable impression of Western and MEDIUM. Mr. Lincks had indeed talked to his late and dearly beloved wife, and now he looked forward to seeing her 'in the great beyond.' He was vague about the details of her description of the afterlife. He had been mainly concerned in finding out if she were happy and in assuring her that he would never be happy until reunited with her and God. He had also spent much time (at $5,000 per half-hour) in telling her how well the automobile agency and his investments were doing. The actual time spent talking to her was about thirty minutes. It had taken two hours to locate her and half an hour to establish her identity, even though he had been sure from the first moment of contact that it was his wife. The FCC required the half-hour of identity-establishing if the session were not free. Even the dead suffered from too much government interference, Mr. Lincks said.

However, despite the heavy hand of the federal government on free enterprise, MEDIUM certainly 'exposed the wrong-ness of those godless atheists who called Mr. Western a crook and established the eternalness and true verity of the Good Book.'

Mr. Lincks had overlooked the fact that the majority of Christian sects denied that it had been proved that MEDIUM could get into contact with the dead.

Carfax, after reading the article, had been swept by fury to the phone. He had called Mr. Lincks at his main office on Lot No. A-1 of the Robert (Bob) Lincks Easy Credit Automobile Agency, told him who he was, and then had said, 'Why didn't you talk to *my* wife and ask her forgiveness for your criminal driving?'

Lincks had sputtered and then had said, 'If she'd been driving an American car instead of that German tin can, she'd be alive today!' And he had hung up.

Carfax felt ashamed of himself, though he did not know why.

Now, drinking the coffee and watching the birds, he thought of Frances. Perhaps the shame had come because he had always felt that if he had gone with her, he would have saved her. He would have insisted on finishing a chapter before they left and that would have altered the timing, and the old man would have sailed through the stop sign and struck no one.

Perhaps he opposed Western's claims because he did not want to believe that it would be possible to talk to Frances again. Perhaps he feared her reproaches.

He rose and took the empty cup into the kitchen, bright with the new paint that Frances had applied only three weeks ago. The wall clock indicated 09:05. Patricia Carfax had said that she would call him back at eleven this morning, Illinois time. She'd be phoning from a public booth, as she had done the first time. But she'd use one that had a viewphone so that he could see her face and be sure that she really was his cousin. He could compare her features with the photographs of her in the family album. The latest showed her at the age of twelve, but she had not changed so much that he would not be able to recognize her.

Carfax had proposed that she use the viewphone. For all he knew, Western had put some girl up to posing as his cousin so that he could, in some way, discredit him. Western was, despite all the publicity, an essentially mysterious person. His vital statistics were available, but the true nature of the man himself eluded even the most perceptive interviewers.

Western had made a good impression on Carfax when he had called. His voice was deep and rich and friendly. His big deep-blue eyes and somewhat aquiline nose and out-thrust, cleft chin gave him strength and sincerity.

Carfax knew too well that appearances meant little. This, plus his prejudice against Western's claims, had made him very wary. Yet he had ended the conversation feeling that he had perhaps made a mistake about the man. Or, at least, he would have to try to be more objective to ensure against making a mistake.

After the spell had worn off, he regained the feeling that Western, despite his seeming frankness, was far from being honest.

Western had not only invited him to come at any time to his place for a free session. He had offered to pay Carfax's roundtrip air fare. Carfax had thanked him and said that he would think about it. He would reply not later than Saturday.

Why was Western offering all this? He was speeding along the road to success with no obstacles of any importance in sight. He had many antagonists but many more friends. Why should he worry because some obscure professor of history had happened to get some publicity about his theory? What could Carfax be to Western other than a minor nuisance?

Or was Western aware that Patricia Carfax had phoned him and so was trying to invalidate anything she might say?

Whatever the real situation, Gordon Carfax had never meant to say no to Western. He was far too curious about MEDIUM. He would have to see for himself what it was all about. And he could never have borrowed enough money to pay for a three-hour session with MEDIUM.

He would, however, wait until after Patricia's call before he called Western. He might even put off phoning until late that evening. He did not want to give Western the impression that he was eager.

To be honest, he told himself, he was somewhat scared of the idea of sitting down before MEDIUM.

He heard a car draw up before his house. A moment later, a car door slammed. A few seconds afterward, the door chimes bonged.

Carfax grimaced and strode through the living room to the front door. Since the lecture, he had been besieged by phone calls and by visitors. He had changed his phone number to an unlisted one, and he had tacked a sign up by the door.

PLEASE DO NOT DISTURB
WRITE IF YOU MUST COMMUNICATE

But many people paid no attention to the notice.

Opening the peephole, he suddenly remembered the case of the private investigator who had looked through a keyhole and received a spray of nitric acid. The man had been a friend of his, and had, in fact, worked on several cases with him.

Carfax was, however, wearing his spectacles at the moment, so that any acid would be diverted.

He shook his head and grinned, told himself he was getting more paranoid every year, and put his eye to the hole.

The woman was about thirty. She had a pretty face, though her nose was a trifle too long and there were spiderleg lines from the corners of her nose to the corners of her mouth. Her reddish-bronze hair was cut short and seemed to be naturally curly, though it was difficult to be sure of that, of course. She was wearing a white somewhat rumpled dress over an attractively curved figure.

He knew then why he had thought the hair was naturally curly. He had seen her before, though not in the flesh.

He swung the door open and saw the two suitcases beside her.

'You were supposed to call me,' he said. 'Come in, anyway.'

FOUR

Patricia Carfax looked like a younger edition of his mother. The differences were that her hair was lighter, her nose longer, her eyes were a deeper blue, and she had legs even longer than his mother's. And his mother had never had that desperate look.

He stepped out to pick up the suitcases.

She said, very softly, 'When we go in it might be best to turn up the radio before we start talking. Your house might be bugged.'

'Oh?' he said. He picked up the cases and followed her in. He set them down and rolled five long-playing Beethoven marbles into the stereo. While the *Eroica* was blasting, he gestured for her to follow him onto the sun porch. Beethoven continued his function of beauty and of ensuring that electronic eavesdroppers, if any, were thwarted.

'I'll get some coffee,' he said. 'Sugar and cream?'

'No, thank you. Black. I'm a purist.'

Returning from the kitchen, he put her cup and saucer on the little table by her chair, put down his own coffee, also black, and then pulled up a chair close to hers.

'Is anybody after you?'

'I don't think anybody was on the plane with me, I mean, no shadow was. If he had been, he surely would have done something to me before I got here.'

'He?'

'Well, I suppose a woman could have been sent to stop me. But I thought all professional killers were men.'

'The fact that you're here shows that nobody meant to kill you,' he said. 'Killing is very easy; especially in crowds or on the city streets. It makes little difference if it's day or night.'

She sighed and leaned back and, suddenly, she gave the impression of being boneless.

'I'll bet you're hungry,' he said. 'Bacon and eggs in a little while sound good?'

'Could you make it a hamburger? I don't like bacon and eggs. But I am hungry! And I'm also very tired!'

She sat up, regaining the appearance of hardness under the rounded flesh.

'But I can't sleep until I get everything off my chest.'

Carfax could not help glancing at her full breasts. She caught the glance, looked down, looked up, saw him smiling, and laughed. The laughter was somewhat thin; the cup shook in her hand; her eyes showed too much white.

She drank the coffee without spilling any and set the cup down with only a slight rattle against the saucer. She said, 'I suppose it was overly cautious of me, maybe cowardly, not to phone and tell you I was coming. But I got to thinking after my call, and it seemed to me that it just might be possible that Western had your house bugged and your line tapped.'

'Why?'

'Because I told him I was going to you for help. I shouldn't have, I know that now. And it was a spur-of-the-moment thing. I didn't know you, except that you were my cousin and you had once been a detective. I just pulled your name out of a pile of rage, you might say. But I'll get to that.

'The thing was, really, I wanted to get out of Los Angeles, and I wanted to talk to you face to face. Even with the viewphone, things are so impersonal, and I was sick to death of impersonality, of hiding with no one to talk to. And I knew that that man had been hanging around the entrance of the apartment building down the street from my motel . . .'

'In Los Angeles?'

'Yes, I'd moved there so I could be close to Western. I mean, not to that motel. I had an apartment just outside Beverly Hills, but I moved out when I knew that Western was after me. My lease wasn't up yet, but I'd paid the rent three months ahead. And I've moved twice since. I left my car with a friend in the Valley so Western couldn't trace me through it.

And I never sent back for it because he may have left somebody to watch it.'

'It takes money to hire a man just to hang around one place
for months on the off-chance you might come back.'

'Oh, Western has it! He has lots of money; he's a multi-
millionaire! By rights, that money should be mine. But he has
it all, and still he wants to kill me! Just like he did my father!'

'You understand that I have to be objective,' he said. 'I just
can't take your word, you know. So please don't take offense
at any of my questions.'

'I won't,' she said. 'I know that I have to prove my accusations.'

'You only have to give me some good grounds for suspecting
Western. I doubt you could prove anything.'

'You're right,' Patricia said, sitting up a little straighter and
smiling. 'You're right. First, I may as well satisfy your curiosity
as to why I didn't go to the police and tell them my suspicions
about Western. Not suspicions. Facts. Only, the police, you see,
would ask me for proof, and I can't give them anything that
would stand up in court. Not enough, really, to make them haul
him in for questioning. Besides, he's such a famous person now,
and so powerful, the police would hesitate doing anything to
him unless they caught him red-handed.'

'I doubt that,' Carfax said. 'They might not *like* to arrest
him, but they would do it if they had sufficient cause.'

'But if I went to them, then Western would know where I
was, and he would get to me. Anyway, I went to a lawyer and
presented my case. He told me I didn't have a chance. If I
would leave my phone number, he would call me later. He
might just change his mind. I said, no, thank you, I would tell
him where I lived only when he became my lawyer.

'I walked out, and I took a taxi straight back to my motel,
and there is where I made a mistake. I think he sent someone
to tail me . . .'

'Who did?'

'The lawyer!'

'Who was he?'

'Roger Hampton. Of Hampton, Thorburr, Roxton, and
Row.'

'They have a very good reputation. Why would Hampton send somebody to tail you?'

'Because he thought I was crazy and would get back at Western even if I had to shoot him to do it! I got pretty emotional when I was in his office! But I'm sure that he called Western and told him where I was.'

'It's true he hadn't taken your case, but what you told him should have been confidential.'

'He may have thought Western was in danger from a maniac and so he told him where I was but didn't say anything about what I'd told him.'

'Or he may have had nothing to do with it,' Carfax said. 'Your shadow, if any, may have been on your trail before you went to Hampton.'

'If any?' she said. 'I *know* he was following me. I saw him go to the desk and ask the clerk there about me. After he left, I asked the clerk if he'd been asking questions about me, and he said he had.'

Carfax waved his hand and said, 'Go on.'

'I packed right away and was out of there in fifteen minutes. I took a taxi to a restaurant in Sherman Oaks and another from there to Tarzana. I rented a car, paid cash, and took off for Route 1. I was going to stay with some friends in Carmel; I didn't think Western would know about them. And then, going down one of those steep hills on Route 1 . . .'

'I know,' he said.

'I was almost killed! The brakes gave out. I rode the car all the way down and around the curves and the only reason I didn't run headlong into cars in the outside lane when I was going around the curves was that no one was coming the other way.

'I made the curve at the bottom, even though I went off on the shoulder, and then a tire blew and the car turned over. I got out without a scratch, but I was terribly scared. The car was completely wrecked. A police car stopped and took me back to the restaurant where I'd parked the car while I ate. Sure enough, there was a pool of brake fluid in my parking space.

'I refused medical aid. I didn't need it, except for a few shots of whiskey. Another policeman came in and said the master cylinder had been tampered with. No doubt of it. And it was done on the parking lot, because the brakes had been all right when I drove in, and there wasn't any traffic when I left so I just drove out without using the brakes. It wasn't until I started going down the hill that I used the brakes, and then it was too late.'

'And nobody but Western would have any desire to kill you?'

'Nobody.'

Fifty points out of a hundred in your favor now, he thought.

He said, 'Tell it from the beginning, or we'll wander all over the place. I'll keep quiet and ask questions later.'

'All right. You know my father was a professor of physics at the University of Big Sur, California?'

'I read it in the papers. By the way, all I know about the case is what I read in the *New York Times*. The local paper barely mentioned it.'

'Before he went to Big Sur, he taught at UCLA. Even then he must've been working on MEDIUM. He spent a lot of his time at home on equations, schematics, diagrams, tiny models of something or other. I saw them now and then when I'd come into his study, and I asked him once what he was working on. He said, in a joking manner, that he was working on something that would be the biggest thing since creation.'

'Western is supposed to have invented that phrase.'

'MEDIUM wasn't the only thing he stole from my father. Dad always kept the papers in his safe. But, after we moved to Big Sur Center, he built an electronic device of some sort. It was small, compared to MEDIUM, but it ate up tremendous quantities of power. You should have seen our electric bills.'

'Any of those bills survive the fire?' Carfax said. Then, hastily, 'I know I said I'd keep quiet, but there are some things . . .'

'No, they were all burned up. Of course, the power company had records. I say had, because when I asked for them, I was told that they had been destroyed. It was six months after the fire, and the company said it didn't keep records of paid bills any longer than that. It was part of their recycling policy.

'Anyway, I knew he was using a staggering amount of power.

We were living together, and I was sharing expenses. I was secretary to the university president then, you know. No, you wouldn't know. I was making good money, but I couldn't afford to split the power bill. He said he'd take care of all of it. But I knew Dad couldn't afford it. And, after a few months, he said he was going to a man from whom he could borrow money at a very low rate of interest. Guess who that was.'

Carfax was determined to say nothing.

'His nephew. My cousin. And yours. Dad got the money, but he must have been forced to tell Western what he was working on. Still, would anybody advance money for a crazy, far-out thing like MEDIUM? It'd be like lending money to build a perpetual-motion machine.'

Which, Carfax thought, was now theoretically possible. MEDIUM had opened the gateway to more things than communication with the dead.

'Dad must've got his machine to the point where he could give a convincing demonstration. I don't know. I never saw Western at our house, nor did Dad ever say anything about his being there. But he could have come there while I was working or maybe when I was off to Europe during the summer.'

Carfax wanted to ask her if she knew for certain that Western had advanced the money to her father.

As if reading his mind, she said, 'Dad suddenly started paying the power bills and buying more equipment. I knew he'd deposited twenty thousand dollars at one time and ten thousand at another.'

Carfax mouthed silently, 'Thirty thousand?'

'A good part went for electronic components and consoles and cabinets. Dad wouldn't tell me where he got the money or what the thing was he was working on. He said it'd all come out in good time, and meantime I wasn't to worry. The deposits were in cash, and receipts never did turn up. If there were any, they were burned. Or taken.

'I don't know why Dad wouldn't tell me what he was doing. I wouldn't have laughed at him or thought he was crazy. At least, I wouldn't have told him so.'

She stopped, frowned, and said, 'I must be honest. Yes, I

would have thought he was losing his mind, and I probably would have been unable to keep quiet about it. I would have told him what I thought. And I might have tried to get psychiatric help for him. I didn't believe in survival after death or, in fact, in anything of a supernatural nature. That's a redundancy, isn't it? Supernatural nature.

'But neither did Dad. Not as far as I knew. But my mother had died four years before, and he took it very hard. That's why I went to live with him. I was afraid he'd grieve himself to death or maybe even kill himself. And, well, I said I'd be honest. I needed him almost as much as he needed me. I loved my mother very much, and I'd just been divorced. I went to him so he could give me comfort and so I could give him comfort.'

She opened her purse, removed a delicate handkerchief, and dabbed at her eyes.

'It's possible that his desire to make sure she wasn't dead, that she did live, that he would see her again some day, be with her . . . didn't A. Conan Doyle take up spiritualism after his son died?'

'I think it was somebody in his family.'

'But, Dad, I'm certain, would want to approach the problem scientifically. He wouldn't go to a medium. And it's possible that Mom's death had little to do with his project. He may have serendipitously stumbled across the principles of MEDIUM. Only it wasn't such a happy discovery, as it turned out.'

Looking at the grass, still dew-wet, and at the birds, Carfax felt no intimations of immortality. If he felt anything, it was an intimation of continuity of life in this world. The dead were dead, and they would never come back unless it was in the form of food for soil. And man's burial customs often assured that he wouldn't even do that.

Now, he doubted even the continuity of life. Man was doing his best to kill off all life, himself included.

'It was the evening of March 17,' she said. 'I had driven up to Santa Cruz to visit some college friends, and I got back to the university about one that morning. I was tired but not unhappy, because I'd had a good time. The tank was almost

24

empty, and Dad would need the car in the morning because his was in the garage. He had to go to a department meeting in the morning, he said, but he didn't say why. So I decided to get a new tank before I went to bed. That probably saved my life. And then, just as I drove away from the service station . . .'

She swallowed audibly and, when she resumed, her voice was tight.

'I heard an explosion. The whole town heard it. The house was five blocks away from the station, but the noise sounded as if it were right beside me. The windows were blown out for blocks around, you know, and the neighbors were thrown out of bed.

'I . . . I had to stop for a couple of minutes. I was so shaken up. Then I drove home, very fast. Somehow, I knew whose house it was.

'The house was blown apart and burning; it was just one great bonfire. The firemen got there a few minutes after I did, and they spent the first hour trying to keep the houses next door from catching on fire, too. I just sat there, unable to move or speak, unable to do anything except watch the flames and the firemen and police and the mob that had gathered. Then one of the neighbors pointed me out to a policeman, or so she told me later, and the next I knew, I was being taken off in an ambulance. The doctor there gave me a sedative, and I woke up the evening of the next day. But I still wasn't thinking very well, and I was weak.

'They told me later what they found. Dad's body was blown out into the backyard, but a mass of flaming wood fell on him, and so he was not only . . . mangled, torn apart, really . . . he was burned beyond recognition. He was identified by his teeth only; our dentist had the records. And . . . and . . .'

She blew into her handkerchief and wiped her eyes with the tip of it. He went into the kitchen and came back with several kleenexes. The tears had ruined her makeup, and after she looked into a pocket mirror, she went upstairs to the bathroom to repair the damage. When she returned, she not only looked better, she managed a smile.

'The wall safe was shut,' she said, 'but it was empty. So it was obvious that it had been opened, the papers removed, everything removed, in fact, including my jewelry, and then it was closed. Whoever took the stuff must have forced Dad to open it for him.

'The police concluded that the explosion was caused by gas. The jets of the artificial log in the fireplace were shut tight, but the police thought that they must have been turned on until the house filled with gas. The windows and doors were all shut, and there was some evidence that they had been taped. The tape would've burned up, of course, but they, the police, I mean, had some way of determining that tape had been used.

'But Dad did not die from breathing in the gas. There wasn't any gas in his lungs. He had died of a blow on his head. At least, he had been hit on the head so hard that he should have died from the blow. But it couldn't be determined that he had been struck with some blunt instrument wielded by a man. It was possible that the explosion had driven some heavy object against his head. It didn't seem likely, however, for then he would have been breathing in the gas. So he must have been hit over the head before the gas was turned on.

'Then the killer turned on the gas – he must have been wearing an oxygen mask – waited until the house was full of gas and then set some device to ignite after he left and so cause the gas to explode. The police didn't find anything they could identify as the igniting device, but that may have been, must've been, destroyed in the explosion.

'The killer slipped out of the back door, closed it, and was gone by the time the gas exploded. The two models of MEDIUM were destroyed by the fire and the explosion. An electronics expert who examined them said that some circuits had been removed from them. He didn't know what the models were supposed to do; he'd never seen anything like them. And without the missing circuits installed, he would never be able to figure them out.

'Since the killer must've forced Dad to open the safe for him so he could get the MEDIUM schematics, Dad must've recognized him.'

Carfax could not restrain himself.

'Not if he wore a mask and disguised his voice.'

'I know. But he knew that there wasn't going to be any witnesses, so why should he bother concealing his identity? Anyway, whoever did it, Western was behind it, if Western didn't do it himself. He was the only one who could possibly have known what Dad was working on. It wasn't just a coincidence that Western announced he'd communicated with the dead only six months after my father died.

'I knew that Western had stolen Dad's plans, but how could I prove it? I didn't have any evidence that could stand up in court. But I wasn't going to fold my hands and let him get away with killing my Dad, not if I could possibly help it. So the first thing I did was to use my insurance money to move to Los Angeles and hire a detective agency to investigate Western.

'The news media have reported a lot about him, so I suppose you know his general background. He's got a B.A. in business administration, and he inherited his father's seven electronic-radio-TV stores. He took a number of technical courses in college, and he's got a first-class radiotelephone operator's license. But he doesn't have the knowledge or the genius to invent . . .'

'I'm sorry to interrupt again,' Carfax said, 'but you don't have to have a Ph.D. to be an inventor or a discoverer of new principles.'

'Yes,' she said, her eyes widening as if she were angry, 'but Western had apparently never done anything after he got out of college except run the business, play the stockmarket, and chase women. I'll tell you the type of man he is! The one time I was alone with him, after Dad's funeral, I went out on a date with him just to find out what he and Dad had been up to. In fact, I practically made sure he would ask me out. I called him and asked to talk to him about Dad. He took me to Scandia's to eat, and we had quite a few drinks. Then he said we could talk better in his apartment, quieter, you know, and I said that would be better. I hoped that, with enough drinks, and, I'll admit it, the tendency for a man to talk more if he's with a good-looking woman – I have little false modesty – that he'd say something he shouldn't.'

Her eyes were even wider, and her voice was no longer thin with grief but was thick with anger.

'He asked me to go to bed with him! His own cousin! And

27

he'd murdered my father! I'm afraid I acted stupidly then, but I was out of my mind! I slapped him, and I yelled at him that he had killed my father so he could steal the plans and that I was going to see that he paid for what he'd done. If the police didn't get him, I would.

'I never saw such a change come over a man. For a minute, I thought he was going to kill me, too, right there. But no, he was too smart, that one. He got his temper back as quick as if he'd turned a cold shower on himself. He said I'd better get out at once, and he didn't ever want to see me again. And if I started talking to other people like I'd done to him, he'd see I was shut up.

'He didn't say he'd kill me or anything like that. He just said he'd shut me up. I'm sure he didn't mean he'd do it in a legal manner. I got out of there as fast as I could.

'I found out later, from my agency, that Western sometimes lets women use MEDIUM even though they don't have enough money to rent it. If they were beautiful, he took it out in trade. The filth of the man!'

Carfax thought that it took two to make that sort of bargain.

'I wonder where your agency got its information?' he said. 'Those women wouldn't be likely to tell stories on themselves.'

'My agency has an inside man working for Western. He was told about those women by one of Western's secretaries. Western's staff is loyal, but she talked about him because she was in love with the agent and she thought it wouldn't go any further since he also claimed to be devoted to Western. The detective business is a dirty business, isn't it?'

'Yes. But few things get done in any business with clean hands.'

'Anyway, the agency got information from women who'd turned him down. *They* didn't mind talking!

'Now, I know you're wondering why, if Western is after me, he didn't get me long ago. It's been eight months since I told him what I suspected. If he wanted to kill me, he should have been able to do it by now. However, he *must* know that I've hired professionals to watch him. The two men who run the agency got anonymous phone calls telling them to drop me as a client. This was shortly after they found that my phone line was tapped and my house bugged. And the agency finally identified several men who'd been tailing me. They were from another agency, and that agency wouldn't, of course, tell who had hired it.'

'What was your agency? And the other one?'

'Fortune and Thorndyke was mine. Western's was the Magnum Security and Investigation Agency.'

Carfax nodded and said, 'Fortune and Thorndyke are in West Hollywood. Magnum is in downtown Los Angeles, and it's owned by Valmont. I know all three men quite well, since I've worked for them at one time or another.'

'Whatever made you decide to be a history professor?' Patricia said. 'I can understand why you'd quit the private-eye business. It must be very sordid and depressing and only occasionally exciting. Of course, your breakdown . . .'

He shrugged, and she continued, 'Well, it was in *Time*. It said you had a nervous breakdown when you were working on a case and that it was aggravated, your breakdown, not the case, I mean, when you were almost killed by a mudslide during those awful rains, and . . .'

'I was in a private sanitarium for a while and then at Mount Sinai in Beverly Hills. I was fortunate, or unfortunate, enough to get a psychotherapist who was a great artist in his profession.'

'Unfortunate?'

'Perhaps. Doctor Sloko convinced me, or got me to convince myself, that I really had been crazy and that I'd been suffering from a series of extraordinary and extremely realistic hallucinations. From then on I recovered fairly rapidly. But I'm still not sure that . . .'

'You must tell me about them some time. But I'm afraid that you have given Western a great advantage against you. If he chooses, he can refer to your breakdown and say, or at least hint, that you're undergoing another and so nobody should pay any attention to your science-fiction theory.'

Carfax made a face and said, 'I was well aware of that and of what my opponents could do with it. Western may use that if the going gets too tough for him. You . . .'

He stopped. He did not want to say that one person who had

definitely had mental trouble and another who might possibly be unbalanced would not make very good allies.

'We'll talk about that later,' she said. 'I came to you because you are my cousin and because you are definitely not pro-Western. And because you have had detective experience. And . . .'

'All right, let's have it,' he said. 'No more bush-beating.'

'What?'

'What are you going to ask me to do when I visit Western?'

'It's logical, isn't it?' she said, leaning even closer to him. 'But I realize I haven't any right to ask you, since you'll get just one session with MEDIUM. You'll probably want to talk to your wife or your parents or somebody dear to you. Or, since you're a history teacher, you might want to find out, oh, say, if Secretary of War Stanton really was behind Lincoln's assassination.'

'Lasalle of Chicago University is already working on that. He has a federal grant.'

He paused and then said, 'But finding out whether or not your father was murdered, and who did it, is far more important than the Lincoln assassination. In fact, this could be the most important murder case ever.'

She let out a deep breath and said, 'You'll do it!'

'I'll think about it.'

The insidious effect of this conversation, he told himself, was that he had been eased into contradicting his own theory. Instead of firmly keeping in mind that the entities were non-human but living, he had started to think of them as dead human beings. Patricia was appealing to him for help, yet she believed Western's claims.

FIVE

Gordon Carfax had intended never to see Los Angeles again.

Here he was, aboard a jet lowering on the flight path into the new Riverside International Airport.

Below, over western Arizona, the air was a thick gray-green. The mountains under them looked like a subterranean range seen through a glass-bottomed submarine. Down there was the Kofa Game Reserve, where, it was reported, the last of the wild North American pumas still roamed, though coughing and watery-eyed.

There were also some saguaro cacti, which had died out except in a few small areas. The polluted air, however, was only partially responsible for the near-extinction of the giant cactus.

The president of the United States had promised that within ten years, no matter what the cost, the smog would be back to the 1973 level.

The plane landed and taxied to its appointed station and was presently joined by a telescoping umbilical to the terminal. Carfax walked into the cavernous air-conditioned building. He recognized at once the tall thin man with the broad face and short gray hair. He had met Edward Tours over the viewphone when he had called Western back.

They shook hands and spoke briefly of the smog. However undesirable smog was, it did provide something to talk about. And to curse.

They continued to speak of such things as increasing taxes, beaches which turned away anybody who could not pass a beauty test, the Philadelphia Massacre, the Iranian crisis, and the declining literacy rate. By the time they had covered these subjects – or at least skimmed over them – Carfax's two suitcases dropped out of the slot. A little four-wheeled turtle moved under the cases as the steel arms lifted them in the air; the cases settled down on the flat back; it rolled up to Carfax and stopped a foot from him. Carfax dropped his plastic tag into its slot as two young men picked up the baggage. The turtle spun around and rolled away.

Tours and his two companions were dressed in bright orange summer afternoon business suits. They wore large silvery ankhs at the ends of silvery chains around their necks. The circles on top of the ankhs contained golden M's (for MEDIUM).

About half the crowd in the terminal was wearing the ankhs.

Tours said, 'We'll have to take the MTO, Doctor Carfax. Sorry about that, but we can't give VIP treatment any more. Not out of an airport, anyway. Besides being listed by the media as ecojerks, we'd be subjected to a fine. But you know . . .'

'I didn't expect a chauffeured limousine nor do I want one,' Carfax said. 'Besides, the MTO is a hell of a lot faster than the freeway.'

They walked to the MTO waiting room. A minute later, the Hollywood express entered with shushing and squeaking noise. They got into one of the egg-shaped cars of the train. A few minutes later, they were traveling at 250 kilometers an hour. Carfax, seated at the window, watched the countryside between the great white arches that supported the overhead rail. The smog didn't look as thick as it had from twelve thousand kilometers. And, so far, it hadn't bothered him, since he had not left a filtered air-conditioned environment.

The metropolis had pushed eastward about thirty-five kilometers, so that the former semidesert was now solid buildings, houses and streets. In the older part there were more high-rises, and some of the streets were now double-decked and multi-ramped. Some of the streets he had once traveled had disappeared under buildings. Many pedestrians carried emergency oxygen masks and tiny cylinders. Otherwise Los Angeles had not changed much.

Five minutes after leaving Riverside, the MTO stopped at the Highland-Sunset Station. The area around here had changed considerably. Many buildings had been torn down, and Sunset and Hollywood were double-decked.

The four men, Tours in the lead, went down the moving steps inside a plastic tunnel to the upper street level. Inside a small airhouse, one of of the new taxicabs waited for them. It was equipped with fuel cells, electric motors for each wheel, and a driver with a shaven head and wearing only electric-blue shorts and a scarlet neckerchief.

They moved slowly through the traffic west to the Nicholls Canyon outlet ramp. The new Nicholls Canyon Via took them directly to the private sideroad that ran along the hillside to Western's mansion. Half a kilometer up, a guardhouse and a drawbridge stopped them. The guardhouse swung out of the way after Tours had presented a coded tag and stuck his right thumb into a hole in an ID box. The drawbridge moved up, and they drove over it.

Massive pylons supported the road, which ran alongside the steep hill, branching out into other avenues which ended in ramps leading to various mansions set into cutbacks in the hillside. The entire hill had been manicured, terraced, and corseted with plastic, metal, and concrete, but the surface was mostly covered with ivy.

Through the heavy railing on the side of the road, Carfax could see a large parking lot at the bottom of the hill. This was beside a tall white apartment building. The many people on the lot seemed to be divided into about four groups, most of which were holding up large signs. A number of police cars were parked around the edge of the lot.

'Westernites and anti-Westernites,' Tours said. 'The large group is Westernite. The others are anti, but they don't like each other. One's Catholic, one's Southern Baptist, one's Church of Scientology, and the other, if I am not mistaken, is Carfaxite, if you'll pardon the term.'

'I haven't authorized any society to use my name,' Carfax said. 'Not yet, anyway.'

'You'd better tell them that, then,' Tours said.

Western's house was on the highest point of the hill. It was a three-story wooden and brick building in antebellum style. Five blacks in all-white clothes were working on the lawn and the flowering bushes by the great porch. Carfax almost ex-

33

pected a goatee-ed colonel and his hoop-skirted lady to come out on the porch.

'The gardeners are really security guards,' Tours said. 'The vegetation looks so green and healthy because it's plastic.'

'The mowers and the clippers?'

'No blades in the mowers; dull edges on the clippers. Mr. Western doesn't like a police-type atmosphere, but he has to have guards. Too many misguided people, like Phillips, for instance, you must have read about him, have tried to kill Mr. Western. Some fanatics think they can keep their religion from being discredited if they kill Mr. Western. They're crazy, of course.'

'I understand that Mr. Western talked to Phillips only six hours after he died.'

'Yes, Phillips was located and queried briefly. He hadn't recovered yet from the shock of becoming a *semb* and so wasn't a good contact. Mr. Western does plan to interview him again, though. He thinks Phillips's testimony now might convince others of Phillips's religion that he isn't a fake.'

The taxi stopped before a heavy metal gate at the end of the ramp. A few seconds later, the gate swung open. The taxi drove around to the side of the house and entered into the basement. The flexible doors swung shut behind them. The passengers got out, Tours gave his credit card to the driver, who stuck it in the meter slot and then returned it. The taxi drove off through the swinging doors. The gray-green smog was blown back from the entrance by the airblast as the doors opened.

Tours led Carfax up a staircase of twenty steps into an enormous and beautifully decorated room. The four men there seemed to have nothing else to do but lounge around and look tough. Carfax was ready to submit to a frisking, but nobody suggested it. He must have passed metal detectors on the way up, he thought.

They went down a high-ceilinged hall with murals which he recognized as copies of Etruscan frescoes. At its end was a small elevator. He and Tours entered and were taken up to the third floor. Tours did not touch the controls. They were probably dummies, and a man was probably watching them through closed-circuit TV while he operated the controls. Carfax wondered if the elevator went down into the garage.

They stepped directly into a large office with twenty desks, behind which were men and women talking over phones, dictating into typewriters, studying papers, or listening to recordings. A handsome middle-aged woman was introduced as Mrs. Morris, Western's private secretary. Smiling, she led them through a short hall and a small office with an unoccupied desk and computer console. Beyond this were a long hall and a narrow entrance into a small room. Tours waved at the TV camera set in the junction of wall and ceiling, and the door slid back into the wall.

The room beyond was very large and very chilly. Its walls were painted off-white and were bare of anything except some large charts, the nature of which he did not recognize. Except for a small desk and chair in one corner, and a few chairs here and there, the room had no furniture.

In its center was Western. Beyond him was MEDIUM.

SIX

Carfax had to give Western credit for one thing. He had made no effort to create a mystical atmosphere. There were none of the exotic trappings so often found in the seance chambers of the human medium. The room was bare and bright. The dull-gray one-decameter cube fronted by a curving console with its many panels, dials, switches, rheostats, indicator lights, and viewscreens and backed by enormous cables running down into the floor spelled out S-C-I-E-N-C-E. Western was not clad in flowing robes covered with astrological symbols. Nor did he look like a laboratory worker; he seemed to have just stepped off a tennis court. He wore white tennis shoes, no socks, light-green shorts, and a white sleeveless shirt. Thick black hair curled out over the deep V of the shirt; his thickly muscled legs were matted with black curly hair.

Carfax had expected him to be wearing the ankh with the M, but even that was lacking.

He smiled as he came toward Gordon and put out a large, powerful, and hairy hand.

When he smiled, he looked much like Patricia.

He talked easily with Carfax for a few minutes, asking him about the trip, making the usual comments about the smog, and remarking that life was tolerable in Los Angeles only if you stayed indoors six months of the year and if you had much money.

'Oh, not by the way,' he said, 'but very definitely relevant – has our cousin gotten in touch with you?'

Carfax had not expected such frankness. His entire campaign was wrecked in a few seconds.

It would be best to tell the truth, or, at least, as much of it as would be needed to convince Western that he was not lying.

36

Western might know that Patricia had been at his house.

'Yes,' he answered, hoping his manner was as easy as Western's. 'In fact, she flew out, unannounced, and was my guest for almost a week.'

Carfax had gone through his house very thoroughly, looking for bugs. He had found no evidence of them or of a phone tap. Patricia could have been followed to Busiris, or her destination could have been gotten from the airline. If the latter were true, it would be obvious whom she was going to see in Busiris.

'I'm not too surprised, Gordon,' Western said. 'I don't know what you think of her, but I think that she was driven off the deep end by her father's death. She loved him very much. Perhaps too much. And the circumstances of his death would be enough to deeply disturb even a well-balanced person.

'But she accused me of having stolen the plans for MEDIUM from her father and, of course, since one follows the other, of having murdered her father. Or did she tell you that? Of course, she did.'

Western certainly knew how to disarm. Who would believe that such openness could conceal a thief and a killer?

'Yes, she did,' Carfax said.

'And you expected, or at least hoped, to use MEDIUM, my own invention, to find out if she was telling the truth?'

'You're very perceptive,' Carfax said. 'To tell the truth, and that seems to be what both of us are doing, I wasn't sure that I would ask you to find my – our – uncle. I have my own interests, you know.'

Western laughed and said, 'I'll give you two sessions. I'll admit it will cost me, but I'm not entirely unselfish. I'm offering two for several reasons. One is that, if you're convinced I'm right, your following will die off. Your theory, and others like it, will be scotched aborning. I'm offering some free time to some of my other opponents, you know. I've got a mob of them coming in tomorrow. A trinity of Jesuits: a prominent physicist, an eminent theologian, and an authority on exorcism. The exorcist has my permission to conduct an exorcism if he wishes to.

'And with the Jesuits will be some prominent Anglican and

Methodist ministers, two rabbis, Orthodox and Reformed, a Christian Scientist, a Mormon, a famous atheist who's also a science writer, and the head of the African Animist Church, a Nigerian, I believe.'

He paused and then said, 'I don't know how objective that committee is going to be. After all, their religions, and that includes the atheists, since atheism is a form of religion, are likely to be shattered. And if that happens, then they may be shattered, too. A man's religion often is part of the deep core of his identity, you know. If that is broken, the self-image is threatened. Very few can stand up to that.

'But I hope you'll be as objective as possible. I don't know where you got your theory, unless it was from reading too many science-fiction books . . .'

Carfax winced. Western smiled and said, 'Pardon me. There's really nothing ridiculous about the premises of your theory, but I believe that the facts invalidate it.'

His voice became louder, and his face became somewhat red.

'Great God! What more do people want? The federal commission made a thoroughly exhaustive inquiry, and you know what its unofficial report was! Like it or not, MEDIUM is a means for communicating with the supernatural, though I prefer my own term, *embu*, meaning *e*lectromagnetic-*b*eing-*u*niverse. The official report has not been published yet, as everybody knows, because the president is afraid of the repercussions. He's damned if he says, yes, it's true, and damned if he says, no, it's not true. But the report will have to be issued soon. There's too much pressure on to keep it back forever.'

'I know,' Carfax said.

'No doubt you do. There's enough talk about it in the news media. However, you're anxious to get going, and I'm anxious to have this cleared up. Not that Patricia could really hurt me, but she could be a nuisance.'

He spoke into a screen in a console panel.

'Harmons!'

A moment later, a short, fat, baldheaded man in white shoes, trousers, and a long white laboratory coat appeared.

'Harmons is our chief first-shift engineer,' Western said. 'He'll stand by in case anything goes wrong with MEDIUM or you need help. MEDIUM is a giant piece of instrumentation, but it's as delicate as a baby kitten. Even the masses of our bodies affect it. When it's in operation, we allow no more than three people to get within a meter of it. And it's better if only one . . .'

A light, on what Carfax had thought was a piece of blank wall, flashed red. Western leaned over the console and said, 'Yes?'

'Mrs. Sharpe calling you, Mr. Western.'

'Tell her I'll call back later.'

'Yes sir, but she says it's urgent.'

'Later!'

'Yes, sir!'

Western straightened up. His voice had been harsh, but he was smiling now and, when he spoke, it was gently.

'The woman's very old and very wealthy. And whom does she want to talk to? Her late husband? Her late parents? Her late children? The late Jesus? No, she wants to talk to her late dog!'

He shook his head.

'She's leaving all her money to an animal hospital, and there are children out there dying . . .'

He stopped, bit his lip, and then said, 'Well, shall we get started?'

Gordon Carfax sat down in the chair indicated by Western. He knew that, according to theory, everything that radiated, or had radiated, electromagnetic energy in this universe also existed in electromagnetic form in the other universe. This justified Western's insistence on calling a dead human by the name of *semb*, an initialization of *s*entient *electrom*agnetic *b*eing. Western had tried to avoid using such emotion-loaded and unscientific terms as spook, ghost, spirit, departed, and so forth. He had invented a vocabulary which, however, the man in the street and the news media were largely ignoring.

He had also stated many times that he could not locate individual animals. It was difficult enough to locate human beings, impossible in many cases, and always impossible for animals. But he still got requests, even demands and threats, from many pet lovers.

Western sat down by Carfax and pressed a START button on a panel to Carfax's right. Most of the several hundred lights on the console lit up.

'We use vacuum tubes in the main circuits,' Western said. 'Transistors and such small stuff can't handle the enormous load of power. Actually, what you see before you is only the tip of the iceberg. The main equipment is on the floor below. It's hooked up to the Four Corners atomic-energy power plants. The only California power we use is for the phones and lights elsewhere in the house.

'The air-conditioning for this room is automatically controlled at an exact 70 plus or minus one degree Fahrenheit. Some of the elements and components are very delicate. There are six circuits enclosed in liquid xenon or liquid hydrogen. And that's all I'm going to tell you about MEDIUM's physical aspects.'

A red light came on over an unmarked dial. Western reached up and turned it counterclockwise 76 degrees. He picked up a keyboard attached to the console by long thin cables and punched about a dozen letters and numerals in rapid succession.

'I'm saving us much time because I've already located Uncle Rufton. I did it for my own purposes some time ago. But I would have done it, anyway, since I suspected you would want to make contact with him. His coordinates are on tape, and we will run them off right now, if you don't object.'

He took an octagonal punched card from the inner pocket of his shirt and inserted it in a slot. The card disappeared as silently and as swiftly as a mouse into a hole.

'You'll get a chance to see how we make a search during your second session,' Western said. 'That's scheduled for two days from now. We never permit a client more than three sessions a week. His nervous system can't stand more than that. There's something about contact with the *embu*, something we can't isolate and identify, that disturbs the client. And the operators, too. We take turns operating MEDIUM. This, by the way, is my first this week, so I'll be able to be with you during your second. I'm saving *my* second for tomorrow's session with the theological-cum-exorcism committee.'

While he was talking, he was watching various lights: PROG ST; SRCH LCK; STTC REP; REPEL.

A yellow light flashed above SRCH END, and a buzz came from one of the panels.

Western punched a button under HOLD just after a large viewscreen in front of Carfax became alive. It was milky and filled with what seemed to be thousands of tiny circling sparks.

'Just remember,' Western said, 'you're not seeing the true form of these . . . creatures. You're seeing an electronic analogy. The shapes are the machine's interpretation of the actual shapes. What they really look like, we don't know. There's much that we don't know, so I won't be able to explain everything in that universe any more than I can in this universe.'

He pressed the RLS button under HOLD. The sparks became fewer, and the spaces between them widened. It was as if Carfax were sitting in a spaceship going faster than light and approaching galaxies which were so far away that each had seemed a single point of light, though composed of millions of stars. There was no Doppler shift affecting the light, of course, since this was not faster-than-light space travel. Nor was the device traveling. It was pouring more power into that 'otherworld' or *embu*, and was, in theory at least, 'attracting' the desired configuration to it.

'Whatever entity, whatever inanimate object, radiates electromagnetic energy in our universe is caught up in a configuration in the *embu*. When the source of radiation dies, or ceases to radiate, in this universe, it becomes final in the *embu*, that is, takes a final form. A lightning streak is an inanimate object. In my theory, anyway. It's true that the lightning streak's energy is not lost in our universe. It's dissipated or undergoes transformation, just as sunshine does. But in the *embu* the lightning streak lives on, you might say. And just so, a cockroach or a man lives on.'

'Sunshine is too diffuse to be an inanimate object,' Carfax said. 'The sun shines at all times. It's the rotation of the earth which brings on night, but on earth only. Even in night, there's a certain amount of light. Does each individual night come to life, as it were, in the *embu*? And how can it, when there is no such thing as an individual night? Where would the dividing line be? Surely our time-zone limitations would have no reflection in the *embu*?'

'That I don't know,' Western said with just a touch of irritation. 'Asking me that is like Queen Isabella asking Columbus to describe everything in the New World when he had just made a few landings on the shores of a few islands off the still unsuspected continent.'

'Sorry,' Carfax said.

'I suppose that the energy of the sun itself, as a flaming sphere, and the energy reflected from objects in space, such as our planet, are both present in the *embu*. At the moment, however, we are concerned only with the human beings of the *embu*. We know, for instance, that each is received at death into a configuration, or a colony, of older beings. This colony is composed of a rigidly determined number. There are eighty-one humans or *sembs* in a colony. Rather, I should say there are only eighty-one potential orbits, since a colony has to have a nucleus of one around which others collect, and there are many new colonies forming and, thus, many incomplete ones.

'Eighty-one is nine times nine, and so the mystics have been having a field day with that. And the communists would be making something ideological out of the *sembs*' communal system too, except that they flatly deny the possibility of an afterlife of any sort. I've invited Russia and China to send over their own investigating committees for free sessions. But they've rejected my offers.'

'They've used my theory,' Carfax said, 'though it wasn't my intention to give them aid and comfort. Or to give the Roman and Orthodox Catholics and Protestant fundamentalists support. But their siding with me makes it difficult for people who would otherwise have accused me of being a godless commie.'

The screen had suddenly shown only one spark, and then, even more suddenly, the spark was revealed as a complex of orbiting sparks.

'Notice the central spark, or *semb*,' Western said. 'The others revolve around it in what looks to the untutored eye like crazy random orbits. But we've analyzed the patterns of several colonies, and the *sembs* follow very complicated but limited and repetitive orbits. We have detected new *sembs*, the recently dead, sometimes displacing the nuclear *semb*. A *semb* becomes finalized – I hate that word but it's part of our jargon here – and when this happens, the finalized being sometimes takes over the nuclear role. What that means, I don't know. But I suspect that force of personality has something to do with it.'

Western turned a rheostat, and the screen was filled with a single spark. At this close range, it was a globe of light. It began to slide off to the right of the screen, and Western pressed an AUT FIX button. The globe drifted back toward the center of the screen.

'Uncle Rufton,' Western said.

Carfax said nothing.

'Heisenberg's principle works in the *embu* somewhat as it does here. The closer the observation, the more power required. The more power, the more we influence both the colony and the individual *semb* contacted. The power upsets the e-m bonds and disturbs the orbits. The *sembs* report an uneasy feeling, and they get panicky if the contact is maintained for over an hour.'

Carfax had to keep reminding himself that he was not to think of *sembs* as the human dead. They were some kind of alien being in a universe 'at right angles' to his. But Western's matter-of-fact attitude was subtly influencing. It overrode his defenses without his being aware of it. He had to fight in order to remember his own theory.

And now, confronted with a thing which Western stated was their uncle, Carfax felt the beginning of dread. His heart was beating swiftly. He was sweating, despite the cold air. A sense of unreality was numbing him. His scalp and the back of his neck seemed to be turning to arctic rock.

'If you're like everybody else that ever sat there, you're experiencing the impact of the numinous,' Western said. 'We live in the age of enlightenment, of freedom from superstition, or so it's claimed. But even the least spiritual of men is suddenly gripped by fear and by awe when he sits there. I've had clients who were as eager as hounds at a hunt to speak to their dead.

But, as soon as they were faced with them, they bolted. Or fainted. Or became paralyzed. The Old Stone Age never really dies in us.'

Carfax could not trust himself to speak. He was sure his voice would be high and trembling.

'If we could get closer, we might see that that globe of light is composed of smaller units,' Western said. 'But there's a definite limit to the nearness we can attain. If we increase the power when we reach that limit, the so-called attraction suddenly becomes a repulsion. The *semb* begins to recede, and the colony feels a sense of disruption.'

The screen was suddenly shot with thin twisting white streaks, behind which the globe became less bright.

Western turned a rheostat marked STTC CNTL, and the threads became black and then drifted off the screen.

'Static. At least, that's my name for the phenomenon. The colony got too close to a center of wild energy. Normally, when that happens, the colony is in trouble. The wild energy threatens the e-m bonds that hold the colony together and causes great mental distress to the *sembs*. The colony can't get away from the static fast enough. And that means that we might lose contact. So the static control circuit of MEDIUM applies more energy to keep a hold on the colony. What it does, we think, is supply the colony with the energy needed to get away from the static, but we still keep our lock on the colony.'

He pressed a button marked CON and said, 'O.K., here goes with the audio.'

The *semb* could not actually speak, of course. Speech required vocal chords, and the *semb* was, as far as anyone knew, a pure energy configuration. But it could move the electrical analog of its lips and its tongue and its vocal chords and its lungs, and the analog of its cerebral-neural system and muscles functioned electronically as it had in life.

The voice that came out of the speaker was not exactly Rufton Carfax's. It resembled it but had a stiffness and metallic quality which made it sound like a robot trying to imitate a human voice.

Patricia had brought along a small recorder and played a tape of her father's voice for Carfax. Carfax had listened to it many times, and now he recognized the voice as that of his uncle's, despite its robotic quality.

'I . . . feel you again,' it – he? – said. 'Don't leave me again. Please! Don't leave me!'

'We'll be with you for some time, uncle,' Western said. 'This is your nephew Raymond this time, uncle. And the next voice you'll hear will be your other nephew. Gordon Carfax. He has some questions, uncle. I hope you'll be cooperative.'

Had Western's voice sheathed a threat? Or was he being overly suspicious and so had supplied the hint of threat himself? What could Western possibly threaten his uncle with? Withdrawal of communication?

It struck him that Western had used his new name. This might or might not mean anything, since it was possible that his uncle had known about his name change before he died. And perhaps Western, during previous contacts, had told him about it. Carfax filed away this item with the intention of asking Western about it later.

Western whispered, 'Go ahead.'

Carfax's throat closed up. He was actually about to talk to a dead man. What do you say to a dead man?

But, according to his own theory, this was not a dead human.

Reminding himself of that did not help him. Whether a dead human or an other-universe sentient, this thing frightened him.

After being nudged by Western, Carfax said, 'Hello, uncle.'

'Hello, Hal,' the semimechanical voice said.

'It's Gordon now, uncle,' Carfax said, his throat beginning to open up.

'Oh, yes, Gordon, that's right. Raymond just reminded me of that again, didn't he?'

Carfax wished his numbness would thaw. He was not thinking as quickly and as clearly as he should.

'I have some questions, uncle,' he said.

'They all do,' the voice said.

Carfax blinked his eyes and shook his head. Was his brain deceiving him, or was the globe expanding and contracting, as if it were a photonic lung working to expel ectoplasmic air for a ghostly voice?

45

(But the human mind had to cast everything into an anthropomorphic mold.)

'How are you, uncle?' said Carfax. (As if he were meeting him on the street!)

'It would take me a long time to tell you exactly how things are here, my boy. When I say time, I don't mean time as you know it. But I don't have the language to tell you what time is here. I'd take time, all of my time, Gordon, if you had the time. But you don't. Raymond tells me that time is money, as far as MEDIUM is concerned, anyway.

'It's lonely here, boy, though I don't lack company. But it's not company that I chose. And it's weird here. They tell me that after a while the strangeness wears off, and then the world we left becomes the strange world. But I don't believe them.'

'I'm sorry if you're unhappy, uncle,' Carfax said. 'But your universe does have some advantages, and where there's life there's hope.'

He stopped. A second later, a flat metallic hooting laughter came from the speaker. It finally stopped, though Carfax had been afraid that it would go on and on.

'Speak up, nephew,' the voice said.

'Yes, uncle. First, did you invent a machine to communicate with, uh, the dead?'

There was a long silence. Then the voice said, loudly, 'I? Of course not! My nephew, Raymond Western, invented it! He's a genius! The greatest man who ever lived! We had no hope before, but we do now be . . .'

Carfax waited a few seconds and then said, 'Because of what, uncle?'

'Because we were cut off forever, we thought, from the world we left behind, what else, you simpleton? You don't seem to understand that we're as wildly excited about MEDIUM as you are!'

Carfax did not believe that that was what his uncle had meant to say, but he had no way of proving it. And he had to be tactful with his questions, because his uncle could not be forced to talk if he did not wish to do so.

His uncle? He must remember that this thing could be of nonterrestrial origin.

His next question caused Western to straighten from his slump. Carfax saw him out of the corner of his eye, and he wished that he could watch both him and the screen at the same time.

'Tell me, uncle, can you, uh, people, ever get through to this world via human mediums? Or are human mediums all fakes?'

There was another silence. Western slumped back into his chair, though his fingers drummed on the console. Carfax looked at his wristwatch. If Patricia had phoned, she wasn't being routed through to Western.

A hand coming into the area of his side vision made him jump. But it was only that of a man who had entered with a note for Western. He unfolded it, read it, frowned, put it back in his pocket, and stood up.

'I'll be back in a few minutes,' he whispered. 'Harmons will take care of you.'

Carfax hoped that it was Patricia's call which had taken him away. Harmons would be listening, and the interview was being taped so that Western could run anything he'd missed. But it might be too late for him to do anything about it.

'Your nephew, Western, is gone now,' Carfax said. 'You can speak freely.'

Harmons sat down in the chair Western had vacated. He did not look at Carfax or even seem aware of what Carfax was saying. But Western may have told him to say nothing.

'What?' the voice said. 'What do you mean? Why shouldn't I speak freely when he's around?'

'Your daughter . . .'

'My daughter! Why hasn't she talked to me? Just because I'm dead and can't do her any good . . .'

'She's afraid to come here. She's afraid of Western. Listen, if you were murdered . . .'

'Didn't Raymond tell you that I don't know how I died?' he said. 'I went to sleep, and awoke, if you can call this awakening, here. I was in shock . . .'

'Yes, Western told me that over the phone. But if you didn't invent MEDIUM, what were you working on that ate up so much power that you had to borrow money from Western?'

47

Carfax shook his head again. The globe seemed to be expanding and contracting at a faster rate.

'Ask Western,' the voice said. 'I've told him the complete details. Don't waste time with such questions.'

'I will ask him,' Carfax said. 'But did you tell him why you kept your work from your daughter, why she couldn't be told?'

'All right. If I'd told her I was building a device to detect and interpret messages from outer space, she would have thought I was crazy. But I thought that I'd found a certain pattern in interstellar *noise*, and if I was right . . . but I wanted to keep it secret until I knew for sure that I wasn't on a false trail.'

'Why would a receiver take so much power?' Carfax said. 'I could understand it if it was a transmitter.'

Carfax tried to think of his original question. He had asked his uncle, or the thing, whatever it was, something about . . . something about . . .

The globe had become much larger; the brightness was suddenly around him.

He reared up off the chair, crying out and trying to push against the light. He turned and ran, stumbling, half-blinded by the brilliance, to the door. It opened automatically for him, and he was out in the hall.

The brightness around him faded and then was gone.

He was sitting slumped against the wall, breathing as hard as if he had run for several blocks at top speed. His heart was thumping, and his chest hurt. He was cold except around his crotch and his thighs. Later, he would realize that he had wet himself.

Western had appeared from nowhere and was leaning over him. He looked very strange.

'What happened?' he said.

Carfax felt very alone, weak, and helpless. He was in a building from which he could leave only by Western's permission.

48

SEVEN

Carfax got onto his feet and leaned against the wall. It felt reassuring at first. But ghosts could come through solid walls, or walls thought to be solid. Actually, there was no such thing as a solid object if you thought of it in terms of molecules and atoms. The spaces among the microcosmos of atoms were vast, and many things could slip through them.

He moved away from the wall, as if glowing tentacles would reach through the interstices of invisible worlds and snatch him back through them.

'I thought that thing – uncle Rufton – had leaped out of the screen and was about to wrap itself around me.'

Western did not laugh. He said, 'Let's get some coffee.'

They walked down the dull white corridor and went around a corner and into a small room. This had bright murals of sea life, derived from some Cretan murals, no doubt, what with its blue octopi and orange dolphins. The rug displayed black bulls dashing at naked brown-red boys and girls who were leaping every which way from the bulls' paths or grabbing the horns preparatory to a forward flip onto the beasts' backs. In one corner a huge silvery urn perked. Western went to it and picked up a large ceramic mug.

'Cream or sugar?' Western said.

'I don't want any coffee, thank you.'

Western added two cubes of sugar and a generous amount of cream to his coffee and stirred it vigorously.

Western blew on the coffee to cool it, took several sips, and then said, 'You can see now why we require our clients to sign papers freeing us of all liability. And why we also required that the records of a physical examination by an M.D. be sent us before we process applications.'

'What about all those old people who've hired MEDIUM?' Carfax said. 'Surely? . . .'

'None of them showed indications of advanced heart trouble or of mental disturbances.'

'The old woman who wants to speak to her dog?'

'She won't be accepted.'

'What about my experience?'

Western raised his thick eyebrows and said, 'I was coming to that. You're not the first to see that globe of light rush at you. But it's a visual hallucination. I can assure you of that. There is no possible way for a *semb* to escape the bonds of its colony or to get through the barrier between this universe and its own universe. I don't know what causes this phenomenon. I don't even have a theory, though I'm sure the effects are purely psychological.'

'Are there any other such phenomena?' Carfax said.

'Yes. Sometimes a client has just the opposite of your experience. He feels that he's being pulled into the screen.'

'Why haven't I read about this?' Carfax said. 'I've read everything about MEDIUM I could get hold of.'

'It's not that we're hiding anything sinister. Nor do we require that our clients keep quiet about such things. We're not publishing anything about it, as yet. We're afraid that such information might suggest to people that they'll experience these phenomena, and so they will. We do plan on publishing sometime in the future. But only after we have a fairly reasonable theory to account for them. That way, we can reassure people before they sit down at MEDIUM. You must not forget that MEDIUM is new, that only about six hundred people have used it so far. There are many things that we could publish, but we prefer to evaluate these before publication.'

Carfax did not find the explanation satisfactory, but he had no definite rebuttals.

'You keep saying *we*,' he said. 'I thought that you were the one who made the decisions here.'

Western smiled and said, 'I am head of the team, yes. And I do own MEDIUM and expect to own it for some time to come. I am keeping its principles and theory of operation a close secret, you know. I haven't even applied for a patent, because

I don't want anyone stealing its schematics from the patent office. Believe me, it would be done. This is, as you are no doubt tired of hearing, the greatest thing since creation.'

'Which is why you won't be able to keep it to yourself,' Carfax said.

'We'll see.'

'I think I'll go now,' Carfax said.

Western put the cup down and said, 'Of course. I'd like to talk to you later about this when I have more time. And when you've recovered enough to think about it with the calmness of retrospect. Perhaps you could tell me by tomorrow, though, whether or not you'll be taking up my offer of a second free session.'

Carfax felt his skin warming up. Western was hinting that he was afraid. Which, he had to admit to himself, he was. But he certainly was not going to pass up another chance.

'I can tell you now,' he said. 'I'm looking forward to another session. And next time, I won't bolt. At least, I don't think I will.'

'Very well,' Western said. He seemed to be looking oddly at Carfax, but Carfax told himself that this might be a reflection of his own disturbed state.

'Do you want to make contact with uncle Rufton again?'

Carfax swallowed and then said, 'No. I'd like to speak to Frances.'

'Your wife.'

'The thing that is pretending to be my wife,' Carfax said.

Western grinned. He said, 'You still cling to your theory that *sembs* are nonhuman, alien entities. Well, why not? You really haven't seen anything to *prove* otherwise.'

'That's a very fair-minded statement,' Carfax said.

'I try to be logical about this. Objectivity isn't easy, since I'm so close to this. But I realize what a scientific proof demands and how little I can really offer. I have demonstrated that a phenomenon does exist, that there is *another* universe and that sentient entities exist in *that* universe. There can be no doubt about that; there's no fakery about MEDIUM.

'But, on the other hand, are these entities really the *souls*, or whatever you wish to call them, really *sembs*, as I call them?

51

If they're not, how do they succeed in knowing so much about the people they claim to be? Why are those who claim to be English-speakers able to speak English with the true accent? Could alien sentients reproduce not only the general English accent but the personal? Everyone contacted by someone who knew the dead when he lived has recognized the voice as being genuine. You heard uncle Rufton. There are certain distortions because of our still-primitive electronic means. But you recognized our uncle's voice didn't you? I certainly did.'

'The greater weight of the evidence is on your side,' Carfax said. 'I'll have to admit that. But it's possible that these *sembs*, as you call them, have means of learning about human beings and of feeding back information about them – of posing as them. How, I don't know. But you can't deny that that's a possibility.'

'No, but I do maintain that it's a very unlikely possibility. And why would they be posing as the spirits of the dead? What could they get out of it? They can't possibly *do* anything to us!'

Carfax felt irritated, but he recognized its source. Western was being too reasonable, and he was too likable. He certainly did not seem to be the person described by Patricia. He could, of course, be an excellent actor. There was no doubt that he was extremely tactful and that he knew how to go about making friends. Or, at least, how to act friendly. Carfax wanted to believe Patricia's story. He was finding it difficult to do so. And this ended in his feeling that he was betraying Patricia and himself.

Western escorted him back to the main office and delivered him into the hands of Mrs. Morris. Carfax had one question before he left. Would the examination by the religious committee be shown on TV?

'If the networks agree not to censor any of it,' Western said. 'I don't want any editing that will give a false impression. You'll notice I didn't say unfavorable. I said false. I just want the truth presented. But there is very powerful resistance to showing this session on TV, you know. You didn't? Oh yes, there are many established religious organizations that have objected to its being put on TV. This, mind you, even though they don't know what the results will be. Or do they suspect the truth and so fight against it? Well, enough of this. See you Thursday at ten.'

Western turned away but stopped, hesitated, and turned back to Carfax. He was smiling.

'Tell Patricia she can come along if she wants to.'

Carfax did not reply. He felt that he was anything but master of the situation. Western had found out that Patricia had flown in on a separate plane from Busiris. In fact, she should be phoning him at his hotel shortly after he got there.

The trip to the hotel on Wilshire did not allow him to think about what had happened. The TV in the cab was set on a news station.

'At 15:35 today, Crawford Goolton, of 6748, Westminster Spiral, apartment 6J, was allegedly killed while selling a Do-It-Yourself Spirit Communication Handypak to Anastasia Rodriguez, 99653, Crewles Castle Towers, apartment 89F. The alleged slayer, Maui Aleakala, of 347A4D, New Paradise Cabañas, is reported to have attacked Goolton with a knife. He is reported to have been in a rage because a Handypak sold to him by Goolton the week before had, allegedly, failed to perform as claimed . . .'

How, Carfax wondered, could a person be allegedly killed? Either they were or they weren't. But the news media had to be very careful about how they phrased their reports. The libel and slander suits were clogging the courts now as much as the marijuana cases had a decade ago. The result was that the news media were using some rather peculiarly phrased statements nowadays. In this age, when full nudity was nothing exceptional on daytime TV and sex education films with views of most of the possible positions and group combinations were being shown after 22.00 (when the kiddies were in bed), censorship was steadily cutting down freedom of speech in other areas.

The people of the United States still had not learned that freedom entails responsibility, and it looked as if they would not learn for a long time. The only ones to teach them would have to be themselves, but no one seemed to know how to get the lessons started.

You had to make a choice between the abuses of democracy and those of totalitarianism.

He reminded himself that he had something more immediate to consider. There was nothing he could do to bring about a swift or even a slow change in the world outside. Nothing that made him feel that he was getting results, anyway. But he could – perhaps – determine whether or not Western was right. He could – perhaps – find out whether or not Patricia was right.

'. . . from now on, the air pollution index should indicate a steady decrease of pollutants. Every day sees at least five hundred vehicles with internal-combustion motors retired, replaced by the battery or fuel-cell vehicles. The ESD is confident that the worst days are over, that the record peak of . . .'

That was welcome news, but it wasn't the first time he'd heard its like. Two years ago, electrohydrodynamic generators were to be a household item in a short time. These would revolutionize society and reduce pollution at once. But the devices were still in the experimental stage, and there were a number of disadvantages to their use which had been overlooked when they were first proposed.

The Hotel La Brea occupied two blocks of what had been a dozen office buildings when Carfax had lived in L.A. It was across the street from the La Brea tar pits. Carfax decided to look again at the leftover of the Pleistocene. He walked across the overpass above Wilshire and then walked down to where the corner of Wilshire and Curson had been. Curson had been removed and made part of the park, and the buildings for a block eastward had also been torn down.

He went around the wire fence and stood within a few feet of the two concrete mammoths at the edge of the tar pit. The gigantic father mammoth and the baby mammoth were watching the mother sink into the thick black waters of the pit. The baby was stretching his little trunk out toward his doomed mother as if he could trumpet her out of the tar and back to safety. The great female was struggling vainly against the oily clutch that had killed so many thousands of beasts large and small.

Many people were surprised and disappointed at the smallness of the pit. Evidently they had expected something covering many acres. But all that was left of the great reaches of tar that had once covered much of Los Angeles in this valley was a pool not as large as a football field. There were several very small pools behind the museum, and these still caught animals, such as gophers and squirrels, even though they had to climb over wire fences to get inside to the pool. If the disappointed tourist walked around the park, however, he would see tar oozing up here and there from the grass. He would, if he had any imagination, get an uneasy feeling. The liquid bitumen lay beneath the grass and the concrete not too far beneath, and it was waiting. Someday, that dark ooze said, someday this thin shield will be gone, and I'll be back. And things will be as they were. The mammoths and the dire wolf and the great lion and the saber-tooth and the camel and the giant sloth won't be here. But there will be other animals for me to pull down. And perhaps a man now and then, a man clad in skins, hunting the animals, unwary enough to get trapped.

Carfax did not stand before the pit very long. His eyes stung and watered, and the lining of his nose and throat felt hot. He hurried back to the hotel and entered its triple doors and the comparatively clean and cool air inside. In the evening, the cloud-seeding activities of the day might bring rain, and the air of the metropolis would be breathable for another three days. It was the seeding, which, though expensive and not always fruitful, made life in L.A. possible. It was this that gave it hope and kept the citizens going until the time would come when the electric cars would bring the air back to the 1973 level.

The world was polluted more than it had been ten years ago, but it should be much cleaner in the next ten. The prophets of doom would be wrong.

Carfax ate supper in the hotel dining room. About ten minutes after he got back to his room, his phone rang. He turned it on and saw Patricia in a booth in the Riverside airport.

'Have a good trip?' he said.

'I couldn't relax,' she said, but she smiled.

'You don't look tense,' he said. 'You look quite relaxed. And lovely.'

'Thank you. Did you find . . . never mind. I'll see you in

55

'. . . your place. Or do you think it'd be wise to stay in the same place?'

'I'm sure our line isn't tapped,' he said. 'Not yet, anyway. Sure, come on as planned. I don't really think that . . .'

She frowned and said, 'Think what?'

'Never mind,' he said. It would probably anger her if he said that he did not really believe that Western was dangerous. Not dangerous in the sense she meant, anyway, though he might be dangerous to humanity in general. Besides, he shouldn't be making any such statements when he did not have any evidence for them.

'Just come on out,' he said. He waited to make sure that she had no other messages, but she said, 'All right,' and the screen went blank.

EIGHT

Patricia phoned him when she checked in. He told her the voice code to open his door. He had ordered a supper for her but it had not yet arrived. The kitchen supervisor had apologized, saying that the meal had been sent out on the robot 'turtle' and had gotten as far as the elevator. Then it had broken down, and it was being repaired by the hotel tech. The other turtles were all in use, but the meal would not be more than half an hour late if the supervisor had to bring it up himself.

The announcer spoke Patricia's open-sesame, and the door opened. She looked lovely in her nina, an outfit consisting of a very short skirt and a stiff triangular fabric suspended from her neck and hanging loosely over her breasts. Both articles looked as if they were fashioned from grass, though they were plastic. They were based on the costume worn by the White Goddess of the Izaga, Nina T—, in the TV series, *Trader Horn*. Carfax was dressed in a 'white explorer's' outfit though he did not wear the pith helmet. Patricia sat down carefully, since she wore nothing under the skirt, and she was careful not to bend over or to turn too suddenly because she would expose her breasts. Carfax thought this modesty ridiculous, since she would appear on the beach in nothing at all. But the mores of clothes-wearing were not based on any sort of rationality, though each item of apparel had its own internal system of consistency.

Patricia showed no evidence of self-consciousness, though she surely must have had some thoughts about the very small amount of covering and the insecurity of fastening even that little. He certainly could not keep his mind off it, just as he could never keep from being sexually aroused by the sight of a

57

good-looking girl in a miniskirt. Which meant that he had been in a continual state of excitement for many years.

However, she was his first cousin, and that should cool him off. Should, he thought, but of course it didn't. Especially when you considered that the tabu against incest had been decaying steadily for the past fifteen years.

He would do better not to think about such things. Which was like the sea telling itself to pay no attention to the pull of the moon.

She lit a cigarette, puffed on it a few times while looking at Carfax through the smoke and then said, 'Won't you tell me what happened at Western's?'

He told her everything that seemed relevant. When he finished, he knew that he had angered her. The long slow puffs of cigarette smoke had become short and quick. But he was mistaken. Neither he nor Western was the object of her anger.

'Why would he *lie* about his invention?' she said loudly. 'Why would he? What's the matter with the man? Can't he stand up for himself even when he's dead?'

'I don't understand,' he said.

'I mean that he was always wishy-washy! He had no backbone! He would do anything rather than make somebody angry; and he could not stand being around an angry person! Why, I only had to look mad, and I got my way at once! It made it easy for me to get whatever I wanted, except the one thing I wanted most and couldn't get!'

Literature was full of descriptions of women whom anger made more beautiful. Patricia certainly wasn't one of them. A bitch on wheels of fire, Carfax thought.

'And what was that one thing you most wanted and couldn't get?' he said, since Patricia evidently expected him to ask.

'What do you think?'

'You wanted him to stand up to you.'

She looked surprised and then pleased.

'You're very perceptive. I like that.'

'It didn't take much intelligence to see that,' he said. He leaned forward. 'To be frank, Patricia, no matter how pathological your father was about anger, he would now have no motive to lie. He's dead, and he can't be hurt by anybody in this world, and he surely would want the credit for MEDIUM if he had in . . .'

'In what?'

He smiled and said, 'Here I am talking as if the entity who calls himself your father really *is* your father. It's difficult to keep from thinking that those things are the dead, however.'

'Gordon, I don't want to get into an argument with you about this. I know that Dad invented a machine to get into contact with the dead, and I know that those *are* the dead! I don't like to agree with Western, because he murdered my father. But he is right in what he claims MEDIUM can do. And you yourself said that it was my father's voice. Now, I wonder if Western doesn't have more power than he says he does. I mean, maybe he can not only talk to the dead and see them, but has some way of controlling them too. Maybe he can inflict pain if they don't do what he says.'

'How could he?'

'How would I know?' she said angrily. 'You told me he said that energy can affect them. Maybe he pours in a lot of energy and this is painful to them.'

'Or maybe . . .'

'Yes?'

She leaned forward and to one side to punch out her cigarette in the tray, and the shield swung aside. Her breasts were shapely and full, neither too small nor too large, much like the ill-starred Edwina Booth's in the original *Trader Horn*.

'I have no evidence whatever to back up this speculation. But maybe Western is offering your father something, and this offer has made him lie.'

'Why would he do that?' she said. Her face had smoothed out, but it was twisted again.

'I don't know,' he said. 'Maybe Western is lying to your father, offering, say, a chance to escape from that place. It may be the afterlife, but it doesn't seem to be heaven. Oh, what am I saying! There I go again, talking as if they are the dead.'

'Why is it you're so strongly opposed to the idea?'

'Don't start that psychological stuff with me,' he said.

She was silent for a minute, then opened her mouth, but closed it when three short whistles came out of the door communicator. Carfax got up, walked to the door, looked through the peephole, and spoke the codeword that released the lock. The dome-shaped turtle wheeled in, stopped when Carfax ordered it to do so, and the top opened up. Carfax removed the tray on which were the dishes and cups and told the turtle to leave. The door swung open for it, and it disappeared. Patricia ate all the food as if she had missed several meals. Carfax got hungry watching her and helped her eat all the dishes and the tableware except for a spoon. The room service had forgotten to refill the solvosauce bottle, and so there was not enough left to melt the spoon.

'It's cherry anyway,' he said, turning the spoon so that the raised word on its handle could be seen in the light. 'I never cared for synthetic cherry, though I do love a home-baked cherry pie.'

The tray was chocolate milkshake flavor, and he would have liked to have eaten it later. But he didn't feel like calling room service again.

He poured out an ounce of Drambuie apiece, and they silently toasted each other.

'You know,' he said, 'it's possible that what I talked to was not your father, but a fake. I suppose that someone could have been imitating his voice. And his seeming to jump out of the screen at me could have been a holograph.'

'But why would Western fake it?'

'Possibly to scare me off. And to stop me asking questions.' He hesitated and then said, 'Uncle Rufton never did answer me when I asked him if human mediums could get through to the dead. To the *sembs*, I mean.'

'You can ask your wife that,' Patricia said.

'And what if she doesn't know? The . . . *sembs* . . . are not ominiscient, you know, not by any means.'

'I've been to a very famous medium,' she said, 'a Mrs. Holles Webster. She seems to be honest. At least, she's been cleared of fakery by the Syracuse University Psychic Research Committee.'

'You went to a medium? Never mind answering, you just said you did. But why? To talk to your? . . .'

She nodded and said, 'Yes, my father.'

'And the result?'

'I went twice, and Mrs. Webster failed both times. But the last time she said she was starting to make contact; she could feel it.'

'*Feel* it?'

'She claims that human mediums, the sincere ones, that is, probably operate on the same principles and in the same manner as MEDIUM. But the human medium uses somewhat different sensors and indicators. Instead of a viewscreen and meters, she uses a neural complex which comes through to her as a feeling. It's almost as reliable as the needle on a meter with its numbered graduations.'

'And she makes contact with the dead, not with *sembs*, right?'

'As a matter of fact,' Patricia said, 'I asked her about that. She said she had no doubt at all that the beings *she* summoned were really the spirits of the departed. But she did say that it was possible that your theory was right. Or at least had some truth in it. She was inclined to think that Western had tapped right into the world of demons. Oh, don't smile! She didn't mean little horned devils with pitchforks and all that. She meant evil spirits. Or evil entities of some sort. Not the ghosts of wicked humans but something like . . . well . . . fallen angels. She claims that they disguise themselves as humans in order to . . .'

She stopped when Carfax sighed heavily.

'What's the matter? I know it sounds ridiculous – to you anyway, and even somewhat to me – but . . .'

'Mrs. Webster's theory is a distortion of mine,' he said. 'She uses the term wicked spirits or fallen angels to account for those entities. And I use the more scientific *semb*, though in a different sense from Western's usage. At least, *semb* sounds more scientific. But it can't stand up to any analysis. I have no evidence to back up my theory, any more than Mrs. Webster has. Except that MEDIUM shows a world that sure as hell isn't like any spiritual universe anybody ever postulated. And if the beings we see on MEDIUM's screen are really the dead, then they're in hell!'

'But Mrs. Webster says that we are only seeing what an

electronic device can show us. We aren't seeing the reality, any more than an electronic wave rising from the beating of a heart shows us the heart itself.'

'That's Western's analogy, but with a different interpretation,' Carfax said gloomily.

He was silent for a few minutes. Patricia sat quite still except for the motions required to smoke her cigarette.

'All right,' he said, 'let's see Mrs. Webster. You make an appointment with her for next week, say, Monday.'

'You sound very skeptical.'

'I am, but if the dead can communicate with us, I don't see why the communication has to be through a machine. Anyway, I'm not so narrow-minded that I won't even give a hypothesis a test.'

'Could I have another drink?'

'Sure.'

He got up and poured her two ounces of Wild Turkey over three ice cubes. When he handed it to her, he felt a shock as if static electricity had leaped between them. But the voltage was psychic, not electrical. It was apparent that some of her thought had paralleled his.

A little shaken, he returned to his chair. She was his first cousin. But he had no idea of making her pregnant, and, anyway, he had not bedded a woman for a long time, and he did feel some affection for her. Maybe more than he wanted to admit to himself.

It was then that his early suspicion that she might have been sent by Western, that her appearance was the first act in a put-up drama, returned to him.

'You bastard,' he told himself. 'You're too cynical. And you're too afraid of having warm feelings for another woman. You're scared to death that something might happen to her and cause you pain again.'

Patricia sipped her drink and said, 'You never told me about your breakdown.'

Was she trying to get information which she could pass on to Western?

'You look funny,' she said. 'I'm sorry if I seem to be nosey. If you don't want to talk about it, O.K.'

'I don't like to talk about it because even I find it unbelievable when I tell it. There is only one explanation, I tell myself, and that is that I was crazy. For a while, anyway. Certain things did happen; there's plenty of objective evidence for that. But my observations of them must have been strained through a very distorted filter. And the witnesses I had depended upon to back my story clammed up. Even those I trusted the most. But then they didn't want to be thought crazy, either.'

She leaned forward and said, eagerly, 'What *did* happen?'

He smiled and said, 'Vampires and werewolves and ghosts and ghoulies and things that went bump in the night. And in the daytime, too. But I had been given LSD or something like it, no doubt of that. They seemed to be genuine objective phenomena to me at the time. And there are times when I still think they were. However, such things couldn't be, so I tell everybody that I was under the influence of a psychedelic.

'Even so, I'm not so sure now that there aren't things happening around us that cannot be explained by big capital S Science.'

'What did happen?'

'I'm certified sane now and I intend to stay that way. Let's drop that subject.'

Patricia looked disappointed.

'I'm sorry,' he said, 'but the details might convince you that I'm unreliable. Maybe I am. In any event, I decided to get out of the investigation business, change my name, and drop out of sight. But here I am, back in L.A. and a private eye again. So much for free will.'

'Just one thing, and I'll quit asking about it,' she said. 'Were you taking LSD?'

'No, it was slipped into my drink.'

And if she were Western's agent, he thought, what is to prevent her putting a psychedelic in my drink and so discrediting me?

If she planned to do that, she certainly had made no move to do so tonight. She hadn't been out of his sight for a second.

He felt ashamed of his suspicions, though logic told him that he should question everyone.

She stood up and said, 'The bathroom calls.'

It was all right to look into her purse, he told himself. He'd be a fool not to. Yet he felt as if he were betraying her, and he felt even more so when he found nothing except what was to be expected. That included a bottle of contraceptive and anti-VD pills.

He made up his mind then. When she came out of the door, he was waiting. She looked up at him quickly and came into his arms.

Afterward, as he was falling asleep, he wondered briefly if the dead could see the living. Frances wouldn't like this, but then she didn't have to hang around. Besides, it took a machine to get them even halfway into this world.

Just before sleep finally pulled him down, he thought: what am I talking about? I don't believe that there is an afterlife; the *sembs* are parallel-world phenomena. Or something.

NINE

'Nothing has been proved or disproved,' Gordon Carfax said. 'The bishop tried to exorcize MEDIUM, and he had a heart attack, that's all.'

'But how could Western have known that Bishop Shallund would pick out a childhood playmate, one who died at the age of eleven, one whom Western could not possibly have known anything about? Besides, Western didn't know who was going to be on the committee until the last moment.'

'We know he's very rich, and we can assume that he's unscrupulous,' Gordon said. 'He may have found out who was chosen some time ago, even if it was supposed to be a deep secret. And he may have put his researchers to digging up everything they could find about the committee members. No, all this committee has done is to make everything even more muddy. And it has increased the tensions. The pro-MEDIUMs are claiming that the dead *resented* the committee and that Everts killed Shallund because he wouldn't believe that he was Everts. Or, rather, he frightened Shallund so much that he had a fatal heart attack.

'And the anti-MEDIUMS are still in two schools. One claims that Western is a fraud; the other believes that he is a witch, a Faust, who is tampering with forces that should be left alone.

'We're right where we were, except that passions are roused even higher.'

'And what do you think about the validity of Western's claims?'

'I haven't changed my mind. Not yet, anyway. I will admit that I am biased. My resistance to the idea that there could be an afterlife may be warping my judgment.'

'You'll talk to Frances today, and no matter how extensively Western has researched her, he won't be able to find out everything. There are some things that only you would know about her.'

Gordon smiled and said, 'Yes, but according to my theory that won't matter. It won't be Frances I'll be talking to; it will be some thing, some entity, that has some means of knowing everything about Frances. Mind reading, maybe. Or perhaps it's observed Frances from her birth and so knows all about her.'

'Oh, for God's sakes!' Patricia said. Her body was certainly beautiful, he thought, but her expression of anger, coupled with a complete lack of makeup, made her face ugly.

He got out of bed and put on his pajamas and a thin dressing robe. He grinned at her and said, 'Maybe some hot coffee will cool you off. Don't get mad just because I'm exercising my male prerogative.'

'What's that?'

'I should have said human not male. Homo sapiens is the rational animal. For everything that needs to be explained, he ignores the facts or, rather, twists them to suit his own beliefs.'

'Well, that may be what you do,' she said, 'but I don't! I know that Western killed my father and stole his invention, and I know that those *are* the dead! I can look at things objectively!'

'Sure you can,' he said. 'Look, I'll make the coffee and you put your makeup on.'

'Does my face jar you that much?' she said. 'You don't . . .'

'. . . look so great myself in the morning,' he said. 'Yes, I know, and apologize. I should have learned from Frances when to keep my opinions to myself.'

He walked around the bed to kiss her, but she turned her back and made for the bathroom. He went into the kitchenette, mentally kicking himself and wondering why he had said things designed to anger her. Doctor Sloko had thought that he had a deep-seated need to get the women he loved angry at him. He had agreed that might be possible, but why did he have that need? Neither he nor Sloko had ever found out.

Patricia came out of the bathroom smiling. Her hair was in

a Psyche knot, but she still had no makeup on. She was going to test him further. He wasn't going to do anything now to upset her, he told himself. He kissed her and this time she did not refuse.

'Let's start all over again,' she said. 'Good morning, Gordon.'

'And a good morning to you,' he said. 'I'll be back in a minute,' and he went to the bathroom.

When he came out, she was seated on the sofa in front of the TV and drinking black coffee. He sat down by her and sipped the hot liquid.

The news was mostly about the events at Western's and their implications. There were shots of a riot on the parking lot below Western's between antis and pros, sluggings, bangings of signs on heads, police firing tear gas and shooting foam over the cement so that no one could stand up, a number being hustled off in vans, and ambulances carrying off the more seriously hurt. There were some scenes of parades by pro-Westernites in New York City and San Francisco. A Senator Gray from Louisiana was interviewed. He proposed that MEDIUMs should be built at government expense and installed in all cities with more than fifty thousand population. Free sessions, or moderately priced sessions, should be provided for the public. Gray had a deep, rich voice and a sincere expression which seemed to have been made for TV; he was becoming well known to the public because of his pro-MEDIUM speeches. This was the first, however, in which he had proposed that MEDIUM be made available to everybody. He was for the common man, the man who did not have the money to buy sessions so that he could talk to his beloved dead. He was outraged that the greatest thing since creation was restricted to the rich.

'He wants to be president,' Gordon said, 'and he may make it. He's shrewd, he knows that many of his constituents are fundamentalists or Catholics who think that MEDIUM is the devil's own machine. But he's willing to stick his neck out, because the majority of people in this country think as he does. Why should the wealthy have not only the best of life but a monopoly on the dead? Gray may get to be president on that platform alone.'

'Western could be president if he wanted to,' Patricia said. 'I'm surprised he hasn't announced his candidacy.'

'Maybe Gray is his man,' Carfax said. 'It's better to be the power behind the throne than to sit on it. But I'm not so sure that MEDIUM shouldn't be reserved as a plaything for the rich. If it becomes available to everybody, its impact on society will be tremendous.'

'Like what?' Patricia said.

'We may become the modern Egyptians, focusing our lives on death. This world will be looked at as only a short stage preparing for the next one, the long one.'

'Isn't that the way it's always been?'

'Theoretically, yes. Practically, never.'

Patricia shuddered and put her hands on her face. 'Oh, it's awful!'

'It could be. It'll be different, anyway, unless MEDIUM turns out to be a gateway to a world different from what most people think. Look at the legal profession. Some lawyers have already published articles extrapolating changes in court and police procedure if MEDIUM becomes legally acceptable. A murdered man might be sworn in as the prosecution's star witness. And what about property? Can a dead man have a legal right to administrate his own business or his own estate? Why should he be cut off from its benefits just because he's in another world? On the other hand, what will the rights of the man who first owned the property be? Will John D. Rockefeller, after a long court battle, regain control of Standard Oil? Will George Washington run for president again? If he did, who could beat him, except maybe Abe Lincoln? And how could George Washington run this country competently? He couldn't, because conditions have changed so vastly and deeply that he could not possibly understand them. And . . .'

'You're being ridiculous!' Patricia said.

'Yes, I know. But if you think about all that could happen, you can see what a mess it could be. And probably will be.'

'Whatever happens, whoever owns MEDIUM is going to be very very rich,' Patricia said. 'Even if the government should take it over, it'd have to lease it from the owner.'

Gordon wanted to make some comment about the dollar bills shining in her eyes, but he refrained. He couldn't blame her for thinking about how wealthy she would be if she proved that she was the rightful owner. She was human, and he had thought about how half of those billions would be his if he should marry Patricia. Was that behind his making love to Patricia? No, he told himself, greed had nothing to do with it. Besides, if it had been driving him, even unconsciously, would he have deliberately angered her this morning? Wouldn't he be doing everything possible to make her pleased with him?

But then his remarks might spring from another unconscious source. The drive to convince himself that money had no part in his interest for her.

Life was complicated enough without bringing in the dead, too. And they were coming in, they were coming in.

At 09:00, he left the hotel. The air was clear, and the skies were blue except for a few clouds left over from the night's seeding. He saw a bus a block to the west but decided to walk to the La Brea MT line. It was only ten blocks to the east, and he needed the exercise. Besides, he wanted to check for shadowers and to see how the neighborhood had changed. He sauntered along the southern walk of Wilshire, pausing now and then to look into the shop windows. If anybody was trailing him on foot or by car, he/she was doing a good job of it. Anyway, he did not think that Western considered him an important enough threat to have him under surveillance all the time. He probably knew that Patricia had stayed in his hotel room all night, but that was not an item he could use to discredit Carfax or Patricia. Nobody cared about such things anymore.

The Miracle Mile, he found, had changed little except for the overhead moving bridges for the pedestrians. The streets to the south of it, Eighth and the others, were no longer single-residence houses. These had been torn down and replaced with high-rise apartment buildings or parking buildings. In the middle of them was an eight-story windowless structure, more or less tastefully decorated, hiding oil-pumping machinery.

On La Brea, he took the elevator to the MT platform, and a moment later boarded an express. It shot him to Sunset, where he descended and got on a bus which took him to Highland. A taxi, steam-powered this time, got him to the entrance to Western's. Tours met him at the gate.

'I suppose you saw yesterday's debacle on TV,' he said.

'Who didn't?' Carfax said.

'Perhaps you haven't heard that Bishop Shallund's niece is suing us,' Tours said. 'She won't have a chance, since the bishop signed our release form, of course. But it's a damnable nuisance. Mr. Western would settle out of court just to get rid of her, but if he did that he'd set a bad precedent. There is one good thing about it. I mean, from our viewpoint,' he added, seeing Carfax's raised eyebrows. 'We plan on interviewing the bishop himself in a few days. The bishop's niece has been invited to attend so there'll be no doubt about its being him. She's refused, but we have several people who knew him well, and they can identify him.'

Carfax accompanied Tours up the front steps of the mansion and onto the porch. Carfax said, 'Why are you doing this?'

Tours opened the door for Carfax to precede him but blocked the entrance.

'What do you mean?'

'Why do you want to speak to the bishop?'

'Oh, I see.' Tours laughed. 'Well, if the bishop isn't in hell or in heaven or purgatory, and he verifies it himself, then what happens to religion?'

Carfax grinned and said. 'You've published a score or so of interviews with Catholics, and with other people of other religions. If the faithful reject the testimony of the popes, John XXII and Pius XI, why should they be bothered by a mere bishop's testimony?'

'Because they've been able to throw some doubt on the identities of the popes. But Shallund himself has just died, and . . .'

He stopped and stared past Carfax. Carfax turned and saw the plane just passing over the hills to the north. It was a twin-jet monoplane, coming so swiftly that it was over the valley and halfway to the hill and diving before Carfax could understand what it was doing. Or, rather, what it looked like it was doing.

'That fool!' Tours said. 'He's going to buzz! . . .'

'No-o-o-o!' Carfax shouted, and he dived over the railing

and into the plastic bushes. He crashed through the rough leaves, hit the main trunk, felt it crumple beneath him, and heard the roar of the jets. And then he was lifted by something gigantic and brutal and he spun, half-senseless, through the air, over and over and over until he struck unconsciousness.

TEN

He awoke lying on his back. He did not hurt – as yet – and he had no idea of what had happened or even where he was. He could not make his arms or legs move, and he could hear nothing. Somebody ran by him, arms up in the air, blackened body naked except for a shredded blouse, and hair a charred mass. Then she was gone, and as far as he knew he was alone. The sky was blue, then became black as smoke drifted over it. Something struck his side but he could not turn his head to see what it was.

After a while a helicopter passed over him, quite low, and he could feel the hot air its vanes whirled at him, though he could not hear it. He tried to cry out; his mouth was open; his head roared; blackness came again.

The second time he awoke, he was lying in a stretcher, blankets over him, his arms and legs tied down. This time, he could move them a little, but he wished he hadn't. They were beginning to hurt, and his head felt like a huge clot of dried blood. Or as he imagined his brain would feel if it had been pounded into a bloody mass. A white-coated man was about to apply a respirator to him.

The third time, he opened his eyes to see Patricia standing over him and crying. He was in a hospital room; a nurse was writing on a piece of paper clipped to a board. He could turn his head, though it cost him pain, and his legs and arms felt as if they were connected to thin wires through which voltages of pain were pulsing.

'That plane,' he said to Patricia. 'It deliberately crashed into the house.' His voice seemed to echo in his head.

The nurse put the board down and walked around the bed toward him. 'Now, Mr. Carfax, don't exert yourself. Just go back to sleep. You're all right.' Her voice sounded as if it were far away.

'Is my back broken?' he said.

'No, but one of your legs was, and you had two ribs broken. Otherwise you're just fine.'

'I was afraid my eardrums were broken,' he said. 'What time is it?'

'Just take it easy, Mr. Carfax. You're not going anyplace for a while.'

'What time is it, Pat?' he said.

Patricia looked at her wristwatch through tears. 'It's almost 24.'

'Midnight?'

'Gordon, do what the nurse says. I'll be here if you wake up.'

'No, I want to know what happened,' he said. But he was gone, and when he woke again, he thought that only a few minutes had passed. He was alone, and he thought, 'So much for Pat's promise,' but she entered the room a moment later. She rushed to him and bent over and kissed him and said, 'You would wake up just now! I had to go to the toilet!'

'I think I already have,' he said. 'Call the nurse, will you?'

By 08:00, he was able to sit up and take note of what had happened. His right leg below the knee was in a splint. Two of his left ribs were taped. The hearing in his left ear was fully restored, but he still had a slight buzzing in his right. He had numerous contusions and bruises on his body and face. He had a headache which felt as if he had been on a three-day drunk. And he tended to shake at loud unexpected noises.

Patricia told him as much as she knew of what had happened. The TV and the papers added details.

At 09:20 of the previous day, a Mr. Christian Houvelle of 13748 Sweetorange Lane, apartment 6H, Augusta Complex, had flown a rented Langer four-passenger jet from the Santa Barbara Seaside Airport. His flight plan called for him to fly over the Pacific to Eureka, a city on the far north coast of California. Instead, Mr. Houvelle had swung south and, despite the orders of Seaside Control and Riverside International, had continued on his illegal path southeastward. In a few minutes he had descended so low that radar could not track him. Eyewitness reports confirmed that he had maintained an altitude of about a hundred meters above the tallest buildings and the mountain ranges.

Mr. Houvelle, on approaching the Nicholls Canyon area, had lifted to three hundred meters, circled twice, apparently to make sure of identification of the Western mansion, and then had descended and headed straight for his target. The plane carried Mr. Houvelle and an estimated fifty pounds of dynamite, which Mr. Houvelle, a chemist, had made himself on company time. The plane, the pilot, the dynamite, and the house disintegrated in a ball of flame and expanding air.

With these also went MEDIUM and thirty employees of Western, including Tours, Mrs. Morris, Harmons, and two clients who were interviewing the late Karl Marx.

Western and two of his bodyguards had survived without serious injury. Mr. Western had been in a subbasement beneath the garage at the time, with another client. What he was doing there or the identity of his client were not known. During the confusion, his client had disappeared, and Mr. Western did not care to name him.

Mr. Houvelle had failed in his mission, which must have been to send Mr. Western on to the great beyond.

Carfax, along with many others, had assumed that Houvelle had belonged to some religious group which loathed Western because he was discrediting its faith.

Not so. Mr. Houvelle was a fanatical atheist. He had ridiculed all religions and once had been beaten up in a Silverlake bar when he had suggested that Christianity was the greatest evil that this planet had ever known.

Why would Mr. Houvelle want to kill the man who was in the process of destroying all established religions and most of the unestablished?

No one knew, but the TV casters thought it probable that Mr. Houvelle hated Western because he was also destroying atheism.

The ruins of the house as seen from a helicopter were shown briefly. There was only a deep black hole with pieces of wood and metal scattered outward like the petals of a flower scattered by a giant reciting forget-me-nots.

Mr. Western, his bodyguards, and the unnamed client had scrambled out of the subbasement a few minutes after the explosion and escaped with some burns on their backs and heads.

There was a shot of Western, part of his body and the top of his head covered with bandages. The casters added that he had stated that a new house would be built on the site and a new MEDIUM installed. Mr. Western had also stated that it would have done no good to kill him, since his followers would carry on his work.

'I'd sure like to know what he was doing in that basement and who his client was,' Gordon Carfax said.

'I wish he had been killed!' Patricia said. 'It would serve him right! And maybe then he might have confessed that he killed my father and stole MEDIUM.'

'Why should he?' Carfax said.

'What would he have to gain by lying after he's dead?'

'Being dead doesn't make you any less hypocritical or spiteful,' Gordon said.

'There you go again,' she said. 'You insist that they are not dead but entities posing as the dead. Yet you talk as if you believed they are the dead.'

'I know. It's too easy to slide into the habit of thinking of them as those who did live. There's a continuity that overwhelms you even if you don't want to believe. A man dies and then you're talking to him. And it's only by a rigid discipline of mind that you can separate the two, the once-living man and the thing that's pretending to be him. If, that is . . .'

'If, that is, they are not really discrete entities, is that what you were going to say?'

'I'm afraid so,' Carfax said, smiling. 'In any event, human or not, they are dangerous. I know, though I can't prove it, that one of them was trying to take me over, possess me, when I was interviewing your father.'

'But how could they do that?'

'How would I know? If I did suggest that to the news media, Western would be sure to stress my mental breakdown. Everybody would conclude that I was crazy. Maybe I am.'

'I don't think so,' Patricia said. 'But what matters now is what we can do. You'll have to forget Frances, for a while, anyway, until a new MEDIUM is built. It's an awful thing to say, but maybe it was a good thing that the house was blown up. Western's going to be too busy rebuilding to pay much attention to us. We can get something done while he's occupied.'

Like what? Carfax thought. But they were going to Mrs. Webster for a seance, though he did not expect much from that, and he could sniff around later at the University of Big Sur.

Just before they turned the TV off that night, the caster announced that the official report of the FCIM would be released within a few days. Apparently, the president had yielded to the public clamor. It was a decision reluctantly taken, since it was going to offend many voters no matter what its conclusions.

ELEVEN

The spook business had always done well, but now it was in its Golden Age. Where there had been one medium before Western, there were now twenty. Some operated according to tradition, despising the use of electromechanical aids, depending solely upon their psychic powers. And upon the gullibility of their clients, Carfax thought. Others had gone modern and used devices of their own make which were supposed to be modeled on Western's. (All of these could be classified as fakes, Carfax assumed. But whatever their means, they took in the clients and the money).

Mrs. Webster was no exception, as far as the money was concerned. She lived in a six-room penthouse on a thirty-six-story apartment building in Santa Monica only two blocks from the Pacific. A security guard checked Gordon and Patricia in the main lobby, and another accompanied them in a private elevator. A third rechecked their credentials before admitting them into the anteroom. A maid who looked as if she came from Arabia (and did) escorted them to the seance room. This had none of the trappings of the seance room which Carfax expected. It was large and airy and bright, its walls were oyster-white with a mural which looked like a Cazetti original (and was) running completely around the room, broken only by several doors. A Matisse and a Renoir which looked like originals (and were) were the only paintings. The furniture was the frail Neo-Cretan style, becoming so popular.

Mrs. Webster herself looked as fragile as the furniture. She rose from a spindly sofa and approached them, her hand out, and smiling. She was about fifty years old and about five feet tall, thin in arms and legs but with large breasts and a posterior that delighted Carfax. Her face was oval, large-eyed, and high-cheeked. Her hair was very black and long, floating free. She wore no jewelry except for a small golden ring set with an azure gem which Carfax could not identify. When he took her hand he saw that the ring itself was in the shape of a serpent.

Mrs. Webster's voice was deep for such a small woman.

'Please sit down. The others will arrive within a few minutes. You can smoke if you wish; there are some Kenyans on the table, but you can use your own if you like. You'll have to excuse me for a moment; I have to change into my working clothes.'

The few minutes stretched out to fifteen. Patricia smoked several of the strong Kenyans while Gordon paced back and forth, looking now and then out of the high and broad window fronting the ocean. He noticed thin wires running from the wall into the lower edge of the window. His eyebrows rose. Windows which could be electrically polarized were very expensive indeed.

He had just glanced at his watch when he heard voices. The maid, now dressed in flowing white robes that made her look even more Arabic, entered. Behind her were three women and three men of various ages but all well-dressed. One of them, a blonde of about twenty, was too well-dressed, he thought. She wore the bell-shaped skirt reaching to the floor and the brocaded jacket which the more daring young girls in the larger cities were wearing in honor of their recently dead idol, the singer Cybele Fidestes (née Lucy Schwartz). For street wear, her breasts were covered with a thin gauze band, but she was now shedding that. Carfax wondered how he was supposed to keep his mind on psychic matters while confronted with such splendidly physical matters. Or were they supposed to distract him, to keep him from observation of fraud?

Patricia's lips, he noted, had tightened when the girl entered, and when she removed the band, Patricia's eyes narrowed. She had looked at him to see if he was looking, but he had only grinned and winked at her.

Mrs. Webster had explained over the phone that these guests were exceptionally psychic and would be present only to expedite communication. She had not said so, but Carfax had assumed that they were actually her part-time employees and would get a cut of her rather high fee. They included a professor of psychics from UCLA, a computer programmer, a retired naval officer, a grip for NBC, the wife of a professional painter, and the secretary of the Finnish consul for Los Angeles. The blonde, Gloriana Szegeti, worked for the Social Security office in Sherman Oaks. (But not in those clothes, surely, he thought.)

Gloriana stood close to Gordon while she talked with him.

'I thought your leg was broken, Mr. Carfax.'

'It was, and is, Ms. Szegeti,' he said. 'But they took the splint off the day after it was put on. The break was injected with epoxy glue and set overnight. So were my ribs. I can, theoretically, anyway, do the 100-meter dash with no trouble. Actually, my muscles hurt like fury, and if an occasional twinge passes over my face, it is pain that is causing it. Or perhaps admiration for you.'

Ms. Szegeti laughed; Patricia made strangled sounds.

'I'd read that they were using the epoxy treatment for broken bones in the East, but I didn't know they were using it here,' Ms. Szegeti said.

'I'm one of the first,' Gordon said.

Mrs. Webster entered, and the group became silent. She was now wearing a white chiton which was so thin that it was obvious she had no underclothing. Her breasts looked so firm they must have been pumped full of clinite. Was she also dressed to distract him? If so, she was succeeding.

'We'll sit down now, if you please,' she said, indicating a large round table of ebony, its top inlaid with bright figures of fish, dolphins, and octopi. All but Ms. Szegeti went at once to the table, as she pressed a panel in the base of the wall. The light from the window dimmed. By the time she was seated, the window was a dark red oblong with the sun a very dark blue near its center. The room quickly filled with a thick reddish light. Ms. Szegeti, who was seated across from Carfax, became a dark blue statue with black nipples. He looked at Patricia and saw a blue ghost. His own hands were blue.

The air-conditioning must have been adjusted for at least ten degrees lower; he was suddenly shivering.

Mrs. Webster, seated at his right, took his hand in her small cool hand and said, 'Everybody form a living link.'

Carfax took the hand of Mrs. Applechard, the painter's wife. It was much warmer than Mrs. Webster's.

'This is merely to establish a vital flow between us,' she said. 'We'll just sit here and meditate, on anything you like, Patricia and Gordon, and feel the current of the living. Think nice warm thoughts, if you can. I suggest that you think of love, since that seems to work better in the preliminaries.'

That wasn't difficult, Carfax thought. Ms. Szegeti was bouncing up and down on her chair, and the blue oscillations proved that she certainly had nothing to do with clinite. He wondered what Patricia was thinking. If she were watching Szegeti, she was not thinking of love.

This seemed a strange prelude to communication with the dead. But psychologists, some anyway, maintained that there was a connection between sex and death in the minds of many Americans. They were, so it was claimed, the reverse and obverse sides of a psychic coin. Carfax considered that to be a depreciated currency.

'Feel the current,' Mrs. Webster said softly. 'Feel it flow from one to one, flow through all, around and around, getting stronger with each circuit.'

Suddenly, Carfax felt a tingling where his skin met Mrs. Webster's. A few seconds later, his hand tingled where it was in contact with Mrs. Applechard's.

Somebody moved, a tiny blue spark cracked, and Patricia gasped.

Carfax was also startled, but he wondered if they were, in fact, hooked up to a generator of electricity. It did not seem likely, since the thin top and the legs of the table were not thick enough to conceal anything but a tiny battery. Of course, there could be wires running through the wood connected to a battery beneath the floor. A thin strip of conducting metal could run underneath the top and make contact with the bare bellies of Szegeti or Webster.

On the other hand, the spark had been more like that generated by static electricity.

Mrs. Webster's hand was cool and dry; Mrs. Applechard's

was warm and sweaty. The latter's hand should be a better electrical contact, yet the former's gave a much stronger tingling.

Mrs. Webster said, 'Break, if you please.'

Mrs. Applechard gave a sigh and moved her hand away. Szegeti stood up, with vibrations everywhere free, and walked over to a highboy. Carfax stood up and walked over to Patricia.

'How'd it go?'

She stood up and said, 'I'd like a drink. But Mrs. Webster said we couldn't even have water during the seance.'

'Was that spark from you?' he said.

'Yes. I started to move my hand away, and the spark leaped between my hand and Commander Gardner's. I wish they'd turn the lights on. Everybody looks so ghastly.'

A match speared the darkness; by its light he could see Szegeti's face, white now, and the cigarette in her lips. A moment later he caught the acrid odor.

Patricia jumped, but it was not Szegeti that had startled her. The maid, a blue nun, had entered silently. She was carrying a bowl which glowed a faint orange.

Mrs. Webster said, 'You can smoke grass or tobacco, if you wish. Grass seems to be a better instrument for tuning.'

He presumed that 'tuning' meant attaining a higher 'vibration', whatever that meant.

The maid put the bowl down on the table before Mrs. Webster's place and glided out, or seemed to glide. He walked over to the table and looked in the bowl. It held three lance-shaped leaves, serrate-edged, black in this light.

'Laurel leaves, Gordon,' Mrs. Webster said behind him. She moved closer so that her breast nudged the back of his right arm. '*Laurus nobilis.* The bay or sweet laurel used by the nymphs, or the priestesses, of the pre-Hellenic religion in their orgiastic rites. These come from a tree near the oracular temple at Delphi. I only use them when the circumstances warrant.'

'You get better results when you chew them?'

'Much better. But it's more dangerous to use them. I lose more control.'

'And why should that be dangerous?' he said, turning.

Mrs. Webster did not move at once, so that she was pressed

against him. Then she stepped back to look up at him. Her teeth were black in a blue face, and her tongue was a dark red flickering.

'I don't want you to get too excited. It's better not to suggest what might happen.'

'I'm overly excited now,' he said, wondering if she guessed the ambiguity.

'All right,' she said in a louder voice. 'Put your cigarettes out and come back to the table. Patricia and Gordon, take the same places and link hands.'

This time, there was no tingling in his hands; the electricity seemed to be in the air. Carfax wondered how she could pick up the leaf and put it in her mouth when her hands were held. An arm came over her shoulder, picked up a leaf, and placed it in her open mouth. He turned his head and saw the maid standing just behind Mrs. Webster.

There was silence eased only by the slight chewing noises from Mrs. Webster. The figures across the table became even more blue-black. His head started to ache. Mrs. Applechard's hand became wetter, but at the same time colder. The air was getting colder, too, and it seemed to him that the drop in temperature was not due to the air-conditioning. But that must be his imagination.

Suddenly, Mrs. Webster spat, and he jumped. The mass of leaf shot out beyond the bowl, and he smelled a pleasant aromatic odor. A hand appeared in the corner of his eye. It dipped into the bowl, and it moved a dim object, another leaf, into her open mouth. Silence again, except for the moist chewing sounds.

A few minutes later, while the noiselessness seemed to grow thick as a cloud, the second leaf shot out. The hand swooped down into the bowl and toward her mouth. Mrs. Webster whispered, 'No! Enough!' and the hand, still holding the leaf, disappeared.

His hand felt now as if it were a corpse's. Something rumbled on his left, making him start slightly. He relaxed a trifle and even grinned when he realized that it was gas in Mrs. Applechard's stomach. A highly nervous woman, he thought, though he didn't blame her. And why was she so nervous if she had been through this before? Was it because she had good reason to be?

'Don't let loose!' Mrs. Webster said sharply.

Silence again except for a panting sound. Was it coming from Patricia?

Mrs. Webster's voice seemed to bellow in his ear.

'Rufton Carfax!'

Gordon Carfax felt as if he were turning into quartz from his inner core outward. He was stone precipitating from a thick liquid of fear. Something, or somebody, had entered the room or, rather, not entered but appeared in it. The air over the table was condensing, it was swirling, and the swirls were blackening. Air moved across his face and hands, air pushed out by a mass hovering over the table.

'Rufton Carfax!'

A pseudopod, long and thin but rounded at the end, slid out of the mass toward Mrs. Webster. Cold preceded it, cold that brought rime to his skin and made the stone shiver.

Someone across the table, dimly seen through the thickening, giggled. It was high-pitched and shaking with fear and not at all funny. Instead of breaking the tension, it hardened it.

'Rufton Carfax! Be still!'

Mrs. Webster's voice, though commanding, had frayed edges. Her hand had become so cold that Gordon wanted to let loose of it, but he was afraid to do so. If he broke the link, he might be helpless before something which would take immediate advantage of any weakness.

'Rufton Carfax! Take your proper shape!'

The woman giggled again; yes, it was Szegeti. And whoever was panting was desperately afraid.

'Let it go!' a man moaned.

'Hold on!' Mrs. Webster said. 'You must not panic!'

'For Christ's sake!' Patricia said. 'That's *not* Father! What have you done?'

'Stay within the bounds!' Mrs. Webster said, her voice cracking. 'Stay! And identify yourself!'

'It's not Father!' Patricia shrieked.

A chair fell over, and a body struck the floor. There was a scramble of feet, a scream, and footsteps racing toward the

door. Gordon jumped up, jerking Mrs. Webster and Applechard back and paining his bruised muscles, but they clung to
his hands, and Mrs. Webster said, 'Don't run!'

Somebody was struggling with somebody – Patricia with the
maid? – at the door. Suddenly Mrs. Webster shouted, 'Be
gone! Back to the pit from which you came!'

The pseudopod lifted, curved like an elephant's trunk, and
then shot out toward Mrs. Webster's face. She yelled, and she
threw herself backward, pulling Gordon with her. They rolled
on the floor while Mrs. Webster, her hands on her face,
screamed. Gordon rose swiftly, though painfully, from the
floor and saw Szegeti at the window, and he knew she was
going to depolarize the window. The mass over the table was
thinning now but thrashing around, pseudopods whirling outward, reaching for the edges of the table but never going past
them. And then the light became redder and redder, and the
sun came in unbarred, and the mass was gone.

He turned to see the door open and the maid and Patricia
running down the hall. Mrs. Webster was sitting up, her hands
over her eyes and moaning, 'I'm blind! I'm blind!'

He leaned over and forced her hands away. 'Of course you
can't see, you fool!' he said savagely. 'Your eyes are closed!'

Her lids opened, and she stared at him, empty of everything
but horror.

'I can't see, I tell you, I can't see! It touched my eyes!'

'It's gone,' he said. 'Whatever it was, it's gone! You're safe
now!'

He leaned down and pulled her up. How light she was, as if
she had been decanted.

TWELVE

'It could all have been caused by suggestion,' Gordon said. 'Mass hysteria.'

He looked out the window. Wilshire was speeding below them. He caught a glimpse through the window of a third-story apartment of a man shaking his finger at a woman. What were they arguing about, if indeed they were arguing? An in-law? Infidelity? Politics? MEDIUM? Their children? Sex? Money, most likely.

'Then why would we all see the same thing?'

'I don't know, Pat. But we've all been conditioned to expect an amorphous mass, a thing of ectoplasm, which then assumes a definite shape. The movies, TV, books have conditioned us even if we don't believe in ghosts.'

'I don't think it was imagination, and I know it wasn't my father,' she said. 'It was evil, evil. My father was good. He was weak, but he was good.'

'You know,' Gordon said slowly, 'it could have been a genuine objective phenomenon. Maybe. But it didn't necessarily have to be what we call a ghost. It might not have come from the same universe as the *embu*. There are a hundred, maybe a thousand, maybe an infinite number of worlds occupying the same space as ours. And maybe we can get through to them, or they to us, under certain circumstances. If this could be, then we could have summoned – I hate that word because of its association with witchcraft – summoned some thing. In any event, I don't intend to visit Mrs. Webster again. Or any medium. Not for a seance, anyway.'

'I'd rather not,' Patricia said.

'La Cienega coming up,' he said, looking at the flashing words on the screen at the end of the car. 'Let's get off and walk to the hotel. Our minds have been stretched; let's stretch our legs. Physical exercise often puts the mind back into shape, too.'

'You're quite a philosopher,' she said, smiling for the first time that day.

'Homespun as they come,' he said, but his mind was only half-engaged with the conversation. He had seen for himself the existence of MEDIUM (which he hadn't really believed despite all the newspaper and TV reports). He had seen nothing to indicate that Western had stolen MEDIUM and killed his uncle. And even if he should prove that Western was guilty, a larger problem remained. If Patricia did get possession of MEDIUM, she was not going to stop its use. She would not be allowed to even if she wished, and she certainly would not wish it.

Nevertheless, he had promised her that he would either prove or disprove her suspicions. And now, while MEDIUM was not available, would be a good time to work on the minor problem.

So it was that he told her he was leaving as soon as possible for Big Sur Center.

'You're welcome to come along if you want to,' he said. 'But I'll be busy, and you'll have to find something, though not someone, I hope, to entertain you.'

'I'll stay here,' Pat said. 'I can look around for some place to live, some place new where Western will have a hard time finding me. How long do you think you'll be gone?'

'At least four days,' he said. He did not think that Western was worrying about her; now that her own father had denied her suspicions, she was no threat. Or, he checked himself, not her father but the thing posing as him. But its true identity made no difference in practice.

He packed, and he kissed her goodby. He checked into a motel off the campus of the University of Big Sur six hours later, which was too late to make phone calls setting up appointments for the next day. He had three books to pass the time. A collection of science-fiction stories by Leo Q. Tincrowdor, a book describing the recent translation of the Etruscan language, and *The Annotated Odyssey*. Since the second

86

book was based on a linguist's interview with an Etruscan of the second century B.C., he decided to read that. The man who had done this was a Professor Archambaud, a Berkeley teacher who was also a good friend of Western's. This explained why he had been given access to the machine without being charged. He had been forced to use it early in the morning, but he had sacrificed sleep for the sake of knowledge. (Not to mention for the sake of advancing his own career, Carfax thought.) He had located a man who was fluent in both Latin and Etruscan and everything had proceeded swimmingly fine from there.

Though Carfax was interested in the linguistic and historical details provided by Menle Arnthal, he was more interested in the vignettes of Western provided by Archambaud. Western had told him of his early experiments with MEDIUM. Apparently, he had had the idea for years but had only begun working on the prototype two years before he announced its success.

Maybe so, Carfax thought, but Archambaud had only Carfax's word for it. Uncle Rufton could have confided in Western several years ago because he needed the financial backing. But why would Western have given him any money unless he had seen some evidence that it would work? Western was no dreamy visionary. He would have been as likely to finance a perpetual-motion machine as a machine for communicating with the dead. That is, not likely at all.

Overall, Western emerged in Archambaud's book as a fiercely dedicated man, a genius. That certainly did not jibe with Patricia's account. But then Patricia could be wrong.

At 22:00, he turned on the news. And he found out that MEDIUM was also a means for free and unlimited energy. It was just what Carfax had derided a few minutes before, a perpetual-motion machine. Or so Western was claiming.

The caster was brief but clear. Western had issued a statement that experiments had proved that electrical energy could be tapped from the same 'place' in which the dead lived. Western's demands for his house and the machine had been supplied by electricity drawn from the *embu*. An iron resistor three meters in diameter had been melted in ten seconds.

87

Theoretically, given the proper equipment, all of Los Angeles could be powered through MEDIUM. All of California. In fact, all of Earth.

So, Carfax thought, Western had lied when he had said he was getting his power from the Four Corners.

The caster looked skeptical. Carfax did not know how he looked himself, but he thought it would be stunned. He turned the TV off and leaned back in his chair, a bourbon in his hand. Well, why not? According to theory, all electromagnetic energy produced in this universe was duplicated in the next. So, if that universe could be tapped, the energy could be withdrawn back to this universe.

But would not the withdrawn energy then be reproduced again in that other 'place'? Would that place be big enough to contain all that energy? Would it, in effect, burst at its seams? And would its wild energy then come ravening into this universe to destroy it?

Nothing was ever done in this universe without work. A price had to be paid for anything gained. So why should that other universe be different? It must operate according to the same principles which apply in this universe. Somebody had to pay, and since this universe was doing the taking without any return, the penalty would have to be paid.

Or would it? Nothing was actually known about that other place. It did have sentient beings, and it did seem to contain energy replicated from this place. And that was all that was known.

But it might be dangerous to find out just how that place did operate, to find out what system of checks and balances existed between the two universes.

He poured himself another drink and contemplated the future. Forget the dangers. If what Western said was true, then MEDIUM was going to have far more of an impact than anybody had thought. Unlimited electrical power! First, pollution would be reduced enormously. Second, a worldwide power grid could be built. No, that wouldn't be necessary, since every country could have its own MEDIUM. But what if the United States kept MEDIUM for itself? It could produce goods much cheaper than any other nation.

No, that situation could last only for a time. Now that it was known that such a device was possible, the best brains of the foreign nations would be tackling the problems. And they would come up with the answer.

The world was going to be changed in ways that he could not even imagine at this moment. Oh, there'd be resistance. The electrical power establishment would see its empires and its profits dissolving, and they'd fight. But they had already lost the battle.

Finishing his drink, he went to bed, his mind grabbing at extrapolations, seizing some, dropping them as new ones flew by. It was some time before he could get to sleep, and it seemed that he had just dropped off when he was hooked by the alarm clock and reeled back up.

While drinking his coffee, he turned on the morning news. The caster had nothing to add to yesterday's report but promised that the evening news would have an hour's special on the implications.

Carfax ate his breakfast in the motel restaurant and went back to his room to make his calls. At nine he was at the Big Sur Center Power and Light Company. Mr. Weissman, the accounting office manager, remembered that Rufton Carfax's bills had been extraordinarily high. Yes, the professor had had equipment installed to handle his massive power requirements. For the six months preceding his death, he had used eight to nine dk-watt-hours per day. The consumptions had been made after midnight, due to the company's requests. It would have strained it to supply them during the day. Carfax thanked Mr. Weissman and left.

His next stops were at the offices of the two trucking companies which might have delivered special equipment to his uncle. Both, as it turned out, had done so. Their records showed that they had brought in a large console and a number of modules. The console had come from an electrical supply house in Los Angeles, and the modules and some parts had been shipped out by two electronic firms in Oakland. Carfax thanked them and visited the three electrical-parts stores. Two had records of vacuum tubes and other components purchased by the professor. None of the tubes, however, seemed large enough to handle the power that his uncle required.

Carfax wondered if his uncle had picked these up himself in San Francisco or Los Angeles. Or perhaps he had gotten them from Western's store. He made a long-distance call to the store. Its manager required that he give identification, which he did, giving the name of a friend of his, the first one he could pick out of his mind.

The manager said he would look up the records. Would Mr. Comas mind holding the line or would he rather call back? Carfax said he'd wait. Five minutes later, just as Carfax's patience was about down to its last thread, the manager spoke.

'Mr. Comas?'

'Still here, though barely.'

'There is no record of any sale to Rufton Carfax.'

'You're sure?'

The manager's voice chilled. 'Of course. I'm aware that Professor Carfax was Mr. Western's uncle, and I would have remembered any purchase by him.'

Carfax thanked him and hung up the phone. The manager might or might not be telling the truth. Whatever the case, Carfax could not find out. He had no intention of breaking into the store and searching through the records. He wasn't a TV private eye, reckless of consequences if caught. Besides, if Western wanted to cover his tracks, he would have no trouble doing so.

His hopes of quickly identifying all the parts and modules of his uncle's machine had not been strong. Now they died. Nevertheless, he would gather all he could and see what he had.

He spent the rest of the day talking to Rufton Carfax's closest colleagues and his neighbors. None of them had heard anything about the experiments or the machine itself. All agreed that he was an amiable man; his colleagues said that he was a good teacher and researcher, a combination not common in universities.

The following day, Gordon took a hovercraft to Oakland, where he got a list of the parts ordered by his uncle and blueprints of the cabinet. He took the 101 MTO express to Los Angeles and got a list of parts from the store there. Then he phoned Mrs. Webster. Her secretary said that she was in conference. But she had a phone number for him.

Carfax wrote it down and said, 'Is Mrs. Webster O.K.? I mean, has she recovered her eyesight?'

The secretary looked surprised. 'I didn't know that there was anything wrong with her eyes.'

Mrs. Webster had made a quick recovery. Her blindness was due solely to hysteria, which was what he had supposed.

'Give her my regards,' he said.

He left his credit card in the slot and spoke the number which the secretary had given him. Patricia's face appeared on the screen.

'You're back so soon!'

'Speedy Carfax,' he said. 'But it didn't take you long to find an apartment.'

'It's a motel. I still haven't found a place. We may have to go to Santa Susana. A new complex is going up there.'

'Too far off,' he said. 'O.K., where are you?'

She gave him a Burbank address and then said, 'Didn't you speak to Mrs. Webster?'

'No. Why?'

'Her secretary just called me. She said that Mrs. Webster wanted to speak to you right away.'

'I must have just missed her,' he said. 'I'll call her back and then I'll come right out.'

Mrs. Webster looked healthy but excited. 'Gordon, I have some startling news for you! It may be just what you're looking for!'

'I need a break,' he said. 'What is it?'

'I think you'd better come out here. I don't want to tell you over the phone.'

He said he'd be there quickly if he could find a taxi and if not he'd take the MT. He phoned Patricia and told her there had been a change of plans. Two minutes later, he had a cab, and fifteen minutes later, he was ushered into Mrs. Webster's office. He sat down before her desk and said, 'Judging from your big round eyes, you must have something big.'

She lit a Kenyan, puffed several times and said, 'I was just talking to a client, a Robert Mifflon. Ever heard of him?'

Carfax shook his head.

'Well, he's a strange young man, a millionaire and very eccentric, very shy. He's been tremendously interested in the occult since he was a boy, and when his mother died, he came to me.

'You raise your eyebrows? You're wondering if we had any success in evoking her? Three times, though Mrs. Mifflon wasn't able to shape the plasm into a satisfactory form and the few words she could transmit were of a rather silly nature. But then she was a silly, selfish woman in life.

'You smile? You shouldn't. You know I'm not a charlatan. Anyway, when Western announced he had a scientific means for communicating with the dead, Robert went to him. But he was terribly embarrassed, poor boy, because he thought I might think he was betraying me. He came to me first and explained, or tried to explain, why he was going to Western. I told him to go ahead; I didn't mind. But I did warn him to be careful. Science has its charlatans, too.

'He apparently had several successful sessions with MEDIUM. Successful, I mean, in that he had full communication with his mother. But they did not, of course, reassure him. His mother was desperately unhappy, and he could do nothing for her.

'Then he joined the Pancosmic Church of the *Embu*-Christ. He found their premise very comforting. You know, that the *embu* is only a sort of purgatory.'

Carfax nodded and said, 'Yes, I know. After the dead have undergone "purification" in their electronic state, they proceed to the next world, where they are restored to their physical bodies. And their bodies and minds are improvements over the ones they had while in this world, and everybody is happy forever after. There's not the slightest bit of evidence for that premise, but when did people ever let lack of data interfere with their religious theories?'

'Or, if there is data, when did the nonreligious ever consider it?' Mrs. Webster said. 'Let's not argue about that. It's irrelevant to what I have to tell you. Robert did not stop using MEDIUM after he joined the church. For one thing, he wanted to convert his mother to the church's faith; he thought she'd feel better if she believed that she was only in a purgatory. And then, several days before Western's house was blown up, Western approached Mifflon with a strange offer.'

She paused, drew more smoke in, expelled it, and said, 'He wanted to sell Robert insurance.'

'Insurance?' Carfax said. 'You mean life insurance?'

'Exactly that, though not the kind that's being peddled by anybody else. It is, in a way, the only genuine life insurance offered.'

'You don't mean Western'll guarantee that Mifflon won't die?'

'In a way. Western calls it repossession insurance.'

Carfax said nothing. He felt even more stunned than when he had heard the announcement the previous evening that MEDIUM was a power source.

'To be brief, Western said that he could bring Robert back from the dead. He will do this by providing a body for Robert which he can take over. Or possess, to use a time-honored term. The premiums are two hundred thousand dollars a year. These are to be paid while the client is living. The client will name one of Western's agents as his heir, and when the client is in his new body, half of the estate will be returned to him through legal means. The premiums thereafter will be ten percent of the client's yearly income.'

'But . . . the body to be possessed?' Carfax said. 'How is Western going to arrange that?'

'Western refused to say. He just told Robert not to worry about the details. And he swore Robert to secrecy. He said that if Robert let it out, he would have no way of proving it and would probably end up in an insane asylum. Or in a worse state, he said. I suppose he meant he'd be dead with no chance at a live body.

'Oh, yes, the payments aren't made under the table. They are receipted as payment for sessions with MEDIUM. That way, the IRS can't make any trouble.'

After a long silence, Carfax said, 'Surely Western must have offered some proof that he could bring about this repossession? Most millionaires are shrewd; they want assurance that they're not giving their money away. Unless Mifflon is the only client, of course. He doesn't sound as if he's very stable.'

'He's not, if having a conscience makes one unstable. And he's not the only client. Western said he'd introduce him to a man who had come back from the dead.'

'How many are there walking among us?'

'I don't know. Robert told him he'd think about it, but he wouldn't say a word to anybody. He worried about it; he wants to live forever, which is practically what Western offers, but he couldn't stand the idea of stealing another man's body. So, after days of wrestling with himself, he came to me. He said that he hated himself because he was breaking his promise to Western. But he just had to tell me. The greater evil cancelled the lesser.'

'And what did you tell him?'

'To put off a final answer until I thought of what to do. I promised him to have an answer in a few days.'

Carfax thought that Mifflon had adopted Mrs. Webster as his mother, but he saw no reason to comment.

'If this is true,' he said slowly, 'then Western is as rotten as Patricia says he is. And we have our first real break. The only question is, what do we do about it?'

'I don't know,' she said. 'What does this do to your theory that the *sembs* are alien entities?'

'It shatters it to hell. Unless . . . unless those *sembs* are not humans but are taking over humans. After all, they can behave like humans, so why couldn't they fool Mifflon? How would he know whether or not he was talking to a human who'd come back or a *semb* that'd come over?'

He remembered, with a shudder, how the *semb* that was supposed to be his uncle had seemed to expand, to leave the machine, to swoop at him. Had it been trying to invade and conquer him?

He sat up straighter and said, 'That's it!'

'What?' Mrs. Webster said.

'That's why uncle Rufton lied! He had to, otherwise Western wouldn't let him come back! He had to agree to go along with his own murderer! That is, if it really was my uncle.'

94

'In either case, what can you do?'

'I don't know, but I'll think of something. I think the first thing to do is to get Mifflon to require that Western let him talk to his repossessor or whatever you want to call him. He can report back to us, and we can go from there. Do you think he could carry it off?'

'I'll ask him,' she said, and she reached for the viewphone button.

THIRTEEN

Mrs. Webster turned the phone off.

'He's either not there or he's told his secretary to say he's not in. He told me he was going straight home, and I can't imagine why he wouldn't speak to me.'

'If he has an uneasy conscience, he may be sorry he told you about Western's offer,' Carfax said. 'I hope he wasn't foolish enough to confess to Western that he'd broken his promise.'

'Oh, no, he wouldn't do that!' Mrs. Webster said. 'Besides, he's hardly had time!'

'One phone call would do it.'

He stood up. 'I have an uneasy feeling about this. I think I'll go to Mifflon's house. What's the address?'

The estate was in North Pacific Palisades, half a mile from the ocean. Once it had been embedded in a score or so of great houses surrounded by acres of broad lawns, woods, and sculptured gardens. Now it was the lone survivor. The others had been sold to apartment-building developers who had erected a dozen high-rises and were building a dozen more. Dust thrown up by bulldozers was thick in the air, coating with gray the grass, trees, and high stone walls surrounding the Mifflon grounds. The mansion itself, on the highest part of the grounds, had been white but was now khaki.

Carfax spoke into the box outside the iron grille gate. The voice that came from it was thick with Bantu pronunciation. It was also heavy with skepticism.

'I have no record of an appointment with a Mr. Carfax, sir.'

'He's forgotten again,' Carfax said.

There was a pause as the servant considered the well-known

absent-mindedness of his employer. At least, according to Mrs. Webster it was well-known.

'Let me speak to Mr. Mifflon,' Carfax said. 'He'll remember then.'

'Sorry, sir, he's not here.'

'He told me he would be,' Carfax said. 'Let me speak to the secretary, then.'

'She isn't here either, sir.'

'Where can I call them?'

'Sorry, sir, that is confidential.'

'He's going to lose a lot of money if I can't talk to him!' Carfax shouted.

'Sorry, sir. I'm forbidden to give out such information.'

'Four million dollars will go down the drain!'

There was a long pause, then the servant said, with awe congealing his voice, 'Four million dollars, sir?'

'Probably more!'

'But I'd lose my position, sir.'

'Some rules are made to be broken,' Carfax said. 'If the situation demands.'

'Sorry, sir.'

'If I don't get to speak to him, and very soon, you won't have a job because Mifflon will have no money!'

'Yes, sir. But there is a servant shortage, as you know, sir.'

'Oh, you wouldn't have any trouble getting a job,' Carfax said. 'If you could stay here, that is. But you were hired by Mr. Mifflon in Kenya, and you'd have to go back there and hope your agency could find you some other wealthy American or European.'

Carfax hated himself for this despicable brow-beating, but he had a job to do.

'That may be, sir, but while I work for Mr. Mifflon, I owe him loyalty. Goodby, sir.'

Carfax was frustrated, but at the same time he felt admiration for the servant. It was good to find a man who could not be scared or corrupted.

He hesitated about calling Mrs. Webster. If Mifflon was in the house, then he would be doing much legwork for nothing.

Short of prowling the house itself, there was no way to find out if Mifflon was home. At one time, he would have done that, but he was older and less agile and more afraid of the consequences if he were caught.

Sighing, he picked up the carphone.

A minute later, he recradled it. Mrs. Webster had a long dossier on Mifflon, as she probably did on all her important clients. She had told him that Mifflon had his own airplane, which he flew out of the private airport at Santa Susana. The next step was to phone the airport.

Yes, Mr. Mifflon and his secretary had taken off only six minutes ago. Their destination was Bonanza Circus, Nevada.

'That was easy,' Carfax said to himself.

His next station was the Beverly Hills Public Library. He drove four blocks, parked in the MT Santa Monica Boulevard lot, and only had to wait three minutes before boarding the express. Six minutes later, he got off the platform of the Beverly Drive stop, and walked to the library. There he spoke his request into the reference computer and was issued a card. This indicated that all the viewers were occupied, and twenty-three people were ahead of him. Since he did not want to wait, he used the huge U.S. atlas and its auxiliary, both chained to lecterns. Both had some pages missing, torn out by vandals or atlasophiles, but the map of Nevada and the auxinfo pages were still there.

Bonanza Circus had been built four years ago in northern Nevada. Its permanent population was 50,000 and growing, since gambling paid all taxes. It was building a college which would become a university in four more years. Though the Mafia had constructed the city and operated the casinos through dummy corporations, the gambling machines were supervised by the state and federal governments. The local officials had to get a bill of moral health from both governments before they could be elected. The machines were set so that the casinos kept only forty percent of the money poured into them, but they were doing very well at this rate.

Carfax found this interesting, but it wasn't what he was looking for.

He noted the construction companies in the city and went to

a phone booth. On the fourth long-distance call, he found it. The Greater Acme Builders and Developers, Inc., had just finished a complex of large buildings in the mountains twelve kilometers to the east of Bonanza Circus. This was owned by the Megistus Research Corporation. Carfax's informant did not even know what the corporation researched, though he thought it was in the electronic and chemical line.

Carfax phoned Fortune and Thorndyke and asked them to track down all they could on Megistus. After taking the MT back to his car, he drove to the Burbank motel, where Patricia and a message from Fortune and Thorndyke waited for him. The conversation with the agency took three minutes.

'You look happy,' Patricia said.

'I shouldn't, considering what I'm being charged,' he said. 'The agency had to use the Washington, D.C. computer. But they did in fifteen minutes what I couldn't have done in fifteen days. They found out that Western owns the company that owns the company that owns the company that owns Megistus. They also found that Megistus has made no efforts to get contracts.'

'What does that mean?'

'Well, Mifflon never gambles, so why should he go to Bonanza Circus? I would surmise that it's to meet Western in the Megistus complex. Or to use the new MEDIUM that Western may have built there.'

'But there's been nothing in the news . . .'

'Western would want to keep it a secret for several reasons. One, he doesn't want another Houvelle blowing up his machine, not to mention him. Two, he may be using MEDIUM for some purpose which requires absolute secrecy. If Mifflon's story is true, Western may be carrying out his repossessions in his Nevada hideout.'

'But why, right after Mifflon told Mrs. Webster about Western, would he go to Western?'

'Mifflon may have suddenly decided that his chance for immortality overrode his conscience. He wants to make the deal before he changes his mind again . . . Or he may not have gone voluntarily.'

'Why do you say that?'

'Two men accompanied him. Roletti and Curts, if they gave their right names.'

Patricia sat down and said, 'I feel scared.'

'It's only conjecture.'

'Why would they take along his secretary if he went unwillingly? Wouldn't that unnecessarily complicate matters?'

'Not if the secretary is being paid by Western. Anyway, Mifflon never goes any place without her; she's a woman about fifty-five, a motherly type, according to Mrs. Webster. It would look strange if she wasn't with him.'

'It just doesn't seem probable that Mifflon would turn right around and confess to Western that he'd told Mrs. Webster. He might be a little out of his mind, but he's not that unbalanced. So how would Western find out so quickly?'

'He must know that Mifflon has been seeing Mrs. Webster. So he's got her place bugged. Maybe. I have some more calls to make to Bonanza Circus.'

Forty-five motels and hotels later, Carfax had his list complete.

'He didn't check in anywhere, unless it was with a fake name and fake credit card. And that doesn't seem likely.'

'What about Mrs. Bronski and those two men?'

'Nothing. You start packing while I make another call.'

Patricia was startled. 'Packing?'

'Yes. If Mrs. Webster's is bugged, then Western knows that we know about Mifflon. And he'll know where we are. Listen, do you have a friend who'd put us up for a few days? It's too easy for Western to locate us if he wants to.'

Patricia was startled again.

'Then why did we sneak up here?'

'I didn't want to make it too easy. Look, do you have a friend?'

She shook her head. 'The two people I could trust no longer live here. They emigrated to Canada.'

'Can't blame them,' he said. 'Very well. I'll have Fortune and Thorndyke send someone to register in his name, and we'll move in. A big place is what we need, one where the manager isn't likely to see us coming and going. And we'll turn the screen off when we use the phone. I should have done that in the first place, but I didn't really think . . .'

'Go on,' she said. 'You didn't really think what?'

He grinned and said, 'That Western was the villain you painted him to be. And I'm still not one hundred percent sure.'

'You bastard, you thought I was a paranoiac!'

'I considered it, but I don't make up my mind until I have a lot of evidence. Get going. We might need every second we can get!'

Stung into urgency by his tone more than his words, she swiftly began packing. The tight lips, though, were more from anger at him than anxiety over Western.

Carfax decided that he could call the agency later from his car. In fact, it might be better to make all the calls later.

He phoned in to the desk and ordered his bill made ready. The clerk said it'd be done before they got to the desk. All he had to do was to add the phone bill to the computer card. Carfax knew this, but evidently the clerk liked to talk.

Five minutes later, with suitcases full of hastily folded clothing, they left the Grand Vivorium. Four minutes after that, they changed taxis, and they drove to another motel. They waited at the entrance until the taxi pulled away, after which they carried their luggage three blocks to a car rental lot. The transaction took ten minutes, and they drove away in a car with a phone. Carfax talked to a Saunders at Fortune and Thorndyke, made the necessary arrangements, and then had the operator switch him to Bonanza Circus.

He confirmed that Mifflon and party had landed there and that they had not then proceeded elsewhere in their plane. His informant did not know where they had gone after checking out.

A call to Western's temporary headquarters at the Beverly-Wilshire, where he had rented two floors, told him nothing except that Western had a new secretary with a very husky and sexy voice. Mr. Western was not available and would not be for several days. No, she couldn't say where he was without authorization from her employer. But she would give a message to him.

'I'll call back, thank you,' Carfax said.

'I'm sure I'll hear from Mr. Western within a few hours,' Ms. Rapport said. 'Could I have your number in case he wants to speak to you directly.'

'No, thanks,' Carfax said.

FOURTEEN

The next five days were spent mostly in the motel room. They consisted almost entirely of waiting and tediousness, reading, watching TV, exercising, and going to three movies. Gordon Carfax was much better at this game than Patricia. She was not, she said, content to sit like a frog on a lily pad and wait for flies. Gordon tried to keep her occupied by talking to her about her past life, her childhood experiences – happy and traumatic – her lovers, her jobs, her ambitions and frustrations, the things which annoyed and exasperated her, the things which made her rejoice; in short, the items which made her a unique human being.

Patricia liked to talk about herself, but she also had to have physical activity. After a few hours of spilling emotional contents, she would pace back and forth and then say that she either had to go for a walk or to bed with Gordon. He was obliging; he would do whichever she preferred. But near the end of the five days, he was more inclined to walk. His fifteen years of seniority told on him. He was beginning to wonder if they should get married. At present, he could satisfy her, but in twenty years she would be fifty and with a lust probably undiminished. He would be sixty-five and bound to be slowing down.

Patricia had said nothing about marriage, and she might not even be thinking of it. Of course, when she was leading a normal life, when she was not so anxiety-ridden, she would be looking at their situation from the long-range view.

He could have asked her if she wanted to make their arrangement permanent, but he saw no reason to do so. He did not want to make any commitments until this was over.

Meanwhile, though their personal events moved slowly, public events moved swiftly.

A Dr. Orenstein of Yeshiva University, a member of the federal committee which had investigated MEDIUM, appeared on the Jack Phillips talk show. During the conversation, he stated that it was possible that the *embu* was not an expanding universe. If this were indeed so, the energy of eons accumulating in it might destroy it. The so-called 'dead,' the *sembs*, would be destroyed along with the rest of that other world. This was regrettable perhaps, but not dangerous to our world. That is, unless a channel between the *embu* and our universe happened to be open when the *embu* 'exploded.' Who knew what enormous energies, perhaps earth-destroying, might raven through the breach between our worlds?

Jack Phillips turned pale and looked as if he was sorry he had brought up the subject. He did manage to rally and ask how that was possible. Wouldn't the first touch of energy destroy MEDIUM and so close the breach?

Dr. Orenstein: 'It might. But some of us have wondered if the heavy use of MEDIUM hasn't created a weak spot in the wall between our worlds. It could be compared to a trickle in a dike. If that trickle is not stopped up at once, the whole dike will, in a short time, become a wide gap. And the sea pours in.'

Cries from the audience: 'You're crazy!'

'What are you trying to do, scare the shit out of us?'

'My God, we're doomed!'

Jack Phillips, after signaling for silence: 'I don't think you should be making public speculations like that, Doctor. It might cause a panic. After all, what evidence do you have for that? It is just a theory, isn't it? A wild theory? A hypothesis, I should say, since you have absolutely no data, I repeat, no data at all.'

Dr. Orenstein: 'That's true. But the mere possibility should make us stop to reflect. Should we continue using MEDIUM when we don't know what its long-term effects will be? Now, I'm a scientist, and what I'm saying will be regarded as heresy by many scientists. Science must explore wherever it can. Many of my colleagues would insist on this principle. But many others would agree with me. The very chance, however slight, that we might be tampering with forces which could wipe this earth clean of life in a few seconds should make us evaluate the continued use of MEDIUM.

'Anyway, I'm only being a little premature in saying this. My speculations and my recommendations are in the official report. And you'll be reading it soon. That is, if the president ever takes the lid off it.'

Jack Phillips: 'Then you definitely recommend that MEDIUM be shut down?'

Dr. Orenstein: 'At once! We must study it carefully, analyze its possible effects!'

Regina Calomela, a guest: 'But Doctor Orenstein, how can you possibly know what its effects will be unless you use it?'

Dr. Orenstein: 'That's a good question. However, I was thinking of an evaluation of the data already derived from MEDIUM's operation, a mathematical analysis.'

Jack Phillips, looking relieved: 'I have to sell some soap now. We'll continue after this commercial.'

The viewers were disappointed. Phillips announced that Dr. Orenstein had received an emergency call and would not be present. What the emergency was, Phillips did not say.

Two days later, Mrs. Webster announced over a local talk show that she agreed with Dr. Orenstein. MEDIUM had weakened the 'wall.' She was finding it far easier to make contact with the spirit world.

Bob Jaspers, another guest, a stand-up comic, added that he hoped not. It would mean that we'd all be haunted, night and day. And he thought he'd gotten rid of his mother-in-law.

The papers and the TV news were full of reports of riots all over the world.

The president of the United States undoubtedly thought that this was a poor time to release the official report. But pressure was too strong. Three days after Orenstein's appearance, newsmen were given the three-thousand-page document.

The same day, the Vatican issued its official opinion of MEDIUM.

Summarized, the federal committee report stated that there was no doubt that MEDIUM had been the means for communicating with the dead. There was no fakery about it. Forty-five interviewees had been identified from voiceprints or personal details which no charlatan could have known.

Extracts from interviews with the Etruscan, Menle Athlan, Louis XIV of France, Hamilcar Barca (the father of Hannibal), and Pericles of ancient Athens were included in the report. The linguistic specialists on the committee affirmed their genuineness. It would be impossible for any modern, no matter how learned, to have imitated the language well enough to have posed as these ancients.

It was true little had been known of Punic and Etruscan, but much about these had been learned from Menle and Barca. No scholar could have built up a grammar and vocabulary, so self-consistent, from the scanty knowledge previously available. Nor could any scholar have provided such intimate details of ancient Carthaginian, Latin, and Etruscan culture and history.

The same day that the report came out, Dr. Orenstein spoke over a New York City radio station. He had been denied any more time on TV but had found a willing sponsor in the owner of the broadcasting company.

Orenstein's charges were grave. The commission's report was not complete. Lengthy sections had been suppressed by the president. He must have known that he could not keep them quiet forever, but he did not want to be responsible for their publication.

The committee had located and interviewed Jesus and Joseph Smith. Jesus had been considerably surprised and disgusted to find that the gentiles were worshipping him as a god. His teachings had been intended for the Jews only.

Joseph Smith had confessed that the famous tablets of gold on which the Book of Mormon had been inscribed had never existed. He did insist, however, that he had penned them while God Himself dictated them. The tablets were a pious fraud, it was true, but God had ordered him to tell people that he had found the tablets so that the true religion would be accepted more quickly.

Dr. Orenstein was shot and killed by two men as he stepped out of the station.

A ricocheting 9mm. bullet also killed a ten-year-old girl on her way home from school.

The two murderers fled in a car, went through a red light at sixty kilometers per hour, and smashed into a truck. Forty thousand people attended their funerals, and a subscription of eighty thousand was raised to support their survivors. Income tax reduced this to twenty thousand.

The statement of the Vatican was ingenious and disprovable. If the *sembs* did exist, as evidence indicated, then they were also duplicates, as the evidence indicated. They were not truly the souls of the dead. They were 'electromagnetic shadows.' God, for His mysterious reasons, had allowed them to come into being. But they were not spirits in heaven, purgatory, or hell. The faithful could be reassured of that.

The Vatican report mentioned Carfax's theory that they might be alien sentients posing as the dead, doubtless for some evil purpose. This theory, the Vatican said, could be valid. Whatever the truth, it would be good if MEDIUM were shut down permanently. And Roman Catholics were forbidden to use it.

The encyclical of the Pope concerning this subject would be forthcoming sometime in the next year.

'Then it'll be a matter of dogma, not discipline,' Carfax told Patricia. 'I wonder what'll happen when they locate Moses and Mohammed? What rationalizations will we hear then?'

'According to you, they're not rationalizations,' she said. 'Or have you changed your mind?'

'Not yet. But I'm weakening.'

And so the days passed. There were great storms outside their motel-room walls and some small storms inside. Gordon irritated Patricia with his habit of mumbling to himself and his fondness for garlic bread. She angered him because she left her clothes lying around and preferred hamburgers to steak and would eat no green foods and thought the president, a hard-nosed conservative, was a great man. Nor did they agree on their TV shows. She liked to watch the game shows and comedy series, but she was bored by anything suggesting the serious. He loved Shakespeare but he also loved Westerns, and she yawned loudly and sighed when he insisted on watching them.

These issues were trifles to which both could adjust themselves under less crowded circumstances, but they might be indicative of deeper and unreconcilable differences.

Three times, he got a report from Fortune and Thorndyke. Their agent in Bonanza Circus had been unable to determine whether or not Western and Mifflon were living in the Megistus complex. The company had a ten-story building with apartments for its employees and guests, but Reynolds, the F&T agent, had not been able to get past the entrance gate. He had bribed a U.S. mail clerk to check on Megistus's incoming mail. No letters for either Western or Mifflon had gone through. This might mean that they were communicating only via phone or sending their mail through the Megistus planes.

Carfax did know, however, that Western was not at the Beverly-Wilshire headquarters. A newspaper man had ascertained that.

Reynold's second call was to report his findings at the Bonanza Circus Power Company. Megistus was using no more electricity than was to be expected. This was negative evidence, since MEDIUM could be drawing power from the *embu*.

On the fifth day, Carfax got a call from Reynolds at 13 : 20, just after he and Patricia had come back from lunch.

'I'm being shadowed, Carfax. My nosing around has caught somebody's attention. I've tagged two men since yesterday, and somebody's been through my room. So what's the next step? You want me to stay here or pull out?'

'Better pull out,' Carfax said. 'There isn't much more you can do there, and those guys might play rough. The stakes are pretty high.'

Carfax wished that he had gone himself. It would have been much less expensive, and he could have kept himself busy. But if Western was there, it wouldn't do for him to find out that Carfax was sniffing around. It would have been too easy to grab him right there and whisk him into the walls of Megistus.

On the other hand, would Western do anything but keep an eye on him? He must know that Mifflon had told Mrs. Webster about the repossession insurance. Yet Mrs. Webster had received no threats or been attacked. Western must feel very secure, and he had reason to be so. Mifflon would just deny anything she said.

He was stymied. There was little he could do until Mifflon himself came out of hiding.

He was impatient and tense during dinner. Even the movie they saw afterward, a powerful and frightening science-fiction drama based on Lem's *Solaris*, could not keep his mind off Mifflon. On entering their room, he saw a light flashing at the base of the phone. He called the desk clerk, who told him he was to phone a number in Bonanza City. Three minutes later, he turned to Patricia with a big smile.

'I owe a flight controller two hundred dollars. He just told me Mifflon and his secretary are about to leave for the Santa Susana airport.'

FIFTEEN

At this time, 13:25, the Santa Susana airport lobby was almost deserted. Gordon and Patricia Carfax sat in the lobby and drank coffee and waited. At 13:50, they saw the lights of a plane circling in the distance. At 14:00, the two-jet mono-plane taxied toward the hangar where Mifflon stored it. Gordon checked its number against that given him by the controller. It was Mifflon's.

Gordon threw his half-full cup into the disposal vent and said, 'Mifflon will go to the tower to check out. But his secretary may come here to wait for him.'

'And then what?'

'She doesn't know us. I'll try to strike up a conversation . . . here she comes.'

A tall woman with a more than ample bosom, very narrow waist, too-wide hips, and long good-looking legs entered. Her gray hair was piled in a high many-ringed coiffure, but she wore no makeup except for false eyelashes. She looked every bit of her fifty-five years, but she must have been a striking beauty when young. She made straight for the coffee canteen with a long hip-swinging stride that made Carfax wonder if she had once been a stripper. Passing Carfax, she left behind a cloud of sandalwood.

Carfax waited until she was reaching for her cup before speaking.

'Mrs. Bronski?'

She jumped, gasped, and sloshed part of the coffee out of the cup. 'For God's sakes! You startled me so!'

'Sorry,' he said. He showed her an I.D. card, a left-over from his L.A. residency. 'Mr. Western phoned me and told me to escort you two home.'

Her face cleared and then she frowned again. 'Oh, but he didn't say anything to us about you, Mr. Childe.'

'Mr. Western called me a little while ago and said he'd decided you needed a bodyguard.'

'And did he say why?' she said, raising her eyebrows.

'You don't ask Mr. Western why.'

'The least the son of a bitch could have done, he could have radioed us you were coming.'

If he learned nothing else, he thought, he had at least ascertained that they had been with Western.

'I'll introduce you to my colleague, Mrs. Childe,' he said. He wanted to keep her busy until Mifflon showed up so she wouldn't start asking too many questions. He also hoped that she would not ask to see Patricia's identification.

'You have a beautiful wife,' Mrs. Bronski said. 'Isn't she *young*-looking?'

'I'm a cradle robber,' he said. He stopped before Patricia, who looked up from her chair. 'Honey, this is Mrs. Bronski, Mr. Mifflon's secretary.'

Mrs. Bronski sat down beside Patricia and said, 'Are you sure Mr. Western didn't say anything about why we'd need you? I wonder what happened? Everything seemed all right when we left. Robert was in fine shape, but I suppose . . .'

Carfax waited for several seconds and then said, 'Suppose what, Mrs. Bronski?'

'Nothing at all.'

'Maybe Mr. Western was afraid that some fanatic might find out Mr. Mifflon was a client,' Carfax said. 'There's been so much violence lately, especially since Orenstein was killed.'

'That's probably it,' she said. 'But who would've found out? It's been very hush-hush.'

'There are a lot of people spying on Mr. Western. The feds, the newsmen, the crackpots.'

Footsteps sounded around the corner, and a tall chubby man of about thirty-five came around the corner. Carfax recognized him from photographs supplied by Fortune and Thorndyke. He switched on the recorder he carried in his coat pocket.

Mifflon stopped suddenly, looking quickly from the Carfaxes

to Mrs. Bronski. He gripped his briefcase as if he thought it might be taken away from him.

'What is it, Mrs. Bronski?'

She rose, smiling, and said, 'Mr. Western's bodyguards, Mr. Mifflon. He sent them in case there was any trouble.'

Mifflon looked alarmed. 'Trouble? What trouble? Western said everything was fine.'

Carfax advanced, holding out his hand. 'I'm Mr. Childe, and this is my wife, my partner in my agency. I'm sorry to disturb you like this, Mr. Mifflon, but Mr. Western roused us out of bed to meet you here. All he said was that he wanted to make sure you got home safely, and we should stay with you until he discharges us. I don't think there's much to worry about, but, as I was telling Mrs. Bronski, there has been a lot of killing lately. The country's in a turmoil. But then you know that.'

'Yeah,' Mifflon said, as if it was news to him. 'Well, it's too late to call Western. He'll be in bed. But I'll phone him first thing in the morning. If he knows something, I want to know it, too.'

'Do you have any luggage?' Carfax said. 'I'll pick it up for you.'

'It'll be shipped in later,' Mifflon said. 'The house should have everything I'll need. Right, Mrs. Bronski?'

'Right,' she said and added, after a pause, 'as if you didn't know that, Mr. Mifflon.'

Carfax watched him curiously. Mifflon was supposed to be a very shy person with a tendency to stutter when he was with strangers. This man had a brisk confident air and spoke smoothly.

Carfax had ridden up on the MT because it was faster than taking a car, and he had wanted to arrive ahead of Mifflon. He had, however, rented a car to drive them back to North Pacific Palisades. He led them out to the Zagreus, saw Mifflon and Bronski into the back seat, and got behind the wheel. Patricia sat beside him.

'You know how to get there?' Mifflon said.

'No, sir,' Carfax said. 'I have the address, of course.'

There was a pause. Carfax, watching him in the overhead mirror, saw him nudge Mrs. Bronski with his elbow.

'Oh, I'll tell you,' she said.

Carfax didn't listen. He knew the route, and he was thinking that Mifflon, or whoever was in Mifflon's body, did not know. And Patricia, judging from her stiff posture, understood and was scared. He did not blame her. He felt a little dissociated from reality. So it was true.

They drew up before the gate of the estate ninety-five minutes later. Mifflon spoke to the servant over the box, and the gates swung open. Carfax drove up the driveway, stopping before the big house. A black man dressed in pajamas and a robe came out to greet Mifflon. He looked strangely at the Carfaxes but only nodded when introduced. Gordon hoped that he would not remember his voice.

The servant, Yohana, led them into a huge room which looked like the lobby of a hotel. Gordon and Patricia, with their nightcases, were conducted to the second story up a broad staircase and down a long hall to a room near the end. When the door was shut, Carfax said, 'Well, so far so good! But when he calls Western in the morning, we'd better move out fast. I hope he doesn't try to stop us.'

'What'll we do if he does?' Patricia said.

Carfax opened his nightcase and took out a 7.92 mm. revolver. 'I'd hate to use this, but I will. I don't think Mifflon, or whoever he is, would hesitate to shoot us. The stakes are too high.'

'Shouldn't we sneak out later?' she said. 'What's the use of staying until morning?'

'He might not call Western at once. The longer we're here, the more we might find out.'

He looked at her sharply. 'Are you getting cold feet? I told you I should tackle this myself.'

'Only my toes are cold, but they are about twenty below zero,' she said. 'Don't worry. I won't let you down. I'm frightened, but I'm glad I didn't stay home. It's a hundred times better than being cooped up in that room and bored to death.'

'Thanks,' he said, 'but I know what you mean. Going into

action is like being released from prison. O.K. Let's go down for the nightcap.'

Mifflon and Mrs. Bronski were waiting for them in the library-study, a large room with walls lined with shelves of books, a big teakwood desk, leather-covered chairs and sofas, and a giant fireplace. Mifflon was in pajamas and a robe; Bronski was wearing a negligee and a thin light-scarlet, yellow-piped robe. Both had drinks in their hands. Mifflon looked as if he was surprised that they were still in their day clothes.

'I thought I'd check out the grounds first,' Carfax said.

'Good idea. What's your desire?' Mifflon waved his hand at the bar, which seemed to have about every liquor in the world.

Carfax went to the bar and looked at the bottles. When he found a brandy that had not been opened, he said, 'Pat and I'll take this.'

He had no intention of drinking from a bottle which might have been doped.

'There's much better stuff there,' Mifflon said.

'This is fine,' Carfax said. 'It's better than I'm used to.'

Mifflon shrugged and opened the bottle while Carfax watched him closely. He handed the glasses to the two, and then he lifted his Scotch in a toast. 'Here's to immortality.'

Mifflon drank and then laughed loudly. Mrs. Bronski frowned.

Carfax said, 'What's the joke?'

'I'm just happy to be alive,' Mifflon said. 'To be able to breathe, to eat and drink, to walk, to make love.'

'I would imagine anybody'd feel that way after talking to those poor creatures,' Carfax said. 'But in the long run it's depressing, isn't it? I mean, you know that sooner or later you'll be one of them. Forever. A thing of energy whirling around other things, locked in a cold dance in a cold universe. It's nothing to look forward to.'

Mifflon sipped his drink and then said, slowly, 'It's only a stage, a temporary stopping off. I'm a member of the Pancosmic Church of the *Embu*-Christ, you know, and we believe that the *embu* is just a sort of purgatory.'

'No, I didn't know that,' Carfax said. He had to pretend an

almost total lack of knowledge about Mifflon. 'It's a comfortable religion, no doubt of that.'

He was trying to think of something to ask Mifflon which his briefing might not have covered. He would have liked to ask him if he intended to visit Mrs. Webster again. But how could he explain how he knew about Mifflon's attendance at her seances?

'I don't have the money to use MEDIUM,' he said. 'But I did go to a human medium once, a Mrs. Webster. My sister thinks she's great, and she talked me into going with her. Webster tried to summon our mother, and something did appear, something so thin you could see right through it. And we heard a sort of whispering. But that was all. I didn't go back; Webster isn't cheap, though her fees don't come near Western's, of course.'

Mifflon stared hard at Carfax and then smiled. 'Oh, I was her client for a long time,' he said. 'She's a very nice woman, a beautiful woman for her age. And she's no fraud. I mean, she's sincere, and she does have certain undeniable powers. Western says that some mediums can open a brief channel to the *embu*. But it's all so uncertain and so unscientific, and the results are seldom worth the effort and the money. I have no intention of going back to her. Or, for that matter, back to MEDIUM. I'm not interested in the dead any more.'

I'll bet you're not, Carfax thought. He touched the recorder in his pocket. Tomorrow he would take it to Fortune and Thorndyke's laboratory. There this man's voice would be matched against Mifflon's. They would be similar, of course, since the oral cavity and the larynx were the same. But if Mifflon's brain was occupied by a *semb*, the rhythm of speech and the choice of vocabulary items might be different.

After that had been established, if it would be established, what could be done? The police could not arrest Mifflon on such evidence. Even if they did, they couldn't get the district attorney to bring Mifflon to trial. And even if he was tried, no judge would permit the case to last long. There just were no precedents, and nobody was going to set any.

Yet Mifflon surely was not the only one to be possessed. Could not others be tracked down and their pattern of speech be matched against the former owners'? If enough such cases were presented to the police, would they then refuse to take action?

The chances were that they would refuse. Very few would believe that such things could be happening.

It looked hopeless. But Carfax did not intend to quit.

What if there was a way to demonstrate even to the most incredulous that a man could be possessed? What if the invader could be exorcized, and the original occupant could then testify? If scientific means could bring about possession, why could not the same means be used to dispossess?

The trouble with that idea was that Western had a monopoly on the only machine that could do the job – if indeed it could be done.

'Well, Mr. Childe,' Mifflon said, putting his empty glass down. 'It is late, and if you think you should check out the grounds, you should do it now. You can lock the door when you come in, and set the alarm system, it's behind the drapery near the front door, and don't bother reporting to me. That is, unless you find something that needs reporting. I'll be asleep before you make your rounds.'

Carfax rose and said, 'It shouldn't take more than ten minutes. Goodnight, everybody.'

Patricia stood up and stretched, and Mifflon watched her with undisguised admiration. Mrs. Bronski said, 'I'm tired, too. But I'll take along an afternightcap, if you don't object, Mr. Mifflon.'

'Have I ever?' he said.

'Oh no, of course not,' she said quickly. 'But I always ask, don't I?'

Mifflon grunted, and Mrs. Bronski poured ten fingers of Wild Turkey over one ice cube, and strode out, inaudible burlesque music and cries of, 'Take it all off!' surging around her.

Carfax went out the front door and down the portico onto the driveway. The lights were bright here, but he had a slim flashlight in his pocket for the dark places. He walked down the drive to the gate, and went along the wall to the left, passing around heavy shrubbery and a number of trees. The circuit took him fifteen minutes, not the ten he had promised. The garage in back of the house also had to be investigated. Carfax sent the flashlight beam in through the windows and saw nothing but two cars, the Zagreus and a Benz, and some worktables and racks of tools. Yohana had put the Zagreus away; he was now sleeping, or at least was in bed, in the apartment over the garage.

Carfax could have made a perfunctory inspection, since he did not expect to run across any prowlers. But he wanted to fix the layout in his mind for future use. It would not be difficult to get into the grounds. The wall was three meters high, but he could jump up and pull himself over. A fencing of three strands of barbed wire ran across the top, but there was, according to Mrs. Bronski, no alarm connected to it. The house and the garage were equipped with an alarm system, but the burglars who had entered it three years ago had by-passed it. Mifflon had not bothered to install a new system. Mrs. Bronski had said that though Mifflon was timid, he had seemed delighted, not upset, after the burglary. It had injected some excitement into an otherwise dull life, and for weeks afterward he had gotten up in the middle of the night and prowled the house with his 9 mm. automatic. Perhaps he had hoped he could shoot an intruder and so give vent to a suppressed desire for violence. That was, however, Carfax's analysis, not Mrs. Bronski's. He surmised that Mifflon's domination by his mother may have caused an unconscious, or perhaps even a conscious, resentment or hatred. Mifflon had been too suppressed to verbalize his hostility. But he must have hated his mother, and he may have wished to explode this hatred against someone whose injury or death would not result in legal punishment.

It was only a theory, but it seemed probable. At least, it was the only explanation Carfax had for Mifflon's behavior. Mrs. Webster had had no theory; she just thought it was rather strange. She had confided to Carfax that 'Robert is a queer kid. Nice but queer.'

He re-entered the house and locked the door, throwing the alarm switch concealed behind the drapery. When he went into his room, he found Patricia pacing back and forth and looking furious.

'What's the matter?'

'That bastard asked me to go to bed with him!'

Carfax paused and then said, 'Did you accept?'

She looked blank and then quickly smiled. 'You're a great kidder, aren't you? Well, for your information, I said yes!'

Carfax was almost fooled. She was trying to give him as much as he had given. But it would take a long time before she caught up.

'Good,' he said. 'You ought to be able to get a lot out of him. In the way of information, I mean.'

'I almost think you mean it,' she said. 'Tell me you don't,' and she put her arms around him.

'Of course, I don't,' he said. If she had been a professional detective, he would have expected her to take Mifflon up on his proposal, though he would not have required her to do so. He was glad that she had not, yet he regretted the lost opportunity.

Patricia kissed him and, releasing him, said, 'He didn't act like the Mifflon described to me. He was very smooth, as if he'd had long practice and was not accustomed to being turned down.'

'That's the clincher,' Carfax said. 'The real Mifflon is – was – impotent.'

'Oh? How'd you find out?'

'I saw Mrs. Webster's dossier on him. She was a mother image, you know, and he told her a lot more than he had to about himself. Of course, Mrs. Webster wouldn't have let me see that part of the dossier if the situation hadn't demanded that I know everything about him.

'I had Fortune and Thorndyke check on it, and they found out that it's true. Or was.'

'Well, he *is* hard up,' Patricia said. 'I opened the door a crack and watched down the hall. He certainly doesn't waste any time. About two minutes after I'd refused him, he was tapping on Mrs. Bronski's door. She let him in, and as far as I know he hasn't come out yet.'

Carfax winked at her and said, 'I'll tippytoe down the hall and make sure.'

He returned a few minutes later, grinning, and said, 'Her

bed springs need oiling. Tell me, how'd he take it? I mean your big loud no?'

'He didn't like it; he looked as if he wanted to kill me. But he recovered quickly enough, smiled like a gargoyle, and asked me, very sweetly, if I'd change my mind if there was enough money. I told him to go to hell, but he said it'd be worth a thousand to him!'

Carfax whistled and said, 'He *must* be hard up!'

'You go to hell, too,' she said.

'I've been there, and I didn't like it. I wonder?'

'What now?'

'If we could make anything out of this. Granted, he might be all pooped out, but then he may be even hornier than most, and the sight of you, young and beautiful, might rejuvenate him.'

Patricia almost spat at him. 'Are you suggesting that I do go to his room, after he gets through with that old hag?'

'Cool down,' he said. 'I'm not thinking of you going through with it. I was wondering if I could burst in and play the heavy husband. If I knocked him out in a fit of jealous rage, then maybe, just maybe, we would get something out of him when he came to.'

'He could have us jailed,' she said. 'He could charge us with fraud, assault and battery, and God knows what else.'

'Yes, I know,' he said. 'I was just thinking out loud. If I thought I could get the true Mifflon to come through, then we'd have our case. But then I don't know if the true one is still in his body. Maybe it's not a case of the *semb* overriding the original possessor. Maybe there's a switch, the original goes into the *embu* and the *semb* moves in.'

'It's too uncertain, too dangerous,' Patricia said. 'Besides, I don't like the idea of using violence.'

'I don't either, but there's too much at stake to get squeamish. It might at least be worth trying. Mifflon isn't going to bring charges, no matter what happens. He doesn't want the police in on this, even if they can't do anything if they should get suspicious.'

Carfax began pacing. After crossing the big room four times, he said, 'If I thought we could scare Bronski, we could work on her. She has to be in on this. But all she has to do is keep her mouth shut, and she looks tough enough to do that. And I'm not sure that even if she thought I was going to kill her if she didn't talk, that she would talk. She knows that Western brought back someone from the dead and put him in Mifflon's body. So why wouldn't he do the same for her? And maybe give her a young body? Probably, he's already promised her one. No, she wouldn't crack.

'And working on Mifflon is no good, either. I don't know how to go about getting down to the real Mifflon. If he's still there, that is, and he may not be.'

'So what do we do?' Patricia said.

'We're getting out of here now. There's no use waiting until Mifflon calls Western. He might shoot us. More probably he'd hold us here until Western sent somebody to take care of us. I now think it's better to be long gone when Mifflon finds out he's been had. If Western was ignoring us before, he sure isn't going to from now on. He'll know we're on to him. But we've found out what we were looking for. That isn't the real Mifflon.'

He could do nothing alone. He needed to find others, people who would want to do something about Western and who had the power to do it. That should not be difficult, but it would, like most projects, become tedious in execution.

Patricia had not unpacked their cases; they only had to pick them up and walk out. Carfax had determined that the garage door was locked, and so they could not drive off in the Zagreus. He phoned to the nearest taxi company and made certain that they would be picked up in fifteen minutes, though not at the gate. They would walk down Firebird Lane to Vista Grange Drive and a block west.

Carfax walked out of the door with Patricia close behind him. The door to Mrs. Bronski's room opened, and Mifflon, naked and smoking a cigarette, came out. Carfax stopped; Patricia bumped into him.

Carfax had turned off the light in his room before opening the door. The only light in the hall came from Bronski's room and a lamp on a table at the far end of the hall. Mifflon was headed toward his own room and was not looking at them. But Patricia, startled, gasped. Mifflon turned his head and saw

Carfax, half-hidden by the opened door. It was too late to swing the nightcase behind the door.

Mifflon opened his mouth, closed it, and ran into his room. Carfax said, 'He knows we're leaving! Run for it, Pat!'

SIXTEEN

Gordon and Patricia ran down the broad staircase, sliding one hand along the banister to guide themselves in the dark. The door was a pale gray oblong across the long floor; it seemed a long way off. And it was. As they were halfway to it, a gun boomed in the hallway above them. It sounded like a 9 mm. to Carfax. He didn't hear the bullet striking anything ahead or behind them, so he presumed that Mifflon had fired it, while still in the hallway upstairs, as a warning. Or he had discharged it accidentally.

In either event, it was evident that Mifflon would be at the top of the staircase before they could get through the door. They would form a good target, silhouetted against the light from the door, which was almost all glass. If Mifflon was not hasty, if he held the automatic in both hands and took his time aiming, he might hit them. The 9 mm. is not accurate except at close range, but they were not far enough away to take a chance.

The lights all over the big room and the adjoining room went on. Mifflon had thrown the switch from upstairs.

Carfax looked back up and saw Mifflon standing at the top of the steps. He shouted at Patricia, grabbed her arm, and pulled her to the right. The automatic bellowed, and bits of the marble floor flew up ahead of him, and a large hole appeared in the frame of the door leading to the adjoining room. Patricia screamed and jerked herself away and dived to the floor. Carfax was close behind her as they rolled behind a large sofa. The gun boomed again, and pieces of stuffing rained down on Carfax's head. These were followed a second later by bits of wood from the frame of a large painting on the wall about six meters behind him. The bullet had passed a few centimeters over Carfax, ricocheted off the floor and hit the painting.

Carfax removed his 7.92 mm. revolver from his belt, crawled to the far end of the sofa, past the hysterically chattering Patricia, and fired quickly at Mifflon. He ducked back, and three bullets tore through the end of the sofa. More pieces of stuffing showered him.

'Shut up and listen!' he said. 'I'm going to shoot at him again, and when I do, you run for the next room.'

'I . . . I . . . I'm scared!'

'So am I,' he said. He crawled back to the shattered end of the sofa, leaned around, and fired at Mifflon, who was halfway down the staircase. Mifflon fell to his side, and rolled down some steps, but Carfax did not think he had hit him. Patricia, yelling, jumped up and, leaving her case behind her, ran a few steps and dived through the door. Mifflon got up and, crouching, ran down the steps and around the end of the staircase. Carfax shot twice and then reloaded with bullets from the pocket of his jacket.

Patricia shouted from the next room, 'What do I do now?'

'I'll meet you at our place!' he shouted back. 'Get going!'

He heard footsteps hitting the floor hard and, a few seconds later, a door slamming. He hoped that she wouldn't run into Yohana. If Mifflon had kept his head, he would have signaled Yohana in his garage-apartment. He supposed that there was an intercom or some sort of signal which could be turned on in Mifflon's bedroom when he wanted the servant.

He also wished that he had not put off relieving himself after arrival. His full bladder was paining him, and if Mifflon shot again, which he was going to do, Carfax would probably piss in his pants; he was scared. Being shot at had always scared him, and he had wet himself a few times while under fire in Korea.

He was in a bad spot now. Mifflon was crouching behind the other side of the marble staircase. He probably had his automatic pointed at the doorway, expecting Carfax to make a run for it. Carfax rose to a crouching position and ran out from the sofa toward a large chair. He dived at it, slid along the marble, burning his hands, and stopped behind the chair. The automatic fired four times, and the chair disintegrated. Carfax had rolled on past it and was up on his feet and diving again.

He slid again, this time by a huge mahogany sideboard. It provided no shield against the bullets, which would tear through it, but Mifflon could not see him unless he stood up. And the hallway to a rear room was only about sixteen meters away.

The trouble was that Mifflon would now be aiming toward the entrance to the hallway.

'Toss your gun out and come on out with your hands behind your neck!' Mifflon shouted. 'I don't want to kill you!'

'O.K.!' Carfax shouted back, wondering if Mifflon really thought he was fool enough to obey him. No doubt Mifflon did not want to kill him, just yet. He wanted to question him first. Carfax could imagine the interrogation. Western and his aides would be there, along with a paraphernalia of little sharp knives and flaming splinters. Oh, he would talk all right – if they caught him.

There was only one thing to do: stand up at least part way, fire at Mifflon to disconcert his aim, and then dive toward the entrance to the hallway. Or, perhaps go in the opposite direction, where Mifflon would not expect him. The disadvantage in that was that he had much more distance to cover.

He would have preferred to stay where he was, but if he did he would only be putting off the inevitable. He clenched his teeth to keep them from chattering, hoped he could control the shaking of his arms and hands, and rose. As his head cleared the top of a chair sitting about ten feet away from him, he saw Mifflon also rising. He lifted the revolver with both hands, while Mifflon, also using both hands, aimed at him.

Later on, he wondered who would have hit whom. But now he was startled as shot after shot boomed out from his right. He fired once at Mifflon, and the shot went over Mifflon's head. He swung around, expecting to see Yohana standing at the door through which Patricia had run and about to shoot at him. He saw no one, though someone was firing from the next room.

The automatic must have been emptied; he was too excited to be counting the shots, but the boomings seemed to go on and on, though they actually took only a few seconds. Then he heard Patricia sobbing uncontrollably.

Mifflon lay on his back, only his bare feet visible. The three lowest stairs were smashed, the floor in front of the feet was chipped, and the wall beyond bore three holes.

Upstairs, Mrs. Bronski screamed. He looked up and saw her, naked and unarmed, leaning on the banister and staring at Mifflon.

He called out, 'Patricia! I'm coming, don't shoot!'

Patricia ran out, threw herself into his arms, and wept. He pushed her away and looked at her. Blood covered the front of her coat, and her two hands were smeared with it. And now his coat was bloodied.

'Are you hurt?'

'Oh God, no,' she said. 'I'm not; it's *his* blood!'

For a minute he did not understand, then he knew that she meant the blood was Yohana's.

'What happened?'

She tried to tell him but could not get all the words out. He said, 'Wait a minute,' and then looked up at the top of the staircase. Mrs. Bronski was gone.

'No, come with me,' he said. 'She may have gone after a gun.'

With the 7.92 mm. in his right hand, he took Patricia's hand with his left and led her cautiously toward the door. He kept his eye on Mifflon because he might not be dead, and he could not see the 9 mm. As they neared the door, the pistol came into sight. It was lying on the floor near Mifflon's outstretched hand.

'Is Yohana dead?'

She nodded and said, 'I'm going to throw up.'

'You do that,' he said. 'I'm going upstairs to check on Bronski.'

'I don't want to go into the kitchen alone.'

She was very pale and trembling and obviously about to vomit.

'He can't hurt you,' Carfax said. 'But stay here. Use that big bowl on the sideboard. Or the floor. I'll apologize to the host.'

She looked at him strangely and then dashed for the bowl.

He walked to the foot of the steps and examined Mifflon. Only one of the twelve bullets Patricia had fired had hit him, but that had been enough. It had torn off his left shoulder, and knocked him back about three meters. The floor around him was a mass of blood and pieces of flesh and bone. Whoever he was, Mifflon had gone back where he had come from. And the Carfaxes would be charged with murder. Who'd believe their story?

He picked up the automatic, unloaded it, and noted that the clip was full. He dropped the gun in his coat pocket and ran up the steps. At the top, he paused, listened, and then stuck his head around the corner at the base of the wall. No one was in sight. He rose and went softly down the hallway, looked into Mifflon's room, which was lit with one lamp, and then put his ear to the door of Bronski's room. He could hear her talking excitedly, though in a low voice. He hoped she wasn't calling the police.

No, she wasn't. She was speaking to Western.

He tried the knob. It was locked. Bronski must have been watching the door, since she had now quit talking. At least, he could not hear her voice.

Shooting out a key lock looks impressive on TV. But the bullet is liable to ricochet, and the lock mechanism may become jammed. Nor is it easy to slam against the door with a shoulder and burst it open. This door was of thick oak and opened inward. Carfax would rebound with no damage to the door and considerable injury to himself.

He raised his foot and kicked hard. His foot hurt, and the lock remained locked.

He stood to one side to consider the situation. A gun banged inside, and a hole appeared in the door at a level which would have caught him in the stomach if he had been in front of it. Its report sounded like that of an 8.1 mm.

He went back to the head of the steps and called to Patricia. She straightened up from the bowl and walked to the foot of the staircase. She did not look at Mifflon. Her face was drawn and was a pale green. An odor of vomit mingled with that of gunpowder.

'Go into the kitchen and get some screwdrivers and a hammer,' he said. 'If there aren't any there, get into the garage, though you may have to break a window to do it.'

'What are you going to do?' she said weakly.

'I'm going to remove the hinges to Bronski's bedroom door. We're not going to leave any witnesses behind.'

'You mean you're going to kill her? You can't do that!'

'I won't if she'll come along with us peaceably,' he said, but he was lying. It would be too difficult to get her to a hiding place, and they did not have much time. Western must have ordered his local agents to get out here on the run.

He went back to Bronski's door and applied his ear to the extreme right-hand side. She was talking again, but he could not distinguish more than a few words.

He stepped back and to one side and said, loudly, 'Come on out, Bronski! I won't hurt you. I just want to ask you a few questions!'

'Go away!' she screamed.

She wasn't a fool, though she was scared. If he had been in her position, he'd be scared, too.

Patricia appeared in the hallway with two screwdrivers, a hammer, and a small crowbar. He put his finger over his lips and motioned for her to come to him. When he had the tools, he whispered, 'Wash that blood off your coat.'

'What about the blood on yours?'

'Yeah, I forgot.'

He took his coat off and handed it to her. She disappeared into Mifflon's room, and he began working on the hinges.

Bronski fired six times, but all were aimed at the door. After jumping away at the first shot, he worked on the hinges. The screws came out, though not easily. He dug the end of the crowbar into the space between the frame and the wall. Four more holes appeared in the door. That would empty her clip. She'd have to reload. That would only take a few seconds, if she knew what she was doing, and she probably did. He stepped in front of the door and worked savagely. The door inched out on the right side and suddenly that edge was free. He would have to stand before the door to pull it out further. He could not get enough purchase to work from the wall side.

He bent low, grabbed the frame with both hands, and heaved

backward. The door came out with a screech, quickly followed by four more shots.

He was, for a moment, half-under the door, and if Bronski had known the situation she could have killed him.

He retreated a few steps and shouted, 'Throw the gun out and then come out with your hands up, Bronski! Otherwise, I'll set fire to the house and wait for you outside!'

Not a bad idea, he thought, except that it would bring the police, and they would sift out the 7.92 mm. bullets, and it wouldn't be long before they would know that they were from his gun. Western's men would be digging them out, but they wouldn't be notifying the police. And they'd have his and Pat's fingerprints as additional clues. He had no time to wipe their prints off.

Let Western's men clean up. They'd be looking for him even if they didn't have the bullets and prints. Bronski did not know who he was, but she must have described him and Pat to Western. They'd get rid of the evidence, and all the police would find would be two bodies and a lot of bullet holes. They might not even find the bodies. He wouldn't put it past Western to bury them somewhere in the desert.

'O.K., Bronski,' he said. 'I've got some kerosene from the garage. I'm going to sprinkle some along the hall and throw some in the doorway and then throw the can into your room.'

He waited. There was no sound within her room. Either she was not going to fall for it at all or she was waiting for him to throw the can in before she decided.

And then it occurred to him that, now the door was open, Patricia would be an easy target for Bronski when she came out of Mifflon's room. He cursed himself for getting so rattled he had not foreseen it. A moment later, the light went out in Mifflon's room. Pat must have finished washing off the coats and then had realized that she would be in the light when she left. She was trapped unless Bronski surrendered.

'I've got the match, Bronski!' he said. 'It won't be necessary to throw the can in. All I have to do is set fire to the hallway!'

'I don't smell any kerosene!' she screeched.

He swore again, but he had to admire her even if it put him in a bad spot. She certainly was a tough old biddy.

'You'll see it quick enough,' he said. 'I'm counting to three! If your gun isn't out in the hall by then, I'm lighting the match!'

He could hear her now, but she was evidently asking Western for advice. He wondered how close Western's thugs were by now.

'One!'

He could no longer hear Bronski.

'Two!'

He moved next to the doorway.

'And . . .'

He leaped through the door, firing at the silhouette outlined against the thin drapes across the window.

Her gun boomed, and flame spurted, and the silhouette disappeared.

His leap had carried him into a chair, and he fell heavily with it beneath him. He slid off it, vaguely aware that his trousers were soaked, and rolled away from the chair. He heard Pat calling from her room, but he could not answer. Bronski would shoot in the area of his voice.

Silence fell. He was breathing so hard that he could not have heard Bronski if she were still breathing. He did not know whether or not he had hit her; she might just be waiting for him to reveal himself.

He removed his wristwatch – it wasn't working now, probably had been damaged sometime during the action – and he threw it across the room. It crashed against something, but the expected reaction did not come. Surely she was not cool enough to have resisted firing at the sound.

He didn't have much time left. He had to make a move or he would be caught by Western's men.

Reluctantly, he rose. The light from the lamp at the end of the hall fell through the door, showing him nothing but the legs of the chair and the rug. It was moonless and cloudy outside, but a faint light came through the windows from a streetlight down Firebird Lane about a quarter of a kilometer. The room was mostly shadow. No, there was something gleaming palely on the floor near the wall by the windows.

Bronski's naked body.

He approached her swiftly, since it was too late for caution. He leaned over her and felt for pulse and heartbeats. There were none. No wonder. The bullet had hit her solar plexus.

He was glad that she had fired at him. If she had surrendered, logic would have demanded that he kill her, and he was not sure that he would have been able to do that. Logic required it, but, like most human beings, he often found it difficult to obey logic.

He went to the hall and said, 'Come on out, Pat. We have to hurry.'

Five minutes later, having gotten the garage keys from Yohana's apartment, they were driving the Zagreus down Firebird Lane. Carfax had hesitated about taking it and so running into Western's agents. A better route might be over the back wall. He had decided to chance the former, since they desperately needed mobility. They would have to walk through the streets of North Pacific Palisades – he wasn't going to meet the taxi – and if Western's men were in any numbers they might send some cars out to look for them.

They drove past the taxi waiting for them, and when they were out of its sight Carfax stepped on the accelerator. It eased up to its maximum sixty kilometers per hour and held it while he sped for five blocks. He slowed down then because he did not want to attract the attention of a police patrol. Before they had quite reached the end of Vista Grange Road, four cars passed them. Each contained four men.

They might be coming home late from a party, but he did not think so. As soon as they had searched through Mifflon's house, they would recall the lone car they had passed, and at least one carful would go out in pursuit.

Carfax had enough time to shake them. Once he hit the freeway, he drove just under the speed limit to the MTO station, abandoned the car, boarded the express to Woodland Hills, transferred to the Sierra Madre express, and got off at the second stop. Twelve minutes later, they were in their motel.

Carfax poured Pat and himself a tall bourbon. 'Good for the nerves,' he said, 'and deadens the conscience. Now tell me what happened in the kitchen?'

'It was terrible,' she said, 'just awful. I went out one of the kitchen doors, just like you told me to. But I saw Yohana coming down the steps outside the garage, and I ran back in. He had a gun, so I knew you'd be in a bad spot if he came in from the other door. I grabbed a big knife off the rack and waited in the hallway outside the kitchen. I was shaking so badly I was afraid I'd drop the knife, and I was so weak I was sure I wouldn't be able to hurt him much with it. I held the handle with both hands, and when he came through the door I drove it as hard as I could into his stomach. He dropped his gun and staggered back, holding onto the knife, but I wouldn't let go, and then he fell back, and the knife came out. He died without making a sound; he didn't even groan.'

'Good girl,' Carfax said. 'I suppose the safety was off?'

'The what?'

'The safety mechanism on the automatic. If he'd left it on, nothing would have happened when you pulled the trigger.'

She looked horrified.

'I've read about such things but I never thought about it. I just held the gun with both hands, pointed it at Mifflon, and squeezed the trigger. I guess I was aiming too low when I first shot, but the gun just pulled itself right on up.'

'One out of twelve isn't bad under such conditions,' Carfax said. 'It only takes one.'

He downed the drink, and the acrid pungent odor of gunsmoke, which had filled his nostrils since the shooting began, cleared away.

'I'm going to take off these stinking wet clothes and take a shower. You want me to leave the water on?'

'Please do,' she said. She had a dreamy faroff expression, which disturbed him. She was retreating from the horrors of the night. When he came from the shower, he found her lying on the bed, fully clothed, and sleeping. Her glass was empty. He poured himself another one and contemplated the future. Whatever happened, it would come swiftly, and he wasn't going to like it.

Patricia awoke him just at dawn with her moaning and crying for help. He awakened her and held her in his arms while she told him of her nightmare. She had been in her bedroom in the house in which she had lived as a child. She had been happily playing with her dolls when she saw the door to the attic slowly opening. She had frozen with terror while the door continued to open, and then she had cried for her mother as something black and shapeless oozed out from the attic.

'It's daylight now, and you're not a child, and you're safe in my arms,' he said.

'I'll never be safe,' she murmured, but she went to sleep at once. Unfortunately, he was too awake, and after lying on his back for half an hour, he got out of bed.

At 09:00, she sat up in bed and looked at him as if she did not quite place him. He offered her a cup of coffee and while she drank it told her what he had seen on the early morning news.

'The cops got an anonymous call about 06:30,' he said. 'The informant told them that three people had been killed at Mifflon's house. The cops went out there and found a lot of blood and bullet holes, but no corpses.'

'But why would Western tell the cops?' she said. 'What does he care?'

He smiled and said, 'He didn't. I went down to the booth on the corner and phoned the North Pacific Palisades PD. I figured that Western's men had cleaned the place up by then and taken off. But I was dying of curiosity. I wanted to find out if Mifflon and the others had been left behind. It might have been several days before the cleaning women and the gardeners showed up.

'We know one thing. Western can't turn us in now without implicating himself. Not that I expected him to. He'll be looking for us himself.

'And now we can present some solid evidence to Western's enemies. The main difficulty there will not be finding them. The list of candidates is very long. What we have to do is pick the most powerful and the most ruthless.'

'You mean, an underground war?'

'Essentially. In the beginning anyhow. They can start collecting evidence and when enough is assembled, then it can be brought out into the open.'

'Yes, if Western isn't so powerful by then that he just crushes us and nobody dares do anything about it.'

'I hope your middle name isn't Cassandra. Have another cup of coffee.'

SEVENTEEN

After breakfast, Carfax went to the booth on the corner and phoned the agency. He arranged to meet an operative at a coffee shop which he designated by a code name. Since it was possible that Western had tapped Fortune and Thorndyke's lines, he had been using a code name for himself. He took the recording of Mifflon's voice, passed it on to the agent, and gave him a message in a sealed envelope.

Two hours later, the waitress told him that he had a call. He answered it and heard Thorndyke's English accent.

'Hello, Ramus?'

'Here.'

'It's definitely not he.'

'That's what I thought. Could you mail me the phonograms at the designated address?'

'I'll do that. Sorry I won't be hearing from you again.'

'I didn't say it wouldn't be *again*. I said for a long time. Well, thanks a lot. You've been very helpful. You know where to send the bill.'

'Of course. Good luck.'

'I'll need it,' Carfax said, and he pressed the OFF button.

Anywhere in the world was unhealthy for them, but Los Angeles was the unhealthiest. At 14:05, they walked out of the motel without signing out. Carfax, however, had arranged for the agency to pay the motel for them. The agency had also picked up the Zagreus at the MTO station and returned it to the rental company. After a short ride in a taxi, they boarded various MTO's, ending up in Sacramento. From there, using I.D. cards provided by Fortune and Thorndyke, they flew to St. Louis. Carfax wrote a letter to the agency, dismissing them. He thanked them for their invaluable services, but he thought it best that not even they know where he was from this point on.

He and Patricia took the MTO to Busiris, Illinois, where he checked them in at the suburban motel under fake I.D.'s. To avoid the processing of the cards, he paid for their rooms in cash. This caused an odd look from the desk clerk, but looks never hurt anyone, according to Carfax's philosophy. He spent one day in Busiris arranging for the further care of his house and lawn and talking over the phone with the president of Traybell University. Chambers was understandably upset because Carfax would not be returning for the fall quarter. Carfax said that he was sorry, but he had to quit for personal reasons. If Chambers wished to blackball him, then he would have to do so.

He almost gave in to the impulse to enter his house while he was in town. It had all the attractiveness of the womb: safety, warmth, coziness, relaxation, and an opportunity to become comparatively mindless for a while. But he resisted. Though it did not seem likely that Western had a man watching the place, he could not afford to take the chance.

He and Patricia got off the MTO at Dayton, Ohio, where he called Richard Emerson of Manhattan and Guilford, Massachusetts. Mr. Emerson was a very rich and well-known Roman Catholic whose opinions of Western were legend. Carfax got through to him without identifying himself. The magic word was MEDIUM. He had some information which would reveal Western to be a murderer and a threat to the world. No, he just could not say who he was at this time because Western would kill him if he discovered his whereabouts.

Emerson may have thought that Carfax was a crackpot, but he did agree to meet him in four days in the new Pieter Stuyvesant Hotel. And he would mention the call to only one other person.

'His son-in-law is Roger Langer, the senator from New York,' Carfax told Patricia. 'If we can convince Langer, we have a very influential man on our side. He and the president are bitter enemies, but the president will listen to him. And, for once, they'll have something in common. Before that happens, we have to get a lot more evidence. Mifflon's case by itself isn't enough to convince the president.'

'But if you tell Langer that we killed Mifflon, won't he have to turn us in to the police?'

'No. This is far above any mere legalities.'

He refrained from telling her that he thought their chances of survival were very small. Western would have no trouble finding assassins who would not care whether or not they were killed after completing their mission. Western could bring them back to life in another body. He was, in many ways, another Old Man of the Mountain. He had the advantage over the original in that he could fulfill his promise to give his assassins immortality.

Carfax wanted to induce Pat to take cover in a faroff place and have nothing more to do with him for a long time. But he also did not want to see her go. He loved her. And he knew that she would refuse to go. So why make her even more worried than she was?

He turned on the TV just in time to hear the tail end of a report on Western. Only an hour before, Western had announced that a new MEDIUM had been built in the Megistus complex and it was open to business.

Carfax heard the complete report during the 21:00 news. In addition to the machine at Megistus, new MEDIUMs would be installed in all the large cities of North America. Negotiations were being made to install them in many foreign cities.

This was followed by a brief interview with Senator Gray of Louisiana.

Interviewer: 'What is your opinion of Western's plans for the building of many new MEDIUMs?'

Senator Gray: 'MEDIUM will still be restricted to the very wealthy. This is, as I have said on many occasions, a blatant injustice. The common man has every right to communicate with his beloved departed ones, and lack of the requisite money should be no obstacle. Every man should have his chance at MEDIUM, even if he has to be federally subsidized. But I have a better idea than that, one which will not cause the federal debt to become even heavier. I am for placing MEDIUM under federal regulations and under federal control and reducing the price for the use of MEDIUM. There is no reason why such exorbitant fees should be charged. Western can't plead that the power requirements force him to make such high charges. By his own admission, MEDIUM can be operated with no cost whatsoever, exclusive of the money needed to pay for the requisite personnel, maintenance, and other related expenses.'

Interviewer: 'That brings up another much more controversial issue, Senator. If MEDIUM can supply free electrical power, as Mr. Western claims, won't the government be forced to control its use? And what about the impact of free power on the economy?'

Senator Gray: 'Mr. Western has yet to validate his claims about so-called free power. Nothing is free, you know. But if MEDIUM can supply almost free, let's call it very cheap, power, then the federal and state governments will bring such a commodity under its regulations. As for the impact, I'm not prepared to make a statement at this moment. My committee is studying its possible influence, and the report will be issued within a few months. Of course, all this is highly speculative.'

Interviewer: 'There have been rumors that the federal government might advocate nationalizing the electrical power industry if MEDIUM can do what Mr. Western claims it can do. In the power field, that is.'

Senator Gray: 'You hear many rumors, many of them fantastic. However, on a global basis, the impact will be tremendous. Underdeveloped nations will have unlimited power, and this would solve many of their problems. America would be at a definite disadvantage if it continued to use a system based on the burning of fossil fuels or on nuclear reactors. We couldn't permit that.'

'Do you plan on telling Gray about Mifflon?' Patricia said.

'He ought to be sounded out,' Carfax said. 'He may be the next president.'

Two days later, Carfax and Patricia were ushered into a suite in the Pieter Stuyvesant. It was midnight, and the two had walked down from the sixteenth floor to the fifteenth. There a guard admitted them and escorted them to Richard Emerson. There were other armed men standing around, making sure that no unauthorized persons got onto the floor, every room of which had been rented by Emerson.

Emerson was a tall portly man with a high forehead and a thin mouth. Carfax recognized Senator Langer, a man of thirty-seven, standing six feet seven and built like a basketball center, his thick hair a flaming red.

They were introduced under the name of Ramus, though both Emerson and Langer knew by now their real identities. Carfax accepted a bourbon and a cigar and then proceeded to tell all he thought relevant. The two men examined his documents while he talked.

There was a long silence from men who were not accustomed to being silent.

Senator Langer was the first to speak. 'I believe you're telling the truth. The evidence here is enough to convince me. But we must get much more before we can make a public case out of it. I'll get to work on it at once. This is the most dangerous thing that mankind has ever been threatened with. We have a record of every client of Western's, in fact, of everyone who has been admitted to the room in which MEDIUM is kept.'

'I'd suggest that you investigate those men whose records show a discrepancy between the number of times they've actually had sessions with MEDIUM and the number of times they've paid for sessions,' Carfax said. 'They'll be the men paying for repossession insurance.'

'We'll also investigate most thoroughly the men who've inherited the property of those clients who've died,' Emerson said. 'If there is anything irregular about such cases, if the inheritors were not the natural inheritors, if they were obscure men who should not have inherited, then we know something's fishy.'

'There must be some who were forcibly possessed, like Mifflon,' Carfax said. 'They'll be difficult to detect, but if you can get speech records and compare them, and if they suddenly develop behavior patterns which they lacked before . . .'

'Don't teach your grandmother to suck eggs,' Langer said.

'I'm just trying to help,' Carfax said. Langer was a whirlwind, a good man to have on your side, but he was also an egomaniac.

'That's all right,' Langer said, waving his hand. 'I wonder, didn't Governor Simons have a few sessions with MEDIUM?'

It was obviously a rhetorical question so Carfax did not answer.

'He's a possible candidate for the presidency,' Langer added.

Emerson looked pale, and he said, 'You don't think that he's been possessed?'

'I don't know,' Langer said. 'As far as I know, he's still the same man. Certainly no one without experience could do his job so well that nobody would notice.'

'Yes, but what if the possessor happened to be a politician?' Carfax said. 'If Western were to place a *semb* in Simons, he certainly wouldn't put a politically inexperienced man in him.'

Emerson said, 'I understand that you maintain the *sembs* aren't dead, that they're nonhuman creatures?'

'Yes, but the point is that they act *as if* they're human. So it's only natural to think of them as if they are human.'

'Whatever they are, Western is a traitor to the living,' Langer said. 'And I'll see to it that he gets the punishment befitting a traitor. The Judas!'

'We don't even have any laws for this situation,' Carfax said.

'Then, by all that's holy, we'll make the laws! Then we will hang him!'

Patricia looked startled. Carfax felt a little uncomfortable, but he was not surprised. Langer was regarded, rightly, as the foremost proponent of civil rights in the legislature. But he was also a human being faced with an ancient terror, one which had its roots in the Old Stone Age. He must think of this coming conflict as one in which the rules of war applied. If you have to kill your enemy to defeat him, then the sooner the better. And there was no doubt that Western was using the same philosophy.

Nevertheless, he didn't like it, and it was evident that Patricia was horrified.

Emerson said, 'You two must stay out of sight until you are needed. You can't do anything while Western is looking for you. So I suggest that you take a long trip, say, Europe or South America.'

Carfax looked at Patricia and said, 'We don't have the money.'

Emerson dismissed this with a wave of his cigar. 'You're on my payroll. A thousand a week apiece and all fares paid.'

'But we wouldn't be doing anything to earn all that money!' she said.

'You'll be earning every penny of it when the time comes.'

'We'd like to be useful,' Carfax said. 'We both are personally involved. And Patricia has a valid claim to MEDIUM.'

'You don't know that she has,' Emerson said. 'Oh, not that I doubt that she's the rightful owner. But as long as her father says she isn't, what can be done about it?'

'I don't think he's in the *embu* any longer,' Carfax said slowly.

Patricia gasped, and Emerson said, 'What?'

'The only way Western could have gotten my uncle to lie for him would have been to promise him a body. He may be working for Western right now – some place.'

Langer said, 'Then you're thinking of letting Patricia's whereabouts be known? That way, there might be a chance that her father would try to get in touch with her?'

'You're very perceptive,' Carfax said. 'But I wasn't going to bring this up unless I was forced to. And it needs study. Would it be fair for Patricia to expose herself to danger just to be a decoy?'

'And would Patricia do it?' Patricia said. 'You three are talking as if I weren't here! Why don't you ask me?'

'All right,' Carfax said. 'Would you?'

'Certainly. If I thought I could see my father again . . . only I wouldn't actually be *seeing* him, would I? He'd be in a different body.'

'You've got something there, Gordon,' Langer said. 'I don't know why I didn't think of that. Patricia's father may have gone along with Western so he could rejoin the living. But he must hate Western. And he'll surely do anything he can to expose Western.'

'I suppose that's true,' Carfax said. 'On the other hand, Western must know that, and he'll be keeping a close watch on my uncle. If he steps out of line, bang, he's dead again.'

'Maybe Western didn't keep his promise,' Emerson said.

'That's possible. But there's only one way to find out,' Carfax said. 'Besides, I think Western could use my uncle in the technological and scientific end. Western doesn't really know much about that, and my uncle, as the inventor, would be invaluable. For all I know, it may have been his idea to use MEDIUM as a power source.'

Emerson said, 'Very well. We won't send you abroad. And you two have just had a raise. Three thousand a week apiece, and your traveling expenses. O.K.?'

'It's O.K. with me if it's O.K. with Patricia,' Carfax said.

'I'm ready to start work,' she said.

'Here's what we'll do,' Langer said.

Carfax listened, but he was thinking that he had been happier when he was the boss.

EIGHTEEN

The Carfaxes were driven that morning to Guilford, where they were given a house near the estate of Emerson. Three men were assigned to guard them every eight-hour shift. The following day, they went to see a lawyer, Arthur Smigly, whom Emerson recommended and whose fee Emerson would pay. A week later, Smigly filed suit against Western.

'We don't have a chance, but that's not the point,' Smigly told the Carfaxes. 'This is just the warning shot across their bows. Their attention is attracted now.'

Smigly knew something of their plans, but he did not know that Rufton Carfax might be alive again. Nobody outside a very select group was to know. If Western had the slightest suspicion that old Carfax was thought to be wedded to the flesh again, he would make sure that Carfax had a quick divorce.

In a meeting in Emerson's home a few days after, Langer told them that his agent in Megistus was checking out all the major personnel. 'He's got a full description of your father's habits and personal idiosyncrasies. He's also recording all voices so we can match them against your father's.'

'How long have you had that agent in Western's employ?' Carfax said.

'The first one died when Houvelle blew the house up,' Langer said. 'She was Mrs. Morris, Western's secretary. The other one was sent in after we found out about Megistus. It wasn't easy. Western has a security system second to none.'

'And how do we know that he doesn't have an agent in your organization?' Carfax said.

'We don't. That's why this particular project is known to only us four.'

'Four? But the agent makes a fifth.'

'He doesn't know who he's checking out. He just has a list of specifications.'

'That's playing it close to the chest,' Carfax said. 'How are the other cases coming along?'

'We've got one certain and three possibles. Two months ago a millionaire, Gerald Grebski, a client of Western's, collapsed during a session. My man saw him carried out on a stretcher. He was put in the Megistus hospital for overnight observation, under a close guard, I might add. The next day he was up and about but did not go home. He stayed in an apartment in the complex and not much was seen of him for a week. My agent managed to find out that Grebski had been suffering from dizziness and uncoordination of legs and arms. He also seemed to be suffering from a speech defect.

'My agent reported that as a matter of routine, since at that time we had no idea that possession was possible. But when I found out about it, I remembered the report. So I put some men on Grebski, and they report that he's in fine shape now; in fact, he went home after a week in Megistus.'

'Like Mifflon,' Carfax said. 'He spent about a week in Megistus, too.'

Langer frowned at the interruption. 'Yes. It's no coincidence. Apparently possession requires some time for the *semb* to integrate with the new body, to learn to drive it, as it were. Anyway, the voice and habits of the new Grebski have been checked against the old. And he is definitely not the Gerald Grebski who went into Megistus. The reports on the other three, two women and a man, aren't complete yet.'

'And when will we get the report on my father?' Patricia said.

'As soon as the agent can get it out. He's only allowed out on weekends, and he's frisked before and after. However, that doesn't mean that the next batch of data will match against your father's specifications. My man is only able to smuggle out a little at a time. And he hasn't checked everybody out.'

'Don't get your hopes too high,' Carfax said. 'We don't know that your father was given a body, and even if he was, he may have been sent elsewhere.'

And it's probably not your father, anyway, Carfax thought. It's some thing that is posing as him.

There was another thing that Patricia had not thought of. Or, if she had, she was keeping it to herself. When, or if, this business came to an end, what would happen to Rufton Carfax? He'd be owner of a body in which he had no right to be. Would he then be forced to unpossess? It would almost be like killing him to force it, but it would have to be done. Or what if it turned out that the *semb* was not merely superimposed on the original owner, but that the original had traded places with the *semb*? It seemed logical that if the switch could be made in the first place, then a reswitch could be effected. Yet nothing was known of the mechanics of *semb* possession. At least, nobody but Western knew, and he wasn't telling. What if a switch could only be done once? What happened to the *semb*? Would he be jailed? As Langer had said, new laws would have to be made. And what good would it do to imprison the offender? The penal system was supposed to be for rehabilitation, not punishment.

The conversation was short, since Senator Langer was a very busy man. Gordon and Patricia wandered around the house and the gardens for a while, but they knew none of the guests, all very important people. Their three guards trailed them and then, when the Carfaxes decided to go home, closed in around them. One of the guards, Szentes, drove. Jardine sat beside him; Gordon and Patricia were in the rear with the third guard, Brecht. Another car containing three men pulled out after them as they drove onto the narrow county highway. This car always followed them when they were traveling between their house and Emerson's.

It was a pleasant afternoon, the sun was shining, the corn in the fields along the road were green pygmy soldiers on parade, and two redbirds flew across the road ahead of them. At another time, Carfax would have exclaimed with pleasure at seeing them. But today he felt dull and dispirited. He wasn't really doing anything useful, and he missed his Busiris friends. He and Patricia had been cut off too long from a normal life. Their guards were not communicative and probably had little to interest them, anyway. He and Patricia were getting edgy from too close contact. If they could get away from each other for a few hours a day, they would enjoy each other's company more. If only he could get an assignment from Langer . . .

The car traveled around a curve at a speed of fifty kilometers per hour, and there, less than a quarter of a kilometer ahead, was a huge steam truck and trailer. It was across the road, blocking it and both shoulders of the road. By it stood two men, the driver and his partner, apparently. Szentes swore and pressed on the brake, and the tires of the automobile behind squealed as it slowed to keep from running into their rear end.

'Stop!' Carfax said. 'It may be a trap!'

He took out his 7.92 mm.; Jardine lifted from the floor a mini-submachine gun, and Brecht held a 9 mm. automatic. Patricia carried a 6 mm. automatic in her handbag, but she made no move to get it. She seemed paralyzed.

The car screamed to a halt, sliding sideways, its front half across the other lane. Carfax looked behind him. The other car was just behind them, and coming around the curve was another huge steam semi.

'It *is* a trap!' he yelled.

He looked ahead again, and saw that the two drivers were running around the other side of their vehicle. Then the brakes and tires of the semi behind them squealed, and the vehicle slid to a halt, neatly jacknifing and blocking their retreat. Its cab door opened. The single driver scrambled out, ran along the side of the semi, and disappeared.

Carfax thought, they don't have enough men to fight us, unless the vans are filled – the Trojan Horse analogy flashed across his mind – or unless the bushes along the road are concealing more men.

Szentes was phoning in to the State Police Headquarters ten kilometers down the road past Emerson's. Jardine and Brecht were out of the car and walking toward the guards in the car behind. These were advancing to meet them.

Carfax started to get out, but Szentes said, 'You stay in here.'

Carfax did not know whether or not that was a good idea. The automobile was supposedly bulletproof, but Western's men would know that. They might have a bazooka aimed at the car right now.

If, however, the vans did contain men, they should be emptying now. They weren't. Both trucks looked deserted, and the drivers were nowhere in sight.

He opened his window, stuck his head out, and said, 'Hey, Szentes! Can you see the truckers?'

Szentes walked to one side of the road and looked down. He swore and scratched his head and said, 'They're going like hell! Running toward some cars that've just pulled up!'

Carfax swung the door open and shot out. 'Run!' he yelled. 'Run for the woods! There must be explosives in those vans!'

He gestured frantically at Patricia, who was scrambling out. The other men looked at him for a second and then they broke. Carfax took Patricia's hand and pulled her along behind him. His goal was the creek which paralleled the road and which was about forty meters to the east. Between its banks and the road was a row of sycamores planted by Emerson's grandfather. Gordon and Patricia ran between two of these, crashed through some bushes, and dived over the edge of the bank. They rolled down a muddy slope, ending in water a foot deep. They lay there for two seconds, panting, and then Patricia opened her mouth. Carfax never heard what she intended to say.

NINETEEN

Carfax regained consciousness the evening of the next day. He was totally deaf, and his head pained him as if a spike had been driven through it. His face was swollen, and after he got his hearing back, he trembled at every sound. By keeping his right ear pressed to the pillow, he could shut out most noise, however. His left ear, previously injured by the explosion at Western's, was now useless. And the doctor did not think he would recover any use of it.

The twin explosions of the vans, each holding an estimated hundred pounds of dynamite, had knocked down the giant sycamores and thrown the upper part of the creek bank over him and Patricia. The police might have missed them if it had not been for Patricia's hand sticking out of the bank. Their heads were covered by a few inches of loose dirt and some uprooted bushes, and Patricia would have soon suffocated.

None of the others had survived. Jardine was the only one whose body was comparatively intact. He had taken refuge in the creek, too, but he must have stuck his head above the bank for some reason just as the explosions occurred. The postmortem had found massive hemorrhages in his brain.

'If the walls of the van hadn't offered some resistance, you two would be dead,' the doctor had said. Carfax could not, of course, hear him then, but he was a fluent lip reader.

Later, he read in the newspaper that the drivers of the trucks had not been caught. He also read of the murder of Emerson and the wounding of Langer, which had taken place two days after the ambush. They had just entered the Pieter Stuyvesant Hotel lobby when two men got off six shots from their 9 mm. automatics before they were killed by the bodyguards. The murderers had been identified as Leo Congdon and Humberto

Corielli, both with long police records and a total of ten years in jail on charges of assault and battery with intent of murder. Langer, visiting the Carfaxes a week later, told them that there was no provable connection between them and Western.

'They must have known they couldn't get away alive,' Carfax said. 'Western must have promised them new bodies.'

'Undoubtedly,' Langer said. 'They would want new bodies. Congdon had a stiff knee from a bullet wound and deep knife wounds on his face. Corielli was suffering from tertiary syphilis and had a face that would frighten Frankenstein's monster. Western chooses his agents well.'

'And so we know now that Western has agents in your organization.'

Langer said grimly, 'Jackson, one of my bodyguards, was absent that day, and Wiener, one of my under-secretaries, disappeared. Neither would know, I hope, what our plans are, but both had seen you with me and my father-in-law. I'm taking it for granted that there are others, and a thorough recheck of everybody who is in a sensitive position is being made.'

Langer rose from the chair, wincing. His arm was in a sling. A ricocheting 9 mm. had only touched his biceps, but it had gouged out skin and muscles. He would have a weak left arm the rest of his life. Which might be short, Carfax thought.

'I'm not waiting any longer to accumulate a large dossier,' Langer said. 'Tomorrow my staff is mailing out to the president and his cabinet and every member of Congress all the evidence we have. These will also go to the news media. I don't know what'll happen after that, but I do know that Western will be summoned to face my investigating committee. And he won't dare try any more assassinations.'

'Don't be too sure of that,' Carfax said. 'If Western doesn't try it, some of those religious nuts may. He's a god to many.'

'And an anti-Christ to many others,' Langer said. 'He isn't safe either. I wouldn't be surprised if a lynch mob didn't go after him.'

'A fat chance they'd have. Megistus is a fortress. He even has an around-the-clock air patrol equipped with machine guns. He got a permit to arm them on the basis that if one maniac has flown an airplane loaded with dynamite into his house, another might.'

'Of course I know,' Langer said. 'Don't teach your grandmother to suck eggs.'

Carfax sighed. He was getting tired of that phrase. However, he had to admit that Langer was the man to lead the fight against Western. He was almost as ruthless as Western. He would stop short of murder, but that was about all. And later he was to wonder if Langer was not capable of even that.

Carfax and Patricia were in a suite in the Pangea Hotel when Langer's documents became public property. The *New York Times* had a special section consisting of the entire Message to the People of the World and editorial comments on it. The TV shows were interrupted by lengthy special bulletins, and the news programs devoted most of their precious time to it. By morning of the next day, the White House and members of Congress had been deluged with letters and telegrams. Half of these, as expected, protested Western's innocence and an abhorrence of his enemies, particularly Langer. The other half demanded that Western be put on trial immediately or be shot or hung, with or without a trial. At the latest count, one-eighth of the letters contained obscenities that were still unprintable in reputable newspapers, even in this permissive age. These came from both anti- and pro-Westernites.

The 22:00 news showed a brief interview with Western conducted inside Megistus.

Western (looking angry and indignant!): 'I repeat! Those documents issued by Senator Langer are fakes! He is out to get me, and he has stooped to a depth of fraud which I find, even now, difficult to believe that any sane man could sink to.'

Carfax (to Patricia): 'He must be furious. How can you stoop and sink at the same time? He's about to foam at the mouth.'

Patricia: 'Shut up, Gordon!'

Western: 'I have said it and will continue to say it. The senator must be at his wits' end to make such a charge! He is indeed desperate if he thinks he can put across a blatant fraud like this! Of course, I understand his situation. He believes that I've discredited, no, demolished his religion. But it has never been my intent to interfere with religious beliefs. MEDIUM is a scientific device, using scientific means to communicate with another world. There is no doubt that this is a cosmos to which so-called souls go when the body and soul are parted. Any other viewpoint is demonstrably wrong. But . . .'

Newsman (interrupting): 'But why have Grebski, Torrance, Swanson, and Simba fled to Brazil? If they are innocent . . .'

Western: 'Of course they've left the country! They know they're innocent but they're afraid for their lives! They're afraid that they'll be murdered by fanatics! Can you blame them?'

Carfax: 'If they think there aren't any homicidal nuts in Brazil, they're due for a shock.'

Patricia: 'Must you always wisecrack?'

Carfax: 'I must when I'm scared.'

Western: '. . . and let him sue! I stand by my words!'

Interviewer (pulling a piece of paper out of his shirt pocket and handing it to Western): 'Here's a subpoena to appear before Senator Langer's committee, sir.'

Carfax: 'I wondered how they were going to serve it to him! The reporter's a fraud! Oh, man!'

A crazy sweep of the camera, ending in a scene of one of Western's guards slugging the newsman. Western, face a dark red, shouting: 'Throw the bastards out!'

Carfax stood up and walked to the bar. 'Now let him defy the committee! The federal marshals will have authority to go in after him!'

'He might take off for South America, too,' Patricia said. 'What's to keep him from taking his jet right now?'

'I think the president would order it forced down. If that didn't work, his plane would be shot down. Obviously, he'd be trying to escape the country.'

'That'd tear this country apart.'

'It's torn. So what's the difference? Besides, as I said, he won't be safe no matter where he goes. The government of Brazil would be under tremendous pressure to extradite him, and the Brazilians are as much if not more upset than we are. The majority are Catholics, you know.'

'Don't you think I know anything?'

'Sorry,' he said. 'You forget that I am a teacher.'

'I'm sorry, too,' she said. 'But I'm so nervous.'

'Who isn't?'

'I'm worried about Daddy, too,' she said. 'If Western gets scared that everything might blow sky-high, he might get rid of Daddy.'

Carfax had thought of that but he had seen no reason to discuss it with her. She would just become more anxious. Besides, there was no proof that his uncle was in Megistus. If only there was a MEDIUM available, it could be used to determine if his uncle was still in the *embu*.

Patricia must have been thinking along the same lines. She said, 'It looks as if I might get the rights to MEDIUM, doesn't it? And when I do, I'll find out just where Daddy is.'

'Or where he isn't,' Carfax said. 'I wish Langer's man had been able to get his last batch of data out. Then we might know.'

Nobody knew what had happened to him. He had not come out of Megistus with the other employees during the weekend. This might indicate something sinister, or might just mean that he had been kept busy. He sometimes had work to do which necessitated his putting off his holidays.

Carfax started to sit down, changed his mind, and began pacing back and forth.

'I'm tired of sitting on my ass. Now's the time to force an issue, while Western's off balance, and I'm going to do it.'

'I suppose it'll get us killed.'

'Aren't you willing to take a chance if you can save your father?'

'What have you got in mind, for God's sake!'

'I'll tell you later.'

He pressed the phone's VO button and punched Langer's number. He had to wait for twelve minutes, since the senator was 'tied up,' but he declined to leave his number. He didn't want Langer to be side-tracked by other affairs.

Langer was in a hurry, but when he heard a few sentences of Carfax's proposal he told his secretary to delay his next outgoing call. After Carfax had finished, Langer said, 'We'll hit him on both flanks then. I'll take care of the judicial business right now. You and Patricia take the next plane out. I'll see that it's held for you.'

Thirty minutes later, the Carfaxes boarded a passenger plane that had been kept waiting fifteen minutes for them. They were conducted to the first-class section, and the double-decker taxied off. It went past ten planes that were lined up, waiting for Carfax's to take off ahead of them. The stewardesses were all smiles, hovering over them to make sure they were quite comfortable. Carfax suspected that behind the overly courteous attitude was irritation. He didn't mind. He'd been delayed too many times when he was a second-class passenger and his plane had been held up by high-priority big shots.

In two hours and three minutes, the huge jet was in the landing pattern for the Las Vegas airport. The Carfaxes disembarked fifteen minutes later and in five minutes were strapping on their seat belts in the twin-jet that Langer had rented for them. Within thirty-five minutes, their plane was landing on the strip of the Bonanza Circus port.

From there they checked into the only completely roofed-over city in the world. No large vehicles were permitted in it; the population traveled on moving sidewalks or used the small electric fare-free taxis. Gordon and Patricia were met by a U.S. Marshal, George Chang, who accompanied them to the Athena Tower, the legislative building. There they were introduced to the judge who had issued the warrant Langer had asked for, another U.S. Marshal, and the county electrical inspector. The latter were, respectively, Amanda Hiekka, a blonde Valkyrie of Finnish descent, and Ricardo Lopez, a short, stocky cigar-smoking red-head whose parents had fled Cuba thirty years ago. Carfax learned all these unnecessary biographical details from Judge Kasner. The judge seemed to be trying to delay the expedition with trivial conversation. When Carfax expressed impatience, Kasner replied, 'I'm not sure that we shouldn't wait until morning, although the senator did indicate extreme haste. He doesn't know the situation here, and when I tried to explain it to him, he said he wasn't interested. He just wanted action. But . . .'

'And what is the situation?' Carfax said.

'Explosive! There are at least three hundred men camped outside the gates of Megistus, armed men, anti-Westernites. They claim they're there to see that Western doesn't flee the country. The sheriff has ordered them to disperse, but they won't pay any attention to him. In the meantime, the pro-Westernites are organizing; they're meeting now at the Pro-facci Hall. It's evident they plan to march out to Megistus and confront the mob there. The mayor has asked the governor to call out the state militia, but he's refused. He says the situation doesn't warrant it.'

Carfax nodded. This was to be expected. The governor was a good friend of Langer's.

'This is no time to play politics,' Judge Kasner said. 'There's going to be bloodshed unless the militia is there. And maybe even then. I was reluctant to issue the warrants because I was afraid that your appearance there will precipitate things.'

Marshal Chang said, 'I've got my orders. I'm not hanging around here a moment longer. The rest of you coming along?'

'That's why we flew out here,' Carfax said. 'Let's go.'

'I strongly advise against it,' Kasner said.

'Then you shouldn't have issued the warrants,' Carfax said. He felt sorry for the judge, since he had been put under such pressure by Langer for Langer's own purposes. On the other hand, the judge should have had enough character to resist Langer, even if it meant his political career. And there was no doubt in Carfax's mind that Langer's agents had stirred up the anti-Westernites and led them out to Megistus. And all this had been done since Carfax had phoned Langer. There were, of course, strong feelings against Western in Bonanza Circus, as there were in every city in the United States. Langer had spoken to the few men needed to organize this sentiment into a crowd and lead them out to Megistus. The leaders were probably a strange mixture of religious and criminal elements, churchmen and Mafia. The latter organization was the secret, or not-so-secret, builder of Bonanza Circus and owner of the giant gambling casinos. Most of them were devout Catholics except when religion interfered with business, and they were implacable enemies of Western. They feared MEDIUM and were opposed to its use. The proposal that the machine be used to extract testimony from dead members of their organization terrified them. It was said that the Mafia had required all its members to take a solemn oath that they would keep silent about their activities even after death. How could they enforce it, since the dead were beyond any retribution?

Langer was a bitter enemy of organized crime. It must have hurt him to ask its chiefs to help him. But in politics usefulness and compromise are the prime movers. Langer would worry later about his debt to criminals. This was war, where you didn't consider the ethics of your allies or, indeed, any ethics at all.

Why did Langer want a mob with heated emotions outside of Megistus? Was it just to scare Western into giving in to the marshals and Lopez? Or did he plan to send the mob in after the gate had been opened to the legal representatives? Carfax thought that the latter was most likely. This scared him, and it also made him sick. Langer was sending men to their death.

These thoughts occupied him with gloominess while the parties rode through the wide walks of Bonanza Circus. There was not much traffic at this time, which was to be expected. The many faces that appeared at the doors and the windows as they rode by the fantastically ornamented buildings showed that a large part of the citizenry and the tourists were up. Word had gotten around, and the people were afraid. They weren't venturing outside, because they must fear a clash between the pros and the antis.

Chang, however, commented that there wasn't much chance of that in the city itself. All the action would be out at Megistus.

'About a half-hour before you got here, the street walks were full of Westernites going to Profacci Hall. They'll be spilling out there as soon as Western's men whip the poor boobs into a vigilante mood. I hope we get to Megistus before that happens.'

'Why don't the police do something?' Patricia said.

'Half of them have resigned and joined the mobs,' Hiekka said. 'And the other half are afraid to stand in anyone's way. They don't want to get trampled.'

TWENTY

They got out of the electric cars at the Number Twelve Exit and walked out into the desert night. Two steam cars waited for them, one bearing the county insignia and the other the U.S. eagle. Lopez and his two assistants got into the former; the others slid into Chang's car. They drove away from the bright lights and the vast conical light-perforated roof of Bonanza Circus and soon were going up a winding mountain road. Their lights struck the firs and pines lining the road and, occasionally, the red eyes of a rabbit, an opossum, a fox, or a deer.

Hiekka commented that the area between the city and Megistus was an animal-refuge. 'Every three years the deer hunting season opens here. I got a large buck myself last year. I love venison. Four years ago I didn't get a thing. I was busy hunting men. You remember it, don't you? You must've seen it on TV? There were two or three beast-lovers up here shooting hunters? Killed three hunters and wounded two? We never did catch them, and I was hoping they'd show up last year. But they never did.'

She laughed and added, 'There weren't many hunters around last year. They were afraid the deer'd be shooting back.'

She patted the butt of the .45 revolver, a collector's item, in her holster. 'Most men would be as happy shooting cows in a corral. They're not real hunters.'

Carfax got the impression that she had liked hunting men.

The twelve kilometers were mainly on a road that had been cut from the face of the mountain. At its end they came down a long pass between steep rocky slopes. They could see below them the broad plateau on which Megistus had been built. Its lights blazed from many towers and buildings and from the tops of the high brick walls that surrounded it. It covered about a square kilometer and contained four buildings about ten stories high and several smaller ones. Guard-towers were spaced along the top of the walls at forty-meter intervals.

Outside the gates were about eighty automobiles and trucks, a number of which mounted searchlights. A dark mass surged back and forth before the gates, a human yeast.

High over the complex, the lights of two planes flashed.

All the makings of a massacre, Carfax thought. But if Western resisted, and blood was shed, he would be arrested and charged with murder. He must know that. If, however, the mob got out of hand and attacked, he would defend himself. He would have to in order to keep from being lynched.

Ten minutes later, they drove out onto the plain. Here several cars blocked their passage, and men with rifles questioned them. Hiekka and Chang showed their badges and explained their mission. A big hairy scar-faced man named Rexter, evidently in charge, got into the car with them and told them to drive on up to the gate. He stank of booze and excitement. About fifty meters from the gate, Rexter ordered Chang to pull over to the side of the road. Everybody got out. Carfax looked around and saw only one police car. Two men in the uniforms of the county police stood by the hood and smoked cigarettes.

There wasn't a man in the mob who didn't carry a rifle and a handgun of some sort. Their faces looked pale or flushed and were either set grimly or distorted with anger. Their voices struck him and surged over him. But they were kept in some order by men who wore black armbands. These stood along the road, yelling at anyone who got onto it.

About seventy meters up the road from Chang's car was a truck with a camper, a steel girder over its bumper. Aside from the county police car, it seemed to be the only one with a running motor. One man sat in its cab, and another man, with an armband, stood just outside, talking to the driver.

Chang, a tall man with short straight black hair and bright hazel eyes, looked over the crowd. Then he picked up a bullhorn and marched up to the gate. Hiekka and Lopez walked behind him, and Carfax, after a few seconds' hesitation, went after them.

Patricia remained in the back seat. Gordon had asked her to stay there unless she was needed. 'And get down on the floor at the first shot,' he had said. 'That is, if there is any.'

Patricia had nodded as if she were too scared to talk.

Chang stopped near the foot of the two heavy steel gates, muttered, 'This is a hell of a situation,' and then put the bullhorn to his lips. At the first blare of the horn, the crowd fell silent.

Chang identified himself and then stated that he had a warrant which gave him entrance to Megistus and authority to search the place. He was looking for Rufton Carfax, whom the United States government believed was being held there against his will.

The guards in the watch towers remained at their posts, pointing their rifles, shotguns, and machine guns at the crowd. The gates did not open.

Chang repeated his demands and handed the bullhorn to Lopez. Lopez bellowed out his identification and his mission. The county of White Pine demanded that its chief electrical inspector be admitted at once so that he could inspect the power system and the wiring. Lopez must determine that the system feeding from MEDIUM was set up according to legal specifications.

Chang and Lopez were the one-two punches that Langer had spoken of.

A guard dressed in the Lincoln green of Western's security police leaned out the right-hand tower. Through a bullhorn he identified himself as Captain Westcott.

'Your warrants are illegal!' he bellowed. 'No one, I repeat, no one, will be admitted! And I order you to disperse your unlawful assembly! You are on private property!'

'I represent the authority of the U.S. government,' Chang bellowed back. 'Open at once, or entrance will be made forcibly!'

'Any force will be met with force!' Westcott said.

Chang wiped his forehead, which was covered with sweat

despite the chill air. 'Son of a bitch! I'll just have to order in more marshals. I didn't think he'd defy me.'

Rexter, who had been standing behind them, said, 'Out of the way, you! All of you! Pronto!'

Chang turned quickly and said, 'This is going to be done legally. You and your mob have no right to be here.'

'So?' Rexter said. 'Get out of the way unless you want to be run over!'

He turned and ran toward the crowd, shouting. They started yelling and running. The marshals, Lopez, and Carfax stood bewildered until Carfax turned and saw the truck speeding toward them. He shouted and ran also. When he got to Chang's car, he stuck his head in its window, and said, 'Come on, Pat! They're going to blow up the gates!'

The door swung open and Pat, her face white in the lights, scrambled out. Carfax took her hand and ran along the road. The truck sped by them, its left-hand door opened, and the driver fell out. Carfax quit looking at it after that and raced desperately up the road.

Then he heard the banging of rifles and the chattering of machine guns, a crash, and a thundering blast. He threw himself down, pulling Pat with him. The noise filled his right ear, the air tore at his clothes, and he smelled dynamite.

He sat up then and looked at the gates or, rather, where they had been. The explosion had disintegrated the truck and ripped the gates from their hinges. They lay about twenty meters inside the walls. The towers on each side of the gates were half-demolished. The great overhead lights for about sixty meters on each side were dark. The figures in the towers beyond them were silent, but he could see that they were still erect. Evidently, they were paralyzed by the blast. But they would start firing in a moment.

A massive shout went up from the crowd. It poured forward like two giant amoebae, fusing just before the gateway. Rifles banged here and there as shots were fired, either up into the air or at the guards in the towers. A few seconds later, the fire was returned from the guards. And the killing had started.

One of the watchtowers went up in flames as a rocket hit

it. Carfax saw four bazooka teams, exposed now by the withdrawal of the crowd. Three other rockets streaked flaming from them, and they struck below the three towers. These disappeared in roars and clouds, and when the smoke had cleared away, they had vanished or become part-rubble. The bazooka men ran forward, the tubes on the shoulders of four, the firers behind them, and behind them about twenty men carrying missiles.

'It's torn now!' Carfax said. He looked upward. The lights of the planes were dropping swiftly, but they weren't going to strafe the few people still outside the walls. Not yet, anyway.

He stood up and pulled Patricia up.

'That Langer set this up,' he said. 'He didn't expect Western to let us in.'

Patricia did not answer.

'Listen,' he said, 'you get in a car and drive back to Bonanza Circus. No, wait a minute! You might run into the Westernites! Come with me! I'll put you in the charge of those county cops. They can take you back!'

He pulled her along toward the silver-and-black car. From the area inside the walls came a roaring and a screaming, the banging of rifles and the rapid-firing of machine guns. Then, three booms as bazooka rockets exploded. Three more towers were enveloped in smoke, out of which pieces of wood and bricks soared into the light of the few lamps that were still illuminated.

The two county policemen were crouching by the side of the car. One was speaking rapidly into the car phone.

'Can you take her back to town?' Gordon yelled.

The man, a slim youth with a face as white as sugar, shook his head. 'No way. We got orders to stay here. Besides, the pro-Westerns are on the way, and we don't want to get caught between them and the ambushers.'

'What ambushers?' Carfax yelled.

'Hell, the hills just back of the pass are alive with men,' the youth said. 'Didn't you see them?'

Carfax shook his head, and the policeman said, 'They must've all hidden themselves before you got there. Man, this is terrible! Those guys are going to walk into a trap!'

'Then don't you think you should warn them?'

'We radioed in already, but they won't let our men near. And they're all on the road now.'

Four more large explosions, one after the other, caused them to duck down on the ground. Carfax looked over the hood a moment later and saw pillars of smoke. He also saw a small two-engined jet, lances of flame spurting from along its wings, diving at the area just within the walls. Then it curved up and was gone, and another had taken its place.

Either the pilot of the second jet had made a mistake, or some of the ground fire had hit it. It struck the top floor of the middle ten-story building, and the crown of the buildings went up in a ball of fire. Patricia screamed and would not quit until Carfax shook her. She collapsed sobbing on his chest. He made her sit in the back of the patrol car, said, 'You stay here,' and went back to the youth. The man on the phone quit talking then and looked at Carfax.

'Did you tell them we *have* to have the militia here now?' Carfax said.

The man nodded and said, 'They're on the way. The governor called them out about ten minutes ago. But it'll be an hour before any of them get here. If they can get through the mess up in the hills.'

Carfax presumed that he meant by that the expected battle between the Westernites and the ambushers.

Carfax stuck his head in the window. 'I'm going in after your father, Pat.'

'You'll be killed!'

'Maybe. But I have to go,' he said. 'If Western doesn't kill him, those maniacs will. They're likely to slaughter everybody.'

'But you won't even know what he looks like.'

'I know,' he said. 'I don't have much chance for success. You might as well face that, Pat.'

Chang and Lopez walked toward them, and Carfax went to meet them.

'Where's Hiekka?'

'She went on in,' Lopez said, grinning sourly. 'She said she had a duty to find your uncle, and she wasn't going to let any men scare her off. She's mucho hombre, that one. She said we didn't have any balls. I told her we did, but we didn't want them shot off.'

'She's crazy,' Carfax said. 'She just wants to knock off a few males. Well, I'm crazy, too. I'm going.'

'Wait a while, and we'll go with you,' Chang said. 'There isn't any percentage doing it now. You're as likely to be shot by the pros as the antis.'

He jumped as two more explosions beat the air around them.

'Talk me into it,' Carfax said.

'They're setting the whole place on fire!' Lopez said.

He was right. There seemed to be fires in the upper stories of all the buildings. He could see men clinging to the edges of the tops of the walls and dropping. The guards were deserting their posts in the towers.

He ran toward the gateway, drawing his automatic, furnished him by Langer. At the gate, he stopped and looked cautiously inside. There were about twenty-five bodies scattered over the grounds. A few of them were in Lincoln green. These seemed to be guards who had fallen inward from the blasted towers. Two men were dragging themselves toward the gateway.

From the buildings themselves came the uproar of many firearms and voices. Carfax slipped around the wall and ran toward the nearest building. As he did so, he heard the scream of a jet's engines, and he dropped to the pavement. The plane zoomed upward without firing. Apparently, the pilot had no way of knowing whether Carfax was one of his own men or not. At least, the pilot wasn't trigger-happy.

He got up and ran to the doorway, outside of which two men were crumpled. Inside, along the hallway, were about six dead and wounded. None of the latter were in a condition to cause him trouble even if they had been so inclined.

Carfax methodically went along the hall, opening doors and looking inside. Some rooms held dead men; most were empty. At the end, a door led to a chemical laboratory. A man in a white smock was on the floor, unconscious from a blow on the head. Two other lab workers lay dead among shattered glass and plastic tubes. The odor of acids and unidentifiable chemicals set him to choking and his eyes to tearing. He stumbled out, coughing, and leaned against the wall to recover his breath. Then he went down a hallway which intersected the first corridor halfway along its length. The rooms along it had the same grisly contents.

After inspecting the rooms along the hallway at the south side of the building, he climbed a flight of steps. Here a man at the end of the hallway yelled at him. Carfax dropped his gun and held up his hands while the man advanced. When the man got closer, he said, 'O.K. I saw you with Rexter.'

Carfax picked up the gun and said, 'Was it necessary to kill all those men? Most of them were unarmed.'

'Couldn't be helped,' the man said. 'Those guys' – he meant the mob from Bonanza Circus – 'aren't professionals. They are just out to kill anybody who works for Western. But I think Rexter's got them in hand now. At least, he did in this building.'

'Come along with me,' Carfax said. 'I have to search the whole building, and I don't want my head blasted off just because nobody knows I'm one of the good guys.'

The man, a heavy-set dark-skinned Mediterranean, looked at him sharply. He said, 'O.K.'

Near the end of his search of the second story, Carfax found a man holding another at the point of a gun. Carfax spoke to the prisoner, a tall thin man of about forty bleeding from a gash on one side of his face

'Are you Rufton Carfax?'

The man shook his head. Carfax said, 'Do you know Rufton Carfax?'

'Never heard of him,' the man said.

'In what building is Western?'

The man hesitated, and the man with Carfax growled, 'Tell him, mister, or it'll be the worst for you.'

'He was in Building Four,' the tall man said. 'He has an apartment there, two stories above MEDIUM.'

'Building Four,' the man with Carfax said. 'That's the one the plane hit.'

Carfax strode away, shouting over his shoulder. 'Come on!'

They ran downstairs and out into the open as the first of the mob poured out of Building Four. The fire had reached down to the fifth story now, and as Carfax ran toward it the heat struck him. It felt as if it were hot enough to fry eggs, but that was an exaggeration, of course. The men staggering out of it could not have gone more than a few steps if it had been that strong. The clothes of the last man out were beginning to smoke, though.

Carfax found Rexter, who was leading a group carrying Hiekka and a man so covered with blood that his features were unrecognizable. Rexter shouted at Carfax to come with him, and they all walked swiftly to the gateway and some meters beyond it. Here the men carrying Hiekka eased her to the ground. She was dead. A bullet had torn off one of her amazonian breasts and another had half-severed her leg at the knee.

'She got four men before they got her,' Rexter shouted.

'I hope she died happy,' Carfax said. He pointed at the bloody man, who had also been put on the ground.

'Who's that?'

'It's Western,' Rexter said.

'Why didn't you tell me before?' Carfax snarled. He got down on his knees and wiped the blood off Western's face with a handkerchief. He felt the neck and detected a slight pulse. He shouted, 'Western! Can you hear me?'

The eyelids fluttered, and the lips opened. Carfax put his good ear down close to the mouth. He could hear only something like '... wasn't long ...'

He said, 'Western? Where's Rufton Carfax?'

Blood bubbled from the mouth, spraying his ear. Carfax said, 'Western! It's me, Gordon Carfax! Where's my uncle?'

'... not Western ...'

Carfax said, 'Hang on, Western. Hang on long enough to do some good, for Christ's sake! Where is my uncle, Rufton Carfax?'

Western coughed, and more blood ran from his mouth. He sighed, and for a moment Carfax thought he was dead.

Then, weakly but distinctly, 'I'm not Western. I'm Rufton Carfax.'

Carfax had to restrain himself from grabbing him by the shoulders and shaking him.

'What did you say?' he shouted.

'I'm your uncle, Gordon.'

And he was dead.

TWENTY-ONE

Carfax got out of jail the next day on bond, and that only because Chang had vouched for him. The cells of the Bonanza Circus jail were crowded with pro-Westernites and anti-Westernites. The overflow had gone to a number of Nevada prisons. One newspaper article said that every jail in Nevada was packed to capacity with those arrested at Megistus and at the ambush, but that was an exaggeration.

The public outcry was hysterical. The followers of Western demanded that the 'vicious murderers' be given a quick trial and hung, preferably at a televised execution. Those opposed to Western demanded that the 'martyrs,' the 'public benefactors,' be released immediately with thanks from the American public. Some letters to the editor even suggested that the stormers of Megistus should be given the Congressional Medal of Honor.

Western's body was claimed by the chief divine of the Pan-Cosmic Church of the *Embu*-Christ (a distant relative). The public funeral in Los Angeles, attended by 500,000 mourners, was marred by a number of riots and injuries and deaths. The body was not released, however, before a thorough post-mortem had been done on Western. Langer received the secret report on this and showed it to Carfax. Particular attention had been given to the brain and the rest of the nervous system. Langer had asked the pathologists to note anything unusual, though he did not tell them why he wanted the information. The report, however, indicated that Western had had a healthy brain, that there was no degeneration beyond that to be expected from a man his age.

'I was hoping that they would find some changes which they could not explain,' Langer said to Carfax. 'Something that would have resulted, perhaps, from the occupation of the brain by a *semb*. Apparently possession doesn't cause physiological changes.'

Carfax had told only Langer about Western's last words. The senator had decided to keep it a secret for the time being.

'I don't understand it,' Langer said. 'Western, or your uncle, I mean, would not have lied. He was dying and knew it, so what would he gain by lying? But how did Rufton Carfax come to possess Western's brain?'

'I don't know,' Carfax said. 'I doubt that it could have been accidental. I can't say that it couldn't have happened accidentally. I don't know enough about the mechanics of *semb* transference. Maybe Western was going to place Uncle Rufton in a man's brain and something slipped up, and Uncle Rufton possessed Western instead. But if that happened, why didn't my uncle say so? What was to keep him from telling the public?

'I think, however, that there are some people, or at least one person, who could tell us. He is among those found in the subbasement.'

Carfax was referring to the twenty employees who had taken refuge in a secret underground complex deep beneath Building Four. They had survived the fire, which had completely destroyed the building above the surface. They had then gone through a tunnel which led to an exit behind the hangar on the airstrip. They might have escaped unnoticed if a National Guardsman had not glimpsed one of them as he fled toward the hills beyond the plateau. A chase had rounded up twenty, all of whom had been put in jail. With the exception of a few, such as Pat, everybody present at the scene had been arrested. Most of them were being held as material witnesses while a grand jury was being formed.

'Of course,' Carfax added, 'we don't know we caught everybody. A few may have escaped. The people who were in the subbasement swear that nobody did. But they might be lying.'

If only a MEDIUM were available, the truth might be ascertained. MEDIUM had burned, and the schematics needed to build another one had also gone up in flames. Two of the men who had hidden in the subbasement were physicists who might be able to rebuild MEDIUM. They, however, denied that possibility, claiming that they had no overall knowledge of the machine. Carfax thought that they were lying and that they intended to put together another as soon as they got their freedom.

'If they should,' Langer said, 'they'll find themselves in a legal battle which will tie them up for years. Western left no will, so it looks as if any right to MEDIUM should go to Patricia.'

'I find it difficult to believe that he made no will,' Carfax said. 'I've got an uneasy feeling about that. I think when this situation is cleared up, a will will suddenly show up. And whoever gets the inheritance is the man to check out.'

'Every one of the twenty is being investigated right now,' Langer said. 'We're checking them out in every detail. But it's going to take time and money.'

Neither of them expected quick action. For one thing, just picking a grand jury seemed almost impossible. Where, in this country where everybody was so fiercely partisan about MEDIUM, could an unprejudiced person be found? The process of selecting unbiased jurors had lasted three weeks and was far from over, despite the pressure to form one quickly. In the meantime, those jailed were released on bail. Rexter died two days after gaining his freedom, gunned down by four masked men who disappeared immediately after. Jones and Dennis, two of the employees who had taken refuge in the sub-basement, were blown apart by a bomb concealed in their car. Their eighteen fellows were at once jailed for their own protection, but they protested so vehemently about violation of their civil rights that they had to be released again.

'You'd think they'd be so scared they'd want to be locked up,' Carfax said to Langer. 'Yet they don't seem to be worried.'

'What do you suspect?' Langer said.

'Well, for one thing, we don't really know that the two men who were in that car were Jones and Dennis. There wasn't enough left of either for a positive identification. Even the teeth were splintered.'

'You think they might not have been Jones and Dennis?'

'The possibility is worth looking into.'

'Why would they want to be thought dead?'

'For one thing, the anti-MEDIUM nuts won't be looking for

them. But I doubt that's it. It wouldn't be worth it to Jones and Dennis to murder two men. No, the stakes would have to be as high as they can get for them to kill two innocents.'

There was a silence, broken when Langer said, impatiently, 'Well?'

'Maybe one of them, Jones or Dennis, is Western.'

Langer sat down as if the strength had drained from his knees.

'Are you serious? Forgive that question. Of course you are. But why would he have traded bodies with your uncle?'

'I think it must have been a last-minute act. He wasn't sure that his hiding place wouldn't be found out. And he knew that he would be killed if he was found. What better way to throw everybody off the track than to become Dennis or Jones and put my uncle in the starring role? My uncle wouldn't be able to talk then, and everybody would believe that Western was dead.'

'I should have thought of that,' Langer said.

'You have a lot on your mind,' Carfax said. 'Of course, that may not be quite the way it happened.'

'Which means what?' Langer said sharply.

'Maybe Western figured that we would guess correctly, and so Dennis and Jones disappeared just to throw us even more off the track. Or maybe he's one of the eighteen left. Or maybe he got away into the hills.'

'But he would think that your uncle died before he could reveal anything. No one except you and I know that he managed to get out a few words. So why would Western go to all the trouble of covering his tracks when no one is looking for him?'

'Western was no scientific genius, but he was a very thorough and crafty man. He knows the details of his death, as reported by the news media, but he may have wondered how much of it was true. What if Rufton had managed to say something revealing? Then we would still be looking for him, for Western that is. So he got out while he could. I think that we should make comparisons of Dennis's and Jones's speech rhythms with those of Western's, if they're available. We should have done it while they were still around, but then we thought that Western was no longer alive.'

Langer gave the order to locate and check the spectograms. Three hours later, his specialists reported back.

Langer swore and threw a book across the room. 'We had him in our hands, and now he's gone! Because we were stupid, stupid, stupid!'

'Not stupid, unthinking,' Carfax said. 'Well, it's safe to assume that those two men blown up were not Jones and Dennis.'

'Not Dennis, anyway,' Langer said. 'He, Western that is, may have killed Jones to cut off all knowledge of his identity. Jones may have been, must have been, the only one who knew of the switch.'

The explosion in the car had taken place at 23:16 in the garage by Jones's house. This was in a suburban development, Minerva Hills, northeast of Altadena, California. The neighbors had poured out into the street after recovering from their shock, but they had seen no strangers, no speeding cars. Doubtless, Dennis-Western and Jones had left some time before the bomb had gone off. Langer sent out a large crew of detectives to comb the whole suburb, and they interviewed every one of the potential eyewitnesses in Minerva Hills. This took two weeks, at the end of which they had failed to find a single person who had seen anything that might conceivably be a suspicious stranger or a getaway vehicle.

Langer set in motion the most massive manhunt in the history of the United States. Every police department in the country was provided with photographs, finger and eye and voice prints of Dennis and Jones, and descriptions of their physical appearances and personal habits. The F.B.I. was also looking for them, although there was no evidence that any federal crime had been committed. The president had been informed of Langer's suspicions and had ordered the F.B.I. to join the hunt. In addition, Langer was employing thirty private agencies.

None of the bulletins issued to the police hinted that Dennis might be Western. This was known to only three men: Langer, Carfax, and the president of the United States.

At the end of a month, when the results had been zero, Langer purchased a half hour of prime time on all ten of the main channels. Dennis's and Jones's photographs and descriptions were given, and the reward for any information leading to the apprehension of either was raised to one million dollars.

'Even the most fanatical Westernite should be tempted by that,' Langer told Carfax.

'I don't know about that,' Carfax said. 'Western can promise more than money. Immortality.'

'And how can he do that without a MEDIUM?'

Carfax forgot to light his cigar. The match burned while he stared, and he remembered it only when it scorched his fingers. He swore and then he said, 'Why didn't I think of that before?'

'What?'

'Wherever he is, he isn't just going to sit around and hope that the cops don't find him. He knows that he's going to be located, sooner or later. But he can't be identified if he's no longer Dennis. And how can he make sure that he isn't in Dennis's body? He builds another MEDIUM, and then he makes a switch!'

'That seems possible,' Langer said. 'But how can knowing that help us?'

'Look. My investigations at Big Sur Center identified a number of the electrical parts, the type of circuit boards used, and the construction of the console and cabinet. The MEDIUM in Megistus was burned, and many of the parts were melted or destroyed. But at least a quarter of them were identified. Put all this together, and you have a partial reconstruction of MEDIUM. It's not nearly enough to recreate one. But we know at least half of the stuff that Western will have to order if he wants to put together another MEDIUM. And that includes some very large vacuum tubes not usually needed by private individuals.

'You get a list from every electrical parts supplier and console and cabinet maker in the United States. And Canada. A list for everything sold in the country since Western disappeared. Run the lists through a computer. It'll tell you where the parts Western needs have been shipped. Go to that address, and you'll find Dennis. I mean, Western.'

'Do you have any idea of the time and money that'll take?'

'I know your personal fortune has suffered,' Carfax said. 'You can get the help of the federal government for this. The president ought to be able to ram through that project.'

'I hope so. The pro-Western congressmen are likely to take notice and start asking questions. And if Western finds out what we're up to, he'll take off again.'

'You can't afford not to take a chance.'

'All right,' the senator said. 'I'll put through a call to the president now. Excuse me.'

The senator closed the doors of the next room behind him. He would be using a private line, so there was nothing untoward if Carfax used the phone in this room. He punched the number of the phone in his house in Busiris, and after three rings Patricia answered.

'I'm sorry, Pat,' he said, 'but I've been too busy to return your call this morning. Langer is working my tail off. Unofficially, I'm his most-private secretary. So what's up?'

'Nothing, except that I miss you very much,' she said. 'And I want to make sure that you will be coming home in two weeks.'

He hesitated and then said, 'I'm not sure now. Things may break all of a sudden.'

'You mean about those two men, Dennis and Jones?'

'You know I can't discuss that over the phone.'

'I'm sorry,' she said.

'You don't sound sorry.'

'I am sorry. For myself. I miss you very much, and I'm terribly lonely. I've joined the Women's League of Voters and the Lakeview Art Lecture Series, I read a lot and see a lot of TV, and I've made a few friends. Women, of course. But that's not enough. And when it's time to go to bed, well . . .'

'Not so well?' he said. 'Maybe you should come back to Washington. We still wouldn't see much of each other. I'm working an eighteen-hour day or more, but we'd see each other now and then. It might be better than a complete severance.'

'No, it'd be worse,' she said. 'And I don't like Washington.'

'If this thing breaks right, we might be with each other all the time,' he said. 'We could have a normal life. Provided I could find a teaching position, that is. I'm probably blackballed. Still, Langer has enough weight to fix that.'

'Oh, I hope so,' she said. 'I don't like to complain, Gordon, but I'm going out of my mind.'

'Look, I'll be there in a week, maybe more, if this works out all right. I can't promise for certain, but I'm not so indispensable that I can't be given a vacation. If things get bad enough, I can quit. I won't, not until this matter is settled. But I'm just waiting for the day that I can get out of here. I don't like this any better than you do, you know.'

'But you're busy and useful, and I'm not. I want you here so I can be busy and useful taking care of you, being a good wife.'

'I know,' he said. 'But it won't be long. Look, I have to punch out now. The senator is coming back.'

'I love you,' she said.

'I love you, too, very much,' he said. 'Goodby. But not for long, I hope.'

Langer entered, stopped, and said, suspiciously, 'Who was that?'

'Patricia. She needs to hear my voice now and then.'

'Anybody giving her any trouble?'

'No. She lives in a conservative neighborhood, all staunch anti-MEDIUMites. But she doesn't have much in common with them.'

'We ought to hear from NIC by tomorrow,' Langer said. 'It has a complete inventory of every electrical part sold from five years ago up to the past forty-eight hours. The specialists will be setting up the scan as soon as they get the data, and that's being rushed to them. I told Harrison, he's head of NIC, that I'd like to have the results by breakfast.'

Which means you'll get it then or there'll be hell to pay, Carfax thought.

'As soon as we know the address, we close in,' Langer said. 'This time, there'll be no escape. I'll have every road blocked, every possible avenue of escape sealed up. But we won't go storming in like a conquering army. I don't want him to have the slightest idea he's about to be caught. I want it to be a complete surprise! I want to take him alive. He's going to be put on trial, and the whole rotten story is going to be made public. By the time I'm through with him, he won't have a follower in the world.'

'The whole story?' Carfax said. 'You don't mean everything involved in his case? You're going to tell everything that *we* did?'

Langer looked surprised. He turned away for a moment to fix himself a drink. Carfax watched his broad back and wondered what would happen to him and Patricia if the events in the Mifflon house became public. Was Langer going to let the defense probe deeply enough to expose the connections between Langer and the massacre of Megistus? Not very likely.

Langer turned again and said, 'Don't be a fool, Gordon. There are some things I did which would ruin my career if they were known. They were done for the best of causes, the salvation of humanity. I have no feeling of guilt about them. Western can make accusations, but he can't prove anything. And I can prove everything about him.'

Carfax looked at his wristwatch and said, 'I'd like to go to bed, if you have no further need of me. It's going to be a short night and a long day tomorrow. If NIC comes up with anything that is.'

'It will,' Langer said. 'Good night, Gordon.'

Carfax said goodnight and went down the hall to his room. He thought he'd have trouble sleeping, but he passed into a dreamless state almost at once. Suddenly, the phone was ringing. He rose up, startled, and punched the button, and Langer's face appeared.

His red hair was tangled, and there were dark rings under his eyes. However, he looked almost satanically happy.

'Get dressed and get right down here,' he said. 'We'll have breakfast on the plane.'

'What's the name and address?' Carfax said.

'Albert Samsel. A house on a farm near Pontiac, Illinois. He purchased the farm two years ago but only moved in recently. The description of Samsel fits Dennis, and the parts were delivered to him.'

'It sounds too easy,' Carfax said. 'But then we haven't caught him yet, have we?'

TWENTY-TWO

The jet bomber carried Langer, his two bodyguards, Carfax, and three tough-looking men from an unnamed agency. It took an hour from takeoff at Washington to the time its wheels touched the pavement of the airport at Busiris, Illinois. The party immediately transferred to a car which was speedily escorted through Busiris and across the Illinois River by motorcycle cops. It headed east on U.S. Route 24, a divided six-lane highway, and turned north on U.S. Route 66, a divided twelve-lane highway. Pontiac was fifty-five kilometers from Busiris; the entire trip from the airport, which was in the country west of Busiris, to Pontiac took forty-five minutes.

At Pontiac the car and its escort turned onto State Route 23 and traveled north thirteen kilometers through farmland. Suddenly, after rounding a curve, they came upon a roadblock. The car slowed down and stopped a few meters from a state highway patrol car. Two men in civilian suits got out of a car to greet them. They were U.S. Marshal Fred Turner and a Mr. Selms. The latter, Carfax suspected, belonged to the same anonymous agency as did the three men who had accompanied the Langer party. These were certainly deferrent to Selms.

'The farmhouse is down the road three kilometers, senator,' Selms reported. 'The other roadblock is three kilometers on the other side. There are sixty men stationed in the fields and the woods around the house. He can't get away by car or on foot.'

Langer said, 'Good,' and looked at the cars lined up on the right side of the road. The occupants were being allowed through but only after they had identified themselves. A few had tooted their horns impatiently, but they were quelled at once by state troopers.

Langer looked at his wristwatch and said, 'We'll move in now. Radio the other roadblock, and tell them to let no more cars through. I want the road kept clear for six kilometers; there might be shooting.'

'By the time you get to the house, the civilians now on the road will have passed through,' Turner said.

Turner gave the signal, and the troopers and marshals stood to one side while Langer's car drove around the patrol cars onto the pavement. Three minutes later, they stopped. Down the road, on the right-hand side, was an old two-story house which badly needed a fresh coat of paint. Behind it was a large barn, also needing paint, and some farm machinery, a small tractor and a large combine. The fields behind it were covered with weeds. The pens near the barn were empty of animals.

Carfax looked around but could see none of the sixty men supposedly surrounding the house.

A pickup truck passed them, its driver looking curiously at them. Turner got out of the car which had pulled up behind them and said, 'That's the last one. All clear now.'

The plan of attack had been formulated during a radiophone conversation between Langer and the authorities while his plane was on its way. Langer said, 'Let's go!' though he himself made no move to advance. Turner, carrying a bullhorn, walked down the road toward the house. The morning sun shone brightly, a gentle wind stirred the weeds in the fields, and a crow flew over him, cawing. Except for the men, the scene was one of rural peace and quiet. If there was anyone in the house, he was not showing himself at the windows, the blinds of which were up.

According to the reports which Langer had received on the plane, 'Albert Samsel' had last been seen in Pontiac two weeks ago. He had purchased enough groceries at a supermarket to stock him for a month. The clerks and the manager did not remember him until they were shown photographs of Dennis, and then they had not been sure. Dennis was now wearing a moustache, if the man described was Dennis. He had only been at the store twice, and the only reason they remembered him was that he used cash. This was such a rare event that it stuck in their memories.

Carfax wondered why Western had not used an I.D. These were easy to fake. If he had a bank account, and the bill was paid within thirty days, there would have been no suspicions about him. He surely must have known that the expenditure of a large amount of cash would make him conspicuous.

He thought of Patricia, only sixty kilometers away from Western. Western would have no way of knowing that she was now in Busiris, and any thought of revenge would have to be foregone. If she was killed, an investigation would be launched that would put him in danger of being located.

Patricia was going to be frightened when she found out how close Western had been.

Turner, with Selms and his men a few paces behind him, stopped at the gravel driveway. He looked around, took a whistle out of his pocket, and blew shrilly. Answering whistles rose from the woods across the road and faintly from a line of trees along the distant edge of the field behind the barn. Men popped out of the shadows of the trees and advanced on a run.

Turner put the whistle back in his pocket and walked across the weedy lawn to the sidewalk. Selms and his men spread out, Selms going to the side of the big front porch and crouching below a window. The other men took positions on the side of the house. If Western wanted to dash out of the back door, no one was in his path, but he would never get to the barn. Selms's men carried submachine guns which would blow his legs off.

Turner put the bullhorn to his mouth and bellowed, 'Ray Dennis! This is the federal marshal! I have a warrant for your arrest! Come out with your hands behind your neck! If you don't, we are authorized to come in after you!'

The men across the road split into two groups. Half of them ran into the yard and took positions near Turner or by the sides of the house. The other half lined up in the ditch that paralleled the road, ready to throw themselves down if fired upon from the house. The men who had hidden at the edge of the field behind the barn were halfway across now. The sun glinted on the barrels of rifles and submachine guns.

Carfax counted to ten slowly. At the end of that time, Turner signaled to two marshals. These aimed their tear gas guns at the two front windows, one on each side of the porch. The projectiles shot forward; the glass broke; a thick white smoke poured out from the jagged edges.

Turner spoke another order, and his men fired four more gas bombs. The men behind the barn had by then reached the yard, and they started to search the barn and to take positions behind the tractor and the combine. A moment later, tear gas bombs shot from the sides of the machines, and more glass broke.

'Well, I suppose he could have a mask,' Langer said. He spoke into the walkie-talkie on his wrist, and Turner answered. Men in gas masks broke down the front and rear doors with axes and disappeared inside. A few minutes later, one came back out of the front doorway. He ran down the porch away from the thick fumes, removed his mask, and said something to Turner. Turner waved at Langer to come to him.

Langer strode toward him with Carfax close behind him.

'What is it?' Langer said.

'Dennis is inside, all right. But he's dead. Been dead for over a week. Geoffreys says he must have been electrocuted!'

Langer was impatient, but he had to wait until the gas fumes had cleared enough to make it endurable. Other windows were smashed to improve the ventilation, and in five minutes Langer and Carfax entered. The gas was still heavy enough to make them cough and to bring tears. Its effects were less upstairs, where they found a half-built MEDIUM and a body. The stench was so sickening that Langer and Carfax had to retreat to put on gas masks.

The corpse lay on its side beside the machine. Though its features were bloated and black, it was still recognizable as Dennis.

Dead flies lay on the face and around the body. Turner pointed at the exposed interior of the machine and then at the streak, darker than that of corruption, on the swollen hand. Carfax understood. Western had accidentally touched a large transformer and had been killed instantly. His creation had killed him.

Another Frankenstein and his monster, Carfax thought.

Carfax looked at the power switch. It was still on, and the

power line was still plugged in. He pulled the plug out, but he motioned to the others not to go near the machine. He walked out into the hallway with Langer and Turner behind him and removed his mask. Even with the door to the room shut, the stench twisted his stomach.

'It won't be difficult to complete the assembly of the machine,' he said to Langer. 'Western's dead, but he's left a legacy. What do you plan to do with it?'

'A legacy?' Langer said. 'You're thinking about your cousin, aren't you? And if you should decide to marry, you'll be sharing the profits with her, right?'

'Of course,' Carfax said. 'But I'm more concerned with the uses to which MEDIUM will be put. Frankly, if – or when, I should say – Pat gets control of MEDIUM, I'm going to do my best to see to it that its use is strictly confined to certain areas. There'll be no more communication with *semb*s except for historical and scientific research. And that'll be with considerable caution.'

'And what about its use as a source of cheap power? The world won't let you prohibit that.'

'I know,' Carfax said. 'But I'd insist on a long and careful study of its effects before it was used for that purpose. How do we know now that its prolonged operation won't weaken the quote walls unquote between the *embu* and our universe?'

'I'm all for that,' Langer said. 'In the meantime, I'm impounding the machine and all documents relative to it, everything in the house, in fact. I'm doing it in the name of the federal government.'

'Let's hope nothing happens to it while it's locked up,' Carfax said. 'Like a fire, for instance, which might destroy MEDIUM and all the schematics.'

Langer laughed and said, 'You're too suspicious.'

'If something did happen like that,' Carfax said, 'it would only delay the inevitable. Now that we know a MEDIUM has been built, you can bet on it that someone will reinvent it.'

'Don't you think I have any ethics at all?'

Carfax did not reply.

Selms drew Langer aside for a few minutes. A number of civilians whom he had not seen before, but who seemed to be

Selms's men, moved into the room. They carried cameras, fingerprint dusting equipment, tapes, and little boxes of other equipment. Carfax followed Langer outside. There were at least thirty cars along the road; the driveway and backyard were filled with vehicles.

'Western's body will be flown to Washington after the whole house has been searched,' Langer said. 'One of Selms's crews will remove MEDIUM and associated stuff. And then it'll all be up to the courts.'

'You mean the disposition of MEDIUM?' Carfax said.

'Yes.'

Langer held out his hand and said, 'You can go home now. I won't be needing you any longer. But I am certainly grateful for the help you gave me.'

'I'm fired?' Carfax said.

'Discharged with honor. You'll receive a month's severance pay.'

'You're not one to shilly-shally,' Carfax said. 'I can depend on you if I get into any trouble at the investigation?'

'At Bonanza Circus? Certainly. I don't desert my people, even after they've quit working for me. As a matter of fact, even though you'll no longer be on the payroll, I'll foot your expenses while you're at the investigation. You might be there for a long time.'

Which means that, in a sense, I'll still be your employee, Carfax thought.

Selms approached Langer. He was carrying four large binders which were crammed with loose-leaf papers. Carfax decided not to leave yet. He wanted to hear Selms's report.

'Dennis's notes,' Selms said. 'And schematics on microfilm. I looked through a few pages of the first one I picked up. I hope you don't mind.'

'Since you'll be looking through them later, I don't see why I should,' Langer said. 'But no one else is to see these unless I authorize it.'

'He had some crazy ideas,' Selms said. 'One was a project to finance research for growing complete individuals from cells taken from their bodies. Another was to research the possibility of making artificial human bodies. The man was a nut!'

'Not so . . .' Langer said, and then he became aware that Carfax had not left.

'Goodby and good luck, Gordon,' he said, shaking his hand again. 'No doubt we'll be seeing each other some day.'

'No doubt,' Carfax said, thinking that it would probably be in court, *Carfax* v. *the People of the United States*. The issue: the ownership of MEDIUM.

He turned and walked away and then became aware that he had no transportation. He was angry at his abrupt dismissal and did not want to ask Langer for transportation. He hitched a ride on a truck that had slowed down while going by the farmhouse. The driver, a young farmer, was very curious about the crowd. Carfax told him that it was federal business. He wasn't in a position to discuss anything. He could read about it in the papers. He got off in the downtown district and walked to the bus station. Before boarding, he phoned Patricia and told her what had happened. Patricia was very happy; but after she had babbled a minute, Carfax chilled her joy.

'It may be a long time, perhaps years, before we can establish your rights to MEDIUM. And maybe not then.'

'What?' Patricia screamed. 'I'm the rightful inheritor! What the hell do those . . . ?'

Carfax interrupted. 'It's no use getting mad about it, Pat. It's the way things are, and patience is what you're going to need a lot of for a long time. I think it'll be all right in the end. Meantime, simmer down. Pick me up at the bus station in an hour, will you? And have a big drink ready so I can just walk in and pick it up. I'm in need of a lot of relaxation and rest. Not to mention love.'

Patricia paused a moment, and then said, 'I'll be there,' and she punched out.

Carfax sighed. He wasn't in a mood to pacify her; scenes were the last thing he wanted now, not that he ever wanted them. He didn't blame her for being upset, though he had discussed the possibility with her before, and by now she should know better than to react so violently.

On the bus to Busiris, he thought about Selms's comments on the notebooks. Selms had seemed puzzled. Langer, though he had said nothing about them, was intelligent enough to realize their implications. Western had intended to launch research into replication of human beings from cells and to make artificial life for one reason only. That would be possession by *sembs* of the bodies so created. People now living would donate cells to be preserved cryogenically. When the donor died, a cell would be put through a process which would result in a body that would be the duplicate of the donor's. Each cell in a person's body contained all the biological apparatus needed for this. That had been known for a long time. The only thing lacking to bring this about was knowledge. And knowledge could be attained if enough money, determination, and time were available. What if the project took a hundred years, or two hundred, to reach its goal? The *semb* would still be around; it wasn't going any place.

Carfax had read in the *Scientific American* about the work being done in this field. Scientists had succeeded in growing complete rabbits from single cells. These were babies, at a stage comparable to that of the new-born.

If a human baby was processed from a single cell, how would the adult *semb* fit into it? A baby was incomplete; its neural system developed slowly. What would the *semb* do about adjusting itself to the undeveloped faculties of the baby? Would it have to endure being fed, bathed, its diapers changed while it was a prisoner in the infant? Would the drives of the adult to master its environment, to be his own master, conflict with the pace of the growing up of the baby's body? Wouldn't that result in neurosis, or even psychosis, of the occupying mind?

It wouldn't be possible to let the body mature until it was advanced enough for the *semb* to possess it without trouble. The body grown from a cell would have its own brain, and, if left unpossessed, it would develop its own persona, and possession then would be criminal. It would be as much a psychic rape as Western's taking over of Dennis.

Now that he considered it, the baby grown from a cell should have its own civil rights. It would have its own *semb*, too. No, that means of providing a body for a *semb* wouldn't work. Physiologically, psychologically, legally, and ethically, it was a wrong.

Perhaps Western had figured that out after he had first thought of it.

The second means, that of making human beings from cells created in the laboratory, was much less open to objection. If the *semb* was an adult, he'd be given an adult body, probably better than that he had known in his first life. If it were a baby, it would go into an infant's body.

But you couldn't, or rather wouldn't, bring back the idiots, the hopelessly insane, and the nonrehabilitable criminal. Or could and would you? The idiot was so because of a disease, an imbalance in body chemistry, or an injured brain. If the *semb* were placed in a healthy body and brain, would its new environment then allow it to change for the better? Nobody knew, which meant that experiments would have to be made to determine what would happen.

But, Carfax thought, the world is overcrowded now. Where would you put all the dead come back to life?

Western must have thought of that, too. Perhaps he had intended to keep the research secret. Only a few bodies would be made, a few for the elite, namely, Western and his gang. While the artificial bodies were still in the experimental stage, Western and company could kidnap people and use their bodies. Once the artificial bodies were available, they would no longer have to use this method and so take the chance that the police might uncover their kidnappings.

In the meantime, Western could dangle the carrot of immortality before the rich and the powerful. He could legally sell repossession insurance.

Nor did Carfax doubt that in a hundred years Western would have a secret control of the world. He and his council would have achieved that dream which was the premise of so many science-fiction novels. The secret master of the world, controlling the use of MEDIUM, Western would become the richest man on Earth in a short time. From there, step by step, he would gain ownership of all the business corporations. And his offer of immortality would be refused by few of the rulers of the world. Or, if they did refuse, they would be disposed of and Western's men put in their place. Western could take his time at his work. He had all the time in the world.

Or he would have had. A single moment of carelessness had put an end to his plans. Electricity didn't care about the rank or the wealth or the dreams of a man. It took the path of least resistance.

Western was gone, but the world would never be the same. MEDIUM would ensure that. The world will never be the same, he thought. And then, it never is and yet it always is.

The bus rolled into its port, and he saw Patricia standing in front of the bus. She smiled when she saw him. He thought that she had never looked so beautiful.

TWENTY-THREE

She questioned him eagerly all the way home. He finally told her to let him finish an answer before she broke in with another question. She laughed and said she'd be silent, but he could understand, couldn't he, how she lusted to know everything that had happened?

'Perfectly,' he said. 'But watch your driving, will you? I'd hate to come through all this and be killed in a dumb traffic accident.'

'I'm just excited,' she said. 'Would you rather drive?'

'No, just take it easy. We'll have a lot of time to go over everything in juicy detail.'

Five minutes later, they pulled into the driveway of his house. Carfax picked up his suitcase and waited while Patricia fumbled with the keys. 'I'm so excited I'm all thumbs!' she said. 'Here, I've got it now.'

He put the suitcase near the foot of the staircase to the second story and headed toward the bar. Two glasses were set out by the ice-cube container, and five bottles: bourbon, Scotch, vodka, gin, and dark Lowenbrau were lined up by them.

'You must be planning on quite a party,' he said. He put an ice cube in a glass and poured out about six ounces of Weller's Special Reserve. He turned to see Patricia in the middle of the room, looking at him with a curious expression.

'Come on!' he said. 'Surely you aren't planning to have people in?'

'Oh, no,' she said, sitting down and taking a package of cigarettes out of her handbag. 'I was just taking inventory of our liquor stock. I wouldn't let anyone else into the house tonight. To tell the truth, I had expected that the first thing you'd grab would be me, not the whiskey.'

He laughed and said, 'Make up your mind. The story first or bed.'

'The story, of course,' she said. She drew in a deep breath of smoke, released it, and said, 'Would you mind making me one, too, darling?'

'Not at all,' he said.

He poured her three ounces of bourbon and carried it across the room to her. As he handed it to her, he leaned down and kissed her on the lips. She responded as passionately as she had at the bus station. For a moment he wondered if he should put off the inquisition until later. But no, no matter how starved she was for sex, her desire to hear about Western would be stronger. He didn't want her mind occupied with that while he was making love.

He sat down by her, smelled the aroma rising from the glass, tasted it with his tongue, said, 'Ah!' and downed half an ounce. 'Now,' he said, 'to begin all over again at the beginning.'

When he had finished, she said, 'It must have been horrible. I mean, seeing that rotting body. I feel sorry for him, even if he was the world's worst bastard.'

'Smelling him was worse than seeing him,' he said. 'No matter. He stank when he was alive.'

'Well, he's gone now, and this time he won't be coming back. So, here's to Western, wherever he is.'

'Here's to the devout wish that he'll stay wherever he is,' Carfax said, lifting his glass. He drained it down, coughed, wiped the tears from his eyes, and stood up. 'Come on, let's go upstairs. I don't want to wait any longer.'

'I can't think of a better way to celebrate,' she said. She rose, and he took her hand and led her across the room and up the steps.

Afterward, he said, 'You must really have been suffering! That's the first time you ever scratched my back. I didn't mind it while it was happening, but it's hurting like hell now.'

He got out of bed and stood sideways to the mirror, looking at the gashes. 'You'd better fix me up, since you did it,' he said. He went into the bathroom and got a bottle of rubbing alcohol and a box of band-aids. Patricia, smoking a cigarette and look-ing not at all contrite, entered a moment later. She applied the alcohol to the gashes and placed the band-aids over them. He turned around, and she moved her naked body against him.

'I'm not completely satisfied,' she said in a low voice.

'The gashed child dreads the nails,' he said. 'Though not necessarily the gash.'

'What?'

'Never mind,' he said. 'You may have conditioned me for-ever against sex.'

A few moments later, dressed, he went downstairs. Patricia, clad in only a robe, followed him down. She started to resume her place on the sofa when he said, 'Would you mind making some coffee? I need a stimulant, not a depressant.'

'Of course,' she said. 'Instant or perked?'

'Perked. And how about a sandwich? That'll keep me until we have dinner.'

She stopped and turned to him. 'I was hoping that you'd take me out to dinner. I don't feel like cooking tonight.'

'You said you were going to be busy being a good wife to me,' he said. 'I don't feel like going out.'

'Couldn't we just this once?'

'No, I'm tired of eating in restaurants.'

'And I'm tired of cooking.'

'All right, dear, I surrender. But only for tonight. Tomorrow you fix my favorites.'

Well, here they were, reunited for only a few hours and already at odds, he thought, although Patricia's request wasn't unreasonable. On the other hand, neither was his.

He heard her running the water into the coffee pot. That was followed by a clang as she dropped the lid of the can on the floor, succeeded by a soft swearing. He smiled at these domestic noises and leaned back, then winced and leaned forward again. He'd have no more of this wild nail-digging, but he and Patricia would work out the other irritations and hurts and disagreements. They did love each other, and they missed each other when they were separated. There was no reason that he could see why they shouldn't get married soon. They'd lived together long enough to know each other well and to know what to expect in the way of unhappiness and happiness. He might as well pop the question now, when she came back from the kitchen. He did not want her, however, to throw her arms around him. Even the pressure of the clothes hurt his back. Damn the woman! The lovely woman.

Pat entered, carrying a cup of steaming coffee on a saucer. She put it down on the coffee table and stood before him, looking as if she were waiting for him to say something.

'What is it?' he said.

'What's wrong?'

'You seem to be expecting something.'

'Oh no, it's nothing. I just can't get my mind off Western. It's so hard to believe that we don't have to worry about him any more.'

She turned and walked toward the kitchen. He opened his mouth to tell her to come back and sit down, then decided to drink his coffee first. There was really no rush about proposing. His hesitation, he thought, might result from a subconscious reluctance to propose. Was it because it was telling him that he was not actually in love with her? Or was it because he was afraid that she might come to a violent end, as his first two wives had? But that was superstition. He didn't carry a fatality for spouses, and things did not always happen in threes.

He heard the refrigerator door close as he lifted the cup to his lips. And then, as he gingerly sipped the hot liquid, he heard a crunching sound. For a few seconds, he listened. The cup shook in his hand so much that some of the coffee sloshed over the edge. He put the cup down and said, 'What are you doing in there, Pat?'

The crunching stopped, there was a pause, and Pat said, 'I'm just taking the edge off my appetite. Why?'

His heart was beating so hard that he thought he would faint, and his head thrummed as if it were being beaten with drum sticks. He rose slowly and walked across the room and around the corner and looked down the room into the kitchen. She was standing by the counter, a cup of coffee before her, and munching on a stalk of celery.

He advanced even more slowly.

Patricia said, 'What's the matter? You look pale.'

He stopped in the doorway.

Her coffee was a pale brown; beside the cup stood a plastic container of cream and a sugar bowl.

'You . . . you . . .' he said, stepping forward.

'What's the matter?' she said, shrinking back and looking wildly around.

He bellowed and sprang at her. She screamed and grabbed the cup and dashed its contents in his face. His yell of pain mingled with her scream, and for a second he was blind. And then, unconsciousness.

TWENTY-FOUR

When he awoke, he was slumped in a chair in the front room. His face burned, and his head ached. His arms were bound tightly to his body with rope, and his ankles were gripped by more rope. Two ropes around his chest and his waist secured him to the chair, which had been removed from the dining room. The drapes had been pulled and three lamps turned on. There was no one else in the room.

Even with only one good ear, he could hear footsteps upstairs. Somebody was working hard, dragging something across the floor. That somebody had to be Patricia. And he could do nothing, absolutely nothing, except endure whatever she had in mind for him.

After a minute or so, something thumped on the steps. She appeared around the corner, her back to him. She was now wearing a pantsuit and was bent over and hauling something. A second later he saw that it was a cardboard box, a cube about two meters wide. Paying no attention to him, she dragged it across the room, past him, and to the outlet at the base of the wall near the French windows that opened onto the sun-porch. She straightened, breathing hard, and said, 'That's the trouble with being a woman. No muscle. But there are compensations.'

He should have expected anything, but her pronunciation startled him. It was a New England twang, and the *there are* came out as *theah ah*.

She must have spoken thus deliberately, because thereafter her speech was standard mid-Western. The rhythm was not quite that of the Patricia he had known. He should have caught on, he told himself, he should have heard it. But then he wasn't looking for it.

She disappeared into the kitchen, returning with a large butcher knife. His bowels constricted at sight of it, but she intended to use it, for the moment anyway, on the box. She hacked away the cardboard, separating the corners down to the bottom and then put her foot against the metal cube it had contained and slid the bottom of the box out from it. When she went into the kitchen again, he saw that it bore a CRT and a control panel.

She entered his view pushing a serving cart. With much huffing and puffing and some swearing, she hoisted the metal cube onto the top of the cart. She unreeled from its back a long power cord. It was not, however, long enough to satisfy her. She went into the kitchen again and came back with a heavy-duty extension cord. After connecting the cord, she plugged it into the wall socket.

She went around to the back of the machine and checked something. Looking up, she saw that he was staring at her. She smiled and said, 'Old Rufton attached an automatic control device to this, but you have to make sure the two wires from it are connected to terminals. This model is jerry-built, a proto-type, but it works.'

She went around to the front and adjusted dials and pressed some buttons. The screen glowed for a minute, but it became dull again when she pressed the off button.

'There. It's working fine. Everything is going fine, except for you. And that's no real problem.'

Carfax said nothing. He glared at her as she sat down on the sofa across the room from him and lit a cigarette.

'All right,' she said. 'How did you find out?'

'Pat . . . Pat,' he said, choking. Tears were suddenly running down his cheeks, and he wept with sorrow for her.

She – he couldn't think of her as male – looked coolly at him and waited until he was able to talk.

'A good cry never hurt anyone,' she said. 'Though it isn't going to do you much good in the long run. Now, how did you find out?'

'Pat hates – hated – celery,' he said. 'And when I went into the kitchen and saw that you were drinking coffee with cream and sugar, I *knew* you couldn't be Pat.'

She shrugged and said, 'That's why I seemed to be expecting something when I served you coffee. I didn't know if you took it black or not. I was ready to cover up with a plea of momentary forgetfulness if you said anything. I didn't know how she liked her coffee, so I drank it in the kitchen. I goofed anyway. I love celery, and it never occurred to me that anyone might not. So much for the best-laid plans of mice and men. But it's going to be all right. My schedule has to be revised, that's all.'

'What'd you hit me with?' he said.

'A hammer I had lying on the counter just in case. I was afraid I'd killed you. That would've been very bad, because I would have had a hell of a hard time explaining your sudden and violent demise. And I'm tired of running. Fortunately, I'm not strong, and you have a thick skull. And a thick brain, too.'

'It doesn't feel like it,' Carfax said. 'I may throw up.'

'I examined you. You only have a slight concussion, as far as I can tell, anyway. You'll live. At least, your body will.'

Carfax knew that he had no chance of escaping, none at all. But he wanted desperately to stave off the inevitable, and the best way to do that was to keep her talking.

'How did you find out that Patricia was living here?'

'It wasn't difficult. I still have an organization, you know. I knew where you all were all the time, you, your cousin, Langer. That's why I went to the house near Pontiac. It's just one of about two dozen hideouts I had ready. I knew you'd track me down through NIC if I ordered parts to build another MEDIUM. So I set it up to look as if I'd been electrocuted accidentally while putting it together. But first I built this mini-MEDIUM, the plans for which were drawn by your uncle, dumb old Rufton. He was a scientific genius, but he was stupid. He really thought I was going to let him live.'

'I doubt that,' Carfax said. 'He went along with you, I'm sure, because he hoped to escape.'

'And look where he is now, back in his colony.'

'In the original colony?'

'Oh yes. If a *semb* is pulled out by MEDIUM, its place isn't taken by another *semb*. It seems to be left open for the original; it rejects a new one. Why, I don't know. I think I'll get some more coffee.'

Though Carfax's mouth was dry, he would be damned if he would ask for anything to drink. Damned was the right term, he thought. He was headed toward damnation.

She came back with a cup of coffee and a glass of water. Seeing Carfax's surprise, she said, 'Have to keep you healthy, you know. Here, drink this, and don't do anything heroic, like spitting it in my face.'

She held the glass to his lips, tipping it back now and then. The water tasted delicious, and with it came hope. It was ridiculous for him to be hopeful in this situation, but then you never knew what would happen in this universe. Whereas, in that other, you knew. You whirled around in a strictly regulated dance, orbiting other hopeless things. What was it like to be without a body, to be a creature of pure energy? He would find out soon enough. Unless . . .

Even if he could get free of his ropes, he might not be able to do anything. He felt weak, and any sudden movement of his head shot pain through it, and his face felt as if it were covered with fire ants.

He watched her sit down on the sofa, and he said, 'How did you get Patricia?'

She laughed and said, 'I drove down here late at night, went around to the back, used a diamond-pointed cutter to remove a pane of glass in the door, reached in, unfastened the lock, cut out another pane of glass in the French window, reached in, unlocked it, unfastened the chain, and presto, I was inside. I went upstairs and found your cousin sleeping away. Judging from the odor of whiskey, she'd been drinking heavily. I injected a moderate amount of morphine to keep her asleep, tied her up, and set up my brand-new, handy-dandy, mostly transistorized, portable mini-MEDIUM, the latest product of your uncle. After she'd recovered, I raped her. I couldn't see all that beauty going to waste. Besides, I wanted to pay her back for turning me down in L.A. I will admit that I did worry about making myself pregnant, but I assumed that she was on the pill.'

'You lousy son of a bitch!'

'You can do better than that, I'm sure,' she said. 'Then I set up the MEDIUM and made the switch. That was tricky, not the actual switching, I mean, but assuring that, once I was in her body, I could take care of her in Dennis's body. While I was still in Dennis's body, I taped my ankles together and tied them to the bed with a heavy rope. Then I taped my left hand to my left leg. That wasn't easy, but I was heavily motivated, as they say nowadays.

'Your cousin was in a chair beside mine. She was doped so she wouldn't struggle too hard, and she may not even have realized what was taking place. I couldn't dope her too heavily. When the switch was made I didn't want to be too sluggish. I had to recover quickly enough to stop her – in Dennis's body then – from freeing herself. Another factor I had to consider was the initial trouble with coordinating. A *semb* always has that difficulty when it first takes over, you know. Or do you?'

'I figured it out,' Carfax said. 'When I got a report of Mifflon's behavior during the first week he was at Megistus. By the way, who was in Mifflon?'

She chuckled and said, 'You'd like me to talk forever, wouldn't you? Anything to stall me. Well, I don't mind. I like an appreciative audience. I had to pick a *semb* who knew how to fly a twin-engine jet. I could have had Mifflon flown in, but it was well-known that he wouldn't permit anyone but himself at the controls. I didn't want him to deviate from his normal behavior. So I got a *semb* who had been an air force general. Travers. You may remember his death from an automobile accident about five years ago. I located him and explained the setup, and he yelled a lot about ethics, but he came through all right. They all do. How did you find out about Mifflon?'

Carfax said, 'You'll never know.'

She smiled and said, 'Very admirable. Noble to the end. You won't squeal on Mrs. Webster. Oh, don't look so shocked. She had to be the source of information. She was the only one Mifflon ever confided in. Mifflon didn't tell me he'd told Webster he was going to confess to me, but it wasn't hard to figure out. I didn't bother to erase Webster, as they say nowadays. She

193

was no danger. Who's going to pay attention to a crazy spiritualist? But I did keep an eye on her. An ear, rather. I had her place bugged.

'Back to your cousin. I was half-doped and subject to dizziness and uncoordination when I changed. But then your cousin was also subject to that, and she didn't have the practice I've had overcoming it. So, with the helmets on and everything set up, I pressed the button that would start an automatic operation. Everything was set up ahead of time, the proper coordinates fixed and the switching done without manual adjustment of the controls. Even so, I hesitated for a few minutes. This was the first time I'd ever worked the automatic device. Due to the attack on Megistus, I had no time to test it. What if Rufton had made an error? What if some especially strong *semb* seized his chance and took over?'

'That can happen?' Carfax said.

'It has happened. I did it. You ought to know that. Western and Rufton were experimenting with a prototype, there were two, you know. No, you wouldn't. One was in your uncle's house and one was in Western's apartment. I think Western had some plans for grabbing the MEDIUM for himself. That may have been why he insisted on building a second one at his place. Perhaps. I don't really know. In any event, I was contacted by them through Western's machine. It was an accident, they weren't looking for me, they were just probing around. But I knew that the way was open, and I took it.'

'How did you know?'

'I just *knew* it. The English language, any language, I suppose, is incapable of describing what it's like to be a *semb*. You can't see, hear, smell, taste, or feel. There are no sensory inputs or outputs at all. There is no sense of time, which is fortunate, otherwise we'd go crazy. And don't ask me how you can exist without a sense of the passage of time. I don't know, but you do exist without it. There is, however, communication among the members of your colony. There is no communication between colonies, though, so you're restricted to eighty people. Forever and forever until MEDIUM was invented. I don't know how we communicated, but we quote heard unquote words. We spoke by some process I don't understand;

perhaps it was a form of telepathy or modulated energy transmission.

'Whatever . . . I was able to understand only three members. One was a woman who spoke some English, a Boer who'd died a few seconds after I did . . .'

'Which was when?' Carfax said.

'Which was January 7, 1872. You'd like to know who I am? I'll tell you in good time. I like to save the best for the last. There was also a Frenchman who was very fluent in English, a poet. I didn't have much in common with him or the Boer. And I had less in common with the other English speaker, an incredibly arrogant and stupid British lord, a veteran of the Crimean War. The rest were either speakers of gibberish, Chinese and the like, or babies. That was the worst part of all, I think, hearing those babies wailing on and on. But I quickly learned to shut them out.'

'That shoots my theory down,' Carfax said. 'The *sembs* really are the dead?'

'Oh, you're talking about that wild idea of yours that they're things pretending to be the dead?'

She laughed and said, 'That may be useful, though. I'm thinking about making an announcement that your theory has been proved after all. That way, I can get rid of all this antagonism from the religious swine. I'll continue to deal with the *sembs*, of course, but in secret. My main revenue will be from MEDIUM as a power source.'

'I don't think you can convince people of that now,' Carfax said.

She shrugged and said, 'Then I'll handle the situation in another way. My, we do get off the subject, don't we? Anyway, I finally punched the automatic-on button, and the switch was transacted as planned. I was in Patricia's mind. I was drowsy, only half-conscious, since the *semb*, when it's integrated with the body, is affected by physical causes. My body wanted to sleep, but I didn't, and so I forced myself to carry out my plan. It wasn't easy, but I have a very strong will. I fumbled around with the knot I'd tied in the rope I'd put around her to keep her from falling out of the chair. I got it loose and tried to stand up, but I fell over, tearing the helmet off my head.

'Meanwhile, your cousin had been struggling like mad, but she'd only succeeded in falling backward with the chair. She had stunned herself. I taped her other arm down, and then I tore the tape off my own mouth. I'd put it on Patricia to keep her from screaming, just as I'd taped my own mouth when in Dennis's body to keep her from screaming when she was switched. I managed to give her an injection to put her under until noon, and I crawled into bed and went to sleep.'

'You left her lying on the floor on her back tied up to that chair?'

'Sure, why not? She was going to die that night anyway. Besides, I didn't have the coordination or the strength to set her back up. I woke about noon and walked around the house and up and down the steps until I mastered myself. It was strange being in a woman's body, but I found I liked it. I got a big thrill from caressing myself. And from thinking about how recently I'd been screwing myself.'

She laughed loudly for a long time. After wiping away the tears, she said, 'You don't know how eager I was to get you to bed and try out my woman's body. I'll admit I found it repulsive in the beginning. I'd never kissed a man before. But I got over that, and let me tell you, women enjoy sex more than a man can. I didn't think it was possible, but I had the living proof of it. I'm going to have to stay in this body a long time, until I get legal ownership of MEDIUM, anyway, and I'm going to get me a stable of young studs you wouldn't believe.'

'I suppose a queer would make the transition to a woman easier,' Carfax said.

She stared at him a moment and then broke out into laughing again.

'You say that to *me*, Old Stallion Dan? Why, man, I was notorious for my string of Broadway beauties. Three-times-a-night-Dan, they called me, among other things not so complimentary. I was keeping the great Josie Mansfield and three other showgirls at the same time. And none of them ever complained. You don't understand, Carfax. I'm an adapter. I can fall into any situation and come out on top, except . . .'

She frowned, and Carfax said, 'Except . . .'

'Well, there's always the crazy nut who goes ape. You can't

foresee him. Old Stokes shot me, and I wasn't expecting that. And then there was that Houvelle with his plane full of dynamite. But I still came back, didn't I?'

'Stokes?'

'Yeah, Stokes. A business associate of mine whom I'd shafted. I had a little talk with him one night in L.A. I told him what had happened and what he was missing. I threatened to bring him back just so I could torture him. I don't intend to, but he'll be sweating it out for eternity!'

'And what happened to Pat? In Dennis's body?'

'I was able to drive by nightfall, though I had to do it carefully. I moved her car out of the garage and drove mine in. I closed the garage doors and shoved her on ahead of me through the door between the house and the garage. I made her get into the trunk, and I doped her up again. I drove back to the farmhouse, took her into the room where MEDIUM was, told her how much trouble you and she had caused me and how I was going to fool you. Then I turned on the power and shoved her so she fell against the exposed transformer. I removed her tapes, washed off the tape-marks with water and alcohol, and rode my motorcycle north to Streator. I had to leave my car at the farmhouse, of course, and I wasn't going to be seen in Pontiac. I didn't want anybody in Pontiac to remember seeing a woman who looked like Patricia Carfax.

'I abandoned the motorcycle, it was registered in a fake name, and took the MTO and a bus back to Busiris. And I took the MT from downtown to the Sheridan Village stop and walked home. Home sweet home. And there you have it.'

And I'm about to get it, Carfax thought.

'You died in 1872?' he said. 'You must have had a hell of a time adjusting. There were no cars, planes, TV, electronics, almost none of the technology of today. Everything must have seemed so strange, even terrifying. You must not have been able to understand half the vocabulary of the people you had to meet.'

'I adjust quickly, fella,' she said. 'I laid doggo for two weeks, playing sick, while I studied things that seem simple to you, like learning how to operate a viewphone. I went down to the L.A. library, what an experience that was, my first time out of the apartment, and I got a lot of books to study up on. I made many mistakes, like I found out when I got to the library that I could have read all the books on my TV with a simple request to the library. But I learned, oh, how I learned!'

'One of the mistakes you made was killing Uncle Rufton,' Carfax said. 'You should have switched him with some co-operating *semb*, and you'd never have had trouble with Pat. That's what started the whole thing.'

'That was a mistake,' she said. 'But it turned out all right, didn't it?'

She stood up and said, 'Well, we might as well get down to business.'

'You haven't told me who you are.'

'You sure like to talk to me, don't you?' she said, grinning. 'I'll tell you in just a minute. First, I have to get the helmet.'

'Helmet?'

She stopped and said, 'Of course. It's for better control. A *semb* can be extracted, or summoned, or whatever you want to call it, through the CRT itself. It's not only a visual apparatus, it's a door-opener. A wall-breacher. But it's a dangerous step to use it for that because it's not one hundred percent certain. The *semb* might possess one of the innocent bystanders instead of the person for whom it's intended. And also, *sembs*, some of them, can't make it through. Only the strong-willed ones, the tigers, can get through. Your uncle almost made it when you were talking to him, but he didn't have the drive. So I had my scientists design a channeling device, the helmet.'

'How the hell can a person's will determine the action of an electronic being?' Carfax said.

'I don't know,' she said. 'But it can, to some extent, anyway. As for the *sembs* being electronic, that's only a term used to cover up our ignorance of their real essence. Remember, what you can see on the screen is only an electronic analog. But enough of talk. This isn't the Thousand and One Nights, Carfax, and you're not Scheherazade.'

She halted again. 'Oh, yes, don't try screaming. Your neighbors on both sides are gone. Old lady Allen is off to visit her sister in Oklahoma, and the Batterdons are on vacation. Besides, with the drapes pulled, I doubt that anyone could hear you.'

Carfax did not answer. As soon as she had disappeared around the corner, he bent his legs as far back as he could get them under the chair. He lifted up and bent over and began a slow and painful hopping toward the machine on the serving cart. The chair on his back was a carapace, and he was a crippled turtle trying to be a kangaroo. The coffee cart was only about two and a half meters away, but at the pace of a decimeter a hop, it seemed as if it were a kilometer. Each effort drained out half his strength. Like Achilles chasing the tortoise, he would never make it. But then Zeno's paradox didn't work in real life, and he only thought he was weakening by halves. Still, each little jump exploded pain in his head, and he was sweating before he had made three hops.

Once, he wondered if she was expecting him to make this attempt. Was she waiting around the corner to spring on him just as he completed his mission? What mission? He wasn't sure he could do what he planned. Worse, he wouldn't know what he had accomplished when he had done it.

It would not take her long to climb the fourteen steps, go down the hallway into the bedroom, and into the attic. At least, he supposed that she had hidden the helmet in the attic. That must have been where she had concealed the MEDIUM.

He did not believe he would have enough time, but he had to try. If only . . . and the phone rang. He *was* given more time. If only it wasn't a wrong number, if only it was someone who insisted on speaking to him. No, if it were, then she would be down at once to stand out of the field of vision of the phone and to hold a gun at his head while he spoke. If she did, then he was going to yell. He would die, but whoever was at the other end would see what was happening. And she would be in an untenable position again.

He resumed his minute progress, went past the side of the machine, turned slowly, and hopped until he was close to its rear. Panting, fearful that his legs would give way, he bent over. His face slid along the cool metal plate and then his lips touched the nearest of the two wires running from the automatic control box to the terminals on the back of MEDIUM. He shoved his head forward to get a better purchase, clamped his teeth on the wire, and jerked upward with his head. The motion sent pain through his head again, and he almost collapsed. But the wire was torn loose from the jack.

He could no longer hear her voice. In a few seconds, she would be down, unless chance favored him again, and that was too much to expect.

He hopped backward until he was clear of the serving cart, turned slowly, and hopped back. Now he could hear the tinkle of water falling into water. Good. Chance had given him another break.

The toilet flushed as he settled back down. But the chair was only in its approximate previous position, and he had to place the ends of the chair legs exactly where they had been. Their pressure had left four square depressions in the nap of the rug. She would see these and would wonder just how far he had managed to move the chair.

It was very difficult to see the depressions, and when he moved one leg of the chair to cover one depression, he missed the others. It was impossible to see the hind depressions made by the rear legs, so he settled for an attempt at covering the front two. Then he heard footsteps, and he had to stop. He did not know whether he had succeeded perfectly, but there was nothing he could do now.

She came around the corner holding a device which looked like a large metal football helmet. Attached to it was an electrical cord about two meters long.

She looked at him as she passed him and said, 'My, we certainly are sweating, aren't we? That's one nice thing about being a *semb*, you don't sweat. Not physically, anyway.'

He said nothing but watched her while she plugged the end of the helmet cord into a receptacle near the base of the front panel. Still holding the helmet, she pushed the cart with one hand to a distance of a meter from him. She put the helmet on the floor, went into the kitchen, and returned a moment later with a strip of tape.

'Any famous last words?' she said, smiling.

'I'll see you in hell.'

'I may drop in on you now and then,' she said. 'But I won't be staying long. And you will.'

'One thing,' he said. 'Your promise. You said you'd tell me who you really are.'

'My name was James Fisk. Do you know who I am now, or must I give my biography?'

'The Barnum of Wall Street, the Prince of Erie?' he said.

'Right!'

She slapped the square of tape over his mouth, smoothed it out, and placed the helmet over his head. It felt very heavy, and his headache increased. It was the weight of doom, he thought.

'That's a nice boy,' she said. 'It wouldn't do any good to struggle.'

And so he was to become one more victim of the no longer late and never lamented James Fisk. Born in 1834, if he remembered correctly. A native of Bennington, Vermont. Oh yes, he had been born on April 1, April Fool's Day. Very appropriate. Fisk was no fool, but he had certainly fooled many. He had started at the lowly job of circus hand, then become, successively, a waiter, a peddler, a salesman of dry goods, and a stockbroker. He had founded the brokerage firm of Fisk and . . . Belden? And then he had gotten into the big time as a stock-market operator for Daniel Drew. Drew was as big a crook and as ruthless a financier as you could find. He and Fisk and the equally corrupt Jay Gould had become partners in taking control of the Erie railroad from Cornelius Vanderbilt. Nobody had cried about this except old Cornelius, who was as rotten as the unholy three who had beaten him out.

Fisk, as vice-president and comptroller of the railroad, had used its funds to bribe public officials, produce Broadway shows, and seduce Broadway actresses and chorus girls. One of his many mistresses had been the famous Josie Mansfield. Fisk was also Gould's assistant in his attempt to corner the gold market. This had resulted in the stock-market crash, the infamous *Black Friday*, of, when was it?, oh yes, September 24, 1869.

And then Fisk, at the age of thirty-seven or thirty-eight, had been shot by E. S. Stokes and he had died the next day. Carfax remembered the exact day on which he had been shot because it was January 6, the day on which members of the Baker Street Irregulars celebrated Sherlock Holmes's birthday.

He watched her finger approach the automatic-on button. Here it comes, he thought. His heart was hammering, and he wondered what Fisk would do if he should drop dead of a heart attack before he could activate MEDIUM. He wished he would. Fisk might be in trouble then. And he thought, no, he wouldn't. The autopsy would show that I died a natural death, and no one would suspect Fisk.

Goodby, Patricia. If only we could have died at the same time, we would at least be in the same colony.

Fisk, his finger only a centimeter away from the button, turned his head and grinned.

Be a sadist for all I care, Carfax thought. Those few more seconds of life are precious, even under these conditions. And maybe the phone will ring again. That's one question I meant to ask him. Who called? A friend of Pat's? One of Fisk's compatriots? Senator Langer? I'll never know, and it doesn't matter.

The finger moved; the button sank inward.

Carfax felt as if he were shrinking inside himself, collapsing, falling down the well of himself.

But nothing happened except that an indicator by the automatic-on button lit up.

Fisk swore and pressed the button again. The light remained illuminated.

If only Fisk would decide not to trace the trouble but to switch over to manual operation.

Fisk had checked the connections of the two wires at the rear just after he had brought the machine down. There was no reason for him to check it again; they could not possibly have come loose. Not as far as he would know.

Carfax groaned inside the tape. Fisk was looking at the rear of the machine.

'Now how the hell did that happen?' Fisk muttered.

He leaned over and looked at the loose wire.

'Wet!'

He looked at Carfax and said, grinning, 'You wily sneaky son of a bitch!'

Fisk plugged the end of the wire back in and returned to the front of the machine. This time, the indicator light did not come on.

And Carfax was sightless, earless, tongueless, deprived of all senses except thought. And the silent scream of horror which seemed to reverberate through nothing and back from nothing.

Fisk was right. There were no words to describe what it was like being a *semb*.

He was an undescribable something in nothingness.

And then he was a familiar something.

He could see, hear, taste, and feel again.

Mrs. Webster, across the table from him, was screaming, and the others were yelling or jumping up.

He looked down. His bare breasts were large and round and the thumbtip-sized nipples were painted yellow. His skirt was bell-shaped Neo-Cretan.

'It went into you, Szegeti!' a man howled.

Carfax wasn't too numb to understand what had happened.

Mrs. Webster was right. The *walls* had been weakened, and he had flashed straight toward the psychical configuration of her seance, the mental analog of MEDIUM. Like a current of electrons, he had taken the path of least resistance; a voltage hole, he had been tunneled into her presence; he had made the quantum jump from his world to *embu* and back to his world.

Mrs. Webster had quit screaming and was now standing up and staring at him.

'You look familiar,' she said. 'Are you an evil spirit?'

'No more than any man,' he said. 'Bring me a phone, and put me through to Senator Langer.'

THE WORLD'S GREATEST NOVELISTS
NOW AVAILABLE IN PANTHER BOOKS

Iris Murdoch

A Word Child	95p ☐
The Unicorn	£1.00 ☐
An Unofficial Rose	£1.25 ☐
The Bell	75p ☐
The Flight From the Enchanter	75p ☐
The Nice and the Good	£1.25 ☐
Bruno's Dream	85p ☐

Doris Lessing

The Golden Notebook	£1.35 ☐
The Black Madonna	80p ☐
Winter in July	50p ☐
Briefing for a Descent into Hell	75p ☐
The Habit of Loving	75p ☐
A Man and Two Women	75p ☐
Going Home (Non-Fiction)	95p ☐
Five	95p ☐

'Children of Violence' Series

Martha Quest	95p ☐
A Proper Marriage	90p ☐
A Ripple From the Storm	95p ☐
Landlocked	95p ☐
The Four-Gated City	£1.50 ☐

John Fowles

The Ebony Tower	75p ☐
The Collector	85p ☐
The French Lieutenant's Woman	£1.25 ☐
The Magus	£1.50 ☐
Daniel Martin	£1.50 ☐

THE WORLD'S GREATEST NOVELISTS
NOW AVAILABLE IN PANTHER BOOKS

Ernest Hemingway

The Old Man and The Sea	50p ☐
Fiesta	75p ☐
For Whom the Bell Tolls	90p ☐
A Farewell to Arms	75p ☐
The Snows of Kilimanjaro	60p ☐
The Essential Hemingway	£1.25 ☐
To Have and Have Not	75p ☐
Death in the Afternoon (Non-Fiction)	£1.25 ☐
Green Hills of Africa	75p ☐
Men Without Women	75p ☐
A Moveable Feast	75p ☐
The Torrents of Spring	75p ☐
Across the River and Into the Trees	75p ☐
Winner Take Nothing	80p ☐

Richard Hughes

A High Wind in Jamaica	60p ☐
In Hazard	60p ☐

James Joyce

Dubliners	75p ☐
A Portrait of the Artist as a Young Man	75p ☐
Stephen Hero	£1.25 ☐
The Essential James Joyce	£1.50 ☐

TRUE CRIME – NOW AVAILABLE IN PANTHER BOOKS

Ludovic Kennedy

A Presumption of Innocence   £1.25 ☐
10 Rillington Place   95p ☐

Stephen Knight

Jack the Ripper: The Final Solution   £1.25 ☐

Peter Maas

The Valachi Papers   75p ☐

John Pearson

The Profession of Violence   95p ☐

Ed Sanders

The Family   95p ☐

Vincent Teresa

My Life in the Mafia   95p ☐

Colin Wilson

Order of Assassins   60p ☐
The Killer   60p ☐